A DEADLY SEVEN NOVEL

WRATH

LANA
PECHERCZYK

also by lana pecherczyk

CARDINAL CITY MAP

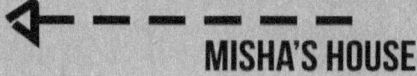

MISHA'S HOUSE

AIRPORT

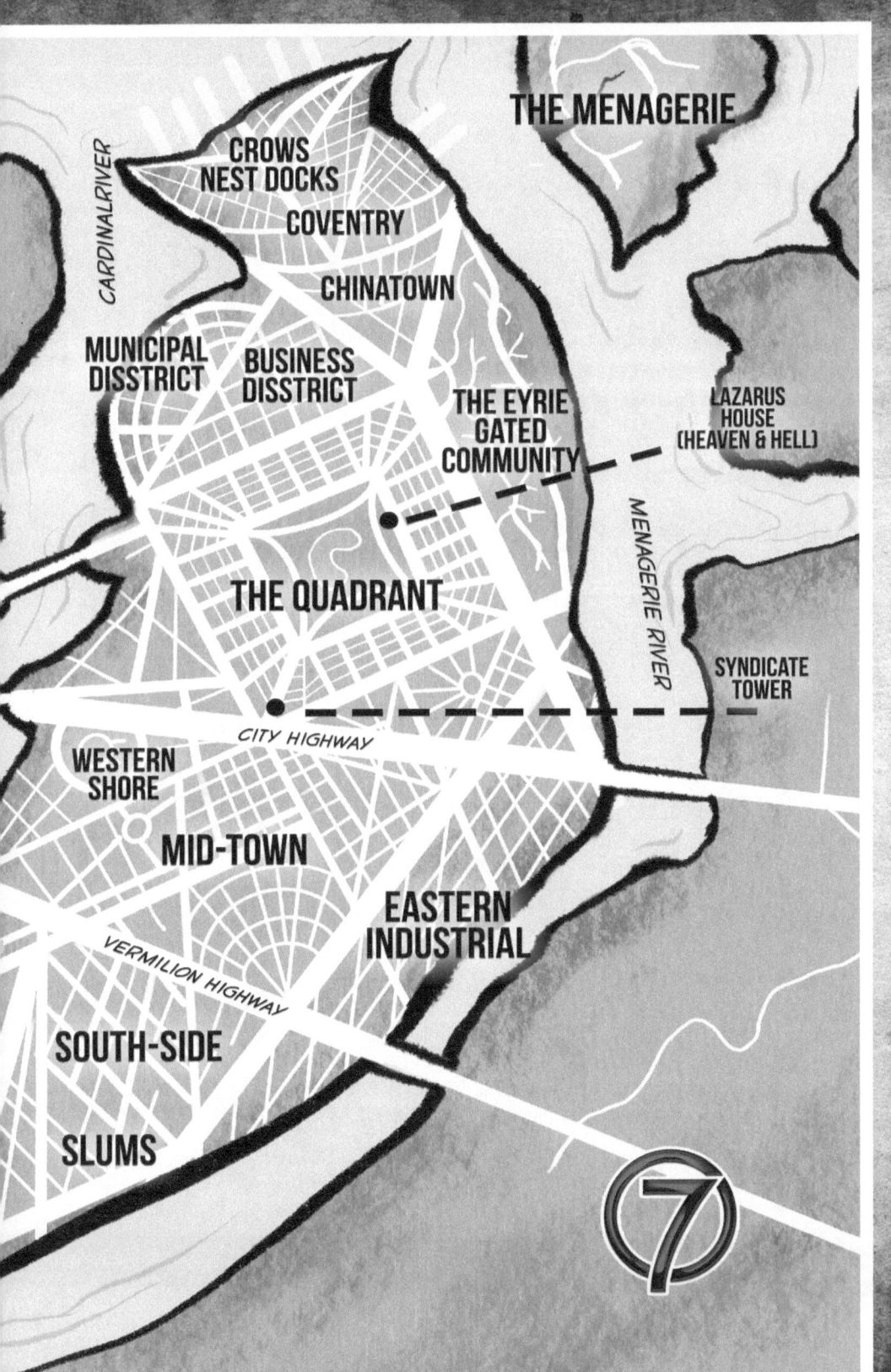

prologue

IN THE DARKNESS of a thirteenth floor in Cardinal City, Julius Allcott stared out over the destitute south-side, contemplating, calculating. Despite being the one who started the Syndicate, he was no closer to being able to replicate the original experiment that created the warriors of sin. This lack of progress was beginning to grate. He barely heard the steps of his most trusted darling as she approached him from behind.

"We have news," she said in a dull voice. Her favored bird mask covered her eyes and nose. Off-white leather hugged her body. A fine mist of red on her collar echoed the same on her fist. She'd come straight from work, then.

"Go on," he prompted, and locked eyes with the city once more.

"One of them has separated from the flock."

He arched an eyebrow, curious. "Which?"

"The one affianced to the Faithful named Sara," she elaborated.

Sara. Julius tapped his chin, trying to remember. *A member of the Syndicate's Faithful… named Sara.* Of course. The one they'd coerced into working undercover for them. She'd gathered important biological samples. "I remember her," he said. "You eliminated her."

"Yes."

"Remind me why."

"She was becoming a liability."

"There's something you're not telling me."

"Recently we learned she failed to disclose the importance of the life-mate to each of the Deadly Seven."

A memory sparked. A conversation he'd had only a week prior. "The surveillance notes we found recently. She'd surmised a woman triggered Envy's full potential."

"Yes. During her time with the warriors, she'd heard rumors that a person embodying the exact opposite of their sin would cancel out the effects of the sin itself, thus helping each warrior resist the dark murderous pull."

Julius turned back to the view of the decrepit streets. But that dark murderous pull was what they needed to destroy all the sinners in the world, leaving it cleansed and free for innocents. Innocents like his wife and daughter.

"First Envy's powers manifesting after meeting someone, then Greed's. Two could be a coincidence."

"But three could be a pattern."

"This warrior who separated from the family. It was Wrath, was it not?

"Correct."

Wrath. Interesting.

"And where is he now?"

"There have been reports of a dark rider haunting the streets at night. He's left a trail of bodies around the country, but has been spotted close to Cardinal City in a small town called Weston Park."

A trail of bodies—the man was slipping then, and sin was taking hold.

Initially, the Deadly Seven were born in a lab—the Syndicate's creations. *His* creations. He tore his gaze from the sinful city and went to his lone desk at the center of the room. Nothing adorned the surface except a family photograph taken almost forty years earlier. His wife and daughter. Both dead from corporate negligence—Sloth. It was for them he fought this battle. For them, he had joined forces with military cells around the world to create the Syndicate, and for them, he financed the lab that created the warriors of sin.

"Weston Park," Julius mused. "So close to Cardinal City. Perhaps the prodigal son is flirting with returning to the fold."

"I have ties with a man in Weston Park."

"Of course you do. Tug on the string. Pull tighter and see what information we can squeeze free."

"And if it is the outlier, Wrath?"

"Then he is alone, desperate and falling under the influence of his sin. Opportunity has never been so ripe for us." He turned to his darling. "Give your man support to stoke the fire. I want this city in flames before the month is out."

"Yes, sir."

"But, darling? Never forget our priority."

His darling bowed. "To complete the puzzle."

"Whatever is begun in anger, ends in shame."

– BENJAMIN FRANKLIN

AFTER SIX MONTHS on the road, Wyatt Lazarus had returned, circling Cardinal City like a hungry shark.

He hated himself for it.

No matter how much distance he'd put between him and his family, he was right back where he started—somewhere between fucked and a place called the Pierogi Palace, about forty clicks from the city where the air smelled like burned oil and garlic.

He polished off a questionable burrito from the Mexican joint across the way while straddling his motorcycle, admiring the tank's glossy shine under his torn jeans and army-grade boots. The black and chromed out vintage '79 Ducati was low slung, sleek and powerful for her age. A badass cruiser that gave him more love than he'd received in years. She outran the cops in Cooperville and helped him evade a disgruntled bar owner in Vegas. After that last one, he'd decided to give her a name: Betty. No reason. He just liked the name.

A few towns back, he'd rescued Betty from some dirtbag owner who'd been wailing on a skinny-assed woman in the bar's bathroom. The fucker wasn't even sorry he'd broken two of her ribs—as if Wyatt would leave Betty in his incapable hands. Since that dirtbag was… well, fuck. He couldn't remember what happened to him. He'd blacked out. Whatever. Point was, Betty was his now.

Wyatt pulled a hip flask from his back pocket, giving it a shake for measurement's sake. Almost empty. Just like his wallet. As he took a burning swig of whiskey dregs, he eyed a commotion brewing at the Polish place. It was a small restaurant. Glass door. Red and white flag in the window. Potted flowers around two empty sidewalk dining tables, each with a little vase holding a poppy. The "Help Wanted" sign in the window looked like a five-year-old drew it, or he supposed, someone who spoke English as a second language. Someone like the stocky gray-haired man getting pushed around by two men in business shirts and long black coats. Two young men against a fifty, maybe sixty, year-old—not exactly fair.

After being shoved, the old man crashed into one of the tables, upending it. Wyatt sent his sin-sense roaming to test for deadly levels of wrath, but found none. He checked the Yin-Yang symbol on his inner wrist. The ancient symbol had been tattooed using a special bio-indicator ink, meaning the more wrath in his system, the blacker the tattoo looked. Today, it was almost black.

Wyatt darted a glance to the Polish restaurant and dismissed the idea of intervening. Any attempt to help would involve his fists, and inevitably wrath. With his blackouts getting more prolonged, and the bodies left in his wake, he couldn't afford attention. Sorry Polish dude. Not wrath, *not my problem*. He put away his hip flask and donned his black helmet, snapping the visor down. He didn't know where he was going at five in the afternoon, but stepped on the kick-starter all the same. It clicked, but no engine fired.

Wyatt exhaled slowly and rubbed Betty's tank.

C'mon, baby. Fire up for me.

He stomped again. Nothing.

Again.

Nothing.

She normally purred like a kitten in his hands, but today...

Shit.

He pulled his helmet off. He'd have to find somewhere to lie low for a few days until he figured out what was wrong with her, but he knew next to nothing about bike repair. Never needed it with the newer model the family had supplied.

The small amount of tinkering he'd done over the past few months had kept her running, barely. But he was more like a blind man in a china shop where Betty was concerned. It was time to give her a proper service, except... he had no money. No transport. No place to stay.

Only a few minutes away in the city, his family would jump at the chance to rescue him from his self-imposed banishment. But the thought of looking his brother Evan in the face, after what Wyatt had done, still made him sick. Admitting he'd been wrong made him feel worse.

The shouts from the Polish restaurant grew louder, and the sense of wrath tickled Wyatt's skin but, fuck it, he didn't want this. Never asked for it. The only thing his sixth sense had been good for lately was giving him an avenue to let his demons out. When all he'd wanted to do lately was rage and scream, he didn't feel so guilty afterwards knowing the people he'd put in the hospital were the worst kind.

Someone had to pay.

It wouldn't be his two brothers with their perfect fucking relationships.

It wouldn't be the Syndicate. They were just as invisible as they'd always been, and Sara was dead in the ground.

And it wouldn't be the rest of his righteous family.

It sure as hell wasn't going to be him. Not after the raw hand he'd been dealt. Nah. Fuck that shit.

The sense of wrath stabbed him like a knife in the gut. He doubled over, clutching Betty's handlebars. Damn, if it didn't feel like a hit of heroin; he was already high on the sick sensation—on the promise the pain made. *Release. Punish. Hurt.* The agony was welcome. It made him feel something other than hate, something other than self-loathing, something *more*. It meant someone out there was a bigger bastard than him.

The thugs hadn't noticed Wyatt sitting there. Too engrossed with their prey... or, more likely, they assumed they were kings of the little town and didn't expect to be challenged by a newcomer on an old motorcycle. A quick glance around the cultural food center's lot showed most restaurant owners and patrons had shut themselves inside the protection of their establishments, as though they were used to this sight.

Wrath wriggled its fingers in his gut and eased its way into his chest, tightening, coiling, ready to release. *Release. Punish. Hurt.*

The two men roughing up the old man, strong-armed him with classic intimidation tactics. But that wasn't where the intense wrath came from... it came from the Polish restaurant as a teenage boy exited. He was tall, lanky, and had longish blond hair. Dressed similarly to the old man in the apron.

Something about the boy reminded Wyatt of his younger brother Evan at that age. An incorrigible fierceness glowed in the teenager's eyes as he defended the older man. His gaze screamed obscenities. With no visible weapons, he approached the men and waved his hands in their face. What the hell was he doing? Realization hit him. The kid was signing.

Shock reverberated in Wyatt's chest.

Can't speak. Like me.

His gloved fingers touched his scarred neck. The hard ridge stretched almost from ear to ear.

Sara. At the thought of her name, acid hit the back of his throat.

The brown-haired thug in a navy shirt backhanded the teenage boy, sending him head first into the thick paned glass behind him. The reflection wobbled from the impact, but didn't break. The boy's eyes rolled back, and he dropped to the ground, stunned.

A raspy snarl ripped from Wyatt. His fingers twitched for his knife but no, he wanted to feel the pain of those fuckers on his skin. He tugged his gloves off and then stalked toward the fallen kid.

Ignoring the men ranting with thick Russian accents—*time for you later*—he crouched and checked on the boy. Two fingers to the carotid told him he was alive. No blood at the back of the head, just a small bump forming. He wore a hearing aid in each ear. Basic model.

"Alek," the old man cried. "Alek. *Ci nie jest?*"

"Shut up, *starikan*," said the youngest Russian. "You need only worry about the money you owe us, old man. Boy's lucky to be alive."

"He is my son. You don't touch him."

"We touch who we want to touch."

"Oi," the second Russian snapped at Wyatt. This thug was older —maybe thirty or so—with a scar running down his face that caved and pulled his lip awkwardly like a one-sided Joker smile. He opened his coat to show Wyatt his concealed weapon, then jerked his head toward the road. "Leave. This is none of your business."

Still crouching, Wyatt gave him a dismissive snort and then patted Alek's face gently. Alek's blue eyes opened and focused on Wyatt. Wyatt pointed with two fingers at the boy's eyes and then back to his own. *Watch me.*

Alek's brows drew together. His attention flicked to the thugs, then back to Wyatt.

Watch me, Wyatt mouthed, hoping Alek understood.

He nodded and Wyatt clapped him on the shoulder. *Good boy.*

Wyatt unfurled himself, straightened to his full six-foot-three height, cracked his neck, and then turned to the Russian thugs. One held Alek's father against the window. Scar-face watched Wyatt with incredulous eyes, as if he couldn't believe someone had the balls to ignore him. He didn't even reach for his weapon.

Fool.

Staring at his opponent, Wyatt exhaled slowly. When all the air was gone, he entered his calm space. The space where wrath dominated. The space where death lived. He pounced. Took the gun from Scar-face. Emptied the magazine clip. Punched his throat with a satisfying crack, then jabbed his face. The man went down, blood spurting from his nose. Wyatt turned to the next thug who came at him with brass knuckles.

He could move out of the way, could step to the side and avoid the hit, but… pain burst in Wyatt's cheek as the Russian connected. Wyatt's head whipped to the side. Tasted blood. That warm, metallic tang—his bitter friend come to make him smile.

Wyatt spat out a wad and, for a moment, his gaze caught on the red splash over the pavement. A memory flashed before his eyes. Blood in the street, Sara's blood, his blood—all mingling. She reached for him. She said she was sorry.

No.

Wyatt shook the memory loose, then his small smile turned into a toothy grin, and he let his feral beast out to play.

He must have blacked out. Must have lost time, or something, because the next thing he remembered was the Russian's bloody face beaten to a pulp, and his fist soaring down for another hit.

"Enough!" The old man shouted behind him. "You will kill him."

With incredible restraint, Wyatt bit the inside of his cheek and stepped back, scrubbing his face. His hands came back covered in tacky dark red. Second-hand blood. *Shit.* The wrath inside had taken over, poisoning his instincts.

He refused to look at the bio-controlled Yin-Yang tattoo on his wrist. He knew it would be entirely black, indicating wrath had intoxicated his bloodstream, making him do evil things. *Yeah, sure, blame the wrath.*

He forced himself to calm. Had to keep control, or else the next time he blacked out and went berserk, he might not come back. Worse—his gaze flicked to Alek—he could take out innocent bystanders.

Scar-face was coming to, and every atom in Wyatt's body wanted to crush him, but he held back and watched the thug help his bloody friend up.

"You shouldn't have done that," Scar-face said, sputtering through a bloody mouth.

Wyatt arched his eyebrow. *Why's that, asshole?*

"Dimitri will hear about this," was his only reply.

It was then Wyatt noticed the man had a tattoo peeking out from the collar of his shirt. Points of a star. *Bratva.* The Russian Mob.

Like he gave a shit. He waited for the two men to drive away in their shiny Volvo Passat, gave them a mocking finger wave, and then walked back to Betty.

"You shouldn't have done that," the old man shouted behind Wyatt, echoing the mobster's earlier words.

Wyatt faced him. The man had gone pale, as was his son.

"Better for us to take a beating than what they will send next," said the old man.

Wyatt shrugged.

"Dimitri. They will send Dimitri." The old man's eyes widened in fear.

A sigh tore from Wyatt's raw throat and he slumped. He was

tired, weary from months on the road, and now he'd fucked up. This family was going to pay for his mistake. He could almost hear his adoptive mother's voice in his ear. *Family first, Wyatt. You protect your own before anything else.* Well, he sucked at helping his family, but perhaps he could do something about this one.

How?

His gaze roved around until it landed on a sign in the window behind the family. *Help Wanted.* Wyatt pointed at it.

The old man's brows winged up. "You want to work here?"

Wyatt nodded.

Alek's expression lit up. Well, he was certainly excited about it, but then: "No," the old man said. "We need a chef."

Wyatt punched his chest. *I am a chef.*

Well, he was. Once.

It was clear the old man wasn't happy, but Alek kept signing erratically at his father, and whatever he said made the man hesitate.

"Why you not speak?" the man asked, his Polish accent thick.

Wyatt touched his scarred throat and then made a break sign with his hands.

"You no' talk?" the man asked again.

He shook his head, then jogged to Betty—*why the fuck was he jogging?*—and opened his duffel bag. There wasn't much inside. A spare change of clothes, his wallet... and his knives. His pride and joys that took him to the heights of being a Michelin starred chef and the lows of the pawn shop, almost. The collection was worth hundreds of dollars, maybe thousands and was his last resort before accessing his old bank accounts, and thus giving away his position to his family. It was either pawn them, or get a job to fix Betty. Well, this was a job. He could kill two birds with one knife. Earn enough to fix the bike and stick around in case those fuckers showed again—and then get the fuck out of Dodge.

He snagged the knife roll out of the bag and walked back to the old man where he unrolled the package. Gleaming metal blades shone in the sun. After a pensive look at the knives, the old man turned to his son who nodded emphatically as he signed.

"Okay," the man said. "Alek thinks you being here will help keep Bratva away. Maybe this is the way we go from here. You can have the job." Then he mumbled, "Let's hope you cook well enough, too."

A coldness dropped in the pit of Wyatt's stomach. He rolled his knives back up and tucked the package under his arm. Was he really doing this?

"My name is Filip. You can call me Vooyek like everyone else—is name for uncle." He nodded at his son. "This is Alek."

The boy stared at Wyatt's throat—at his scar. When he looked up, his eyes widened at having been caught, but Vooyek didn't seem to notice.

"Come, Alek. We have to prepare for dinner." He tugged his son by the collar, then shot Wyatt a concerned look over his shoulder. "We see you in the morning at seven. We open at eleven for lunch."

Um. Wyatt looked back at Betty, and then at the Polish pair. Alek must have caught the uncertainty on Wyatt's face because he shrugged away from his father and pointed at the bike.

It's broken. Wyatt made the broken sign again.

"Is not working?" Vooyek asked.

Wyatt nodded, hand on hip. Or should he shake his head? Fuck.

Alek signed something to his father and Vooyek scratched his head. "Do you not have a place to stay?"

Wyatt shook his head.

A young woman burst out of the restaurant doors. She had curly red hair and looked not much older than Alek. Maybe eighteen. They had the same bright blue eyes and freckles on their noses.

"He can stay at Misha's place," she said. "She hasn't been there for weeks. Hi"—she smiled at Wyatt—"I'm Roksana."

Another woman, an older one about the same age as Vooyek, came bursting out. A brown floral scarf tied her long graying hair away. Under her flour dusted apron, she wore a long skirt and flowing top. If Wyatt didn't know any better, he would say she was still stuck in the Woodstock era with her beads around her neck holding a peace symbol pendant.

"He stay," she said, eyeing him appreciatively.

Before Wyatt knew what was happening, it appeared as if the entire Polish community spilled out of the restaurant and were weighing in on the decision—at least four more people, two old and two in their thirties—until finally Vooyek put up his hand and shouted, "Enough."

Then he waved his hand at Wyatt. "Okay. You have a place to stay if you like. Room over our garage."

two

MISHA MINSKI

A WARM, lilac scented breeze ruffled Misha Minski's hair as she locked her street-side yoga studio after a hard day's work. A full class did wonders for her anemic bank account. If only she didn't have to close early to go to her next job, adding another class to her roster might have been worthwhile.

A tap on her shoulder brought her attention to the bright blue-haired woman standing next to her in the city street. Bev was around sixty and never missed a class. She had the body of a forty-year-old, and Misha was happy to say she'd had a hand in creating it. That shiny blue leotard looked great on her—better than some malnourished and drug addicted girls Misha worked with at the club.

"Thanks for the class, hon," Bev said, flicking her sweaty blue curls from her shoulder. "I'll see you on the weekend for Bikram?"

"You betcha!" Misha grinned. "Bring your A-Game. It's going to be a tough one."

"Got a hot date with Morty on Saturday night, so you know I will." Bev waved goodbye.

"Thanks for a great class, Misha," said Cassy, another student. She winked at Misha from underneath her black bangs. "Oh, and by the way, you were right about that pose doing wonders for my sex life."

"Right?" Misha laughed. "I told you! Next time, crank the heat—it really gets your blood flowing. See ya."

"Bye!"

Misha sighed and went back to her studio lock. She loved teaching yoga. The students were so varied; from the older, limber ladies like Bev, to the younger shy girls, to the hipster boys. There was nothing sexier than seeing a man work to keep his body in shape, especially when it was so easy these days to get what you wanted with a pill or the flick of a button.

She slung her bag over her shoulder and headed toward the city central monorail. There had been an attack on the rail a few months ago where a train derailed and people almost lost their lives. If it weren't for one of the Deadly Seven, things would be very different. Seeing the news story her best-friend Lilo broke was still hard to digest. One of the Seven had used some sort of paranormal power to stop the train falling. He'd moved metal around with a thought.

It was a new age they were living in, a strange one, and it excited Misha with a sense of adventure. Reading the story had reminded her that life was not only finite, but full of endless possibilities.

When she arrived, the train platform was a little on the light side. With the memory of the almost-tragedy still sharp, most people preferred to take the subway or other modes of transport.

Not her.

Misha's bag buzzed. The sound of Snoop Dog's *Drop it Like it's Hot* came from deep within. While she dug around for her vibrating cell, she copped a few wolf-whistles from a group of horny teenagers ogling her yoga attire—more specifically the areas on her body that lacked yoga attire. She wore black cut-off pants and a colorful midriff top that flashed her tanned abs. The spring sun was perfect for catching some vitamin D. Unfazed, she smiled and waved back cheekily.

She'd sort them out in a minute, but first... she answered her insistent phone and walked toward the edge of the platform to wait for the approaching train.

"Tata, is everything okay?" She hadn't heard from her father in weeks, which was virtually unheard of.

"Mishka," he stated. "You must come home."

"Is everything okay?" It better not be something to do with Dimitri. He'd promised her current working arrangement was enough to cover the protection fee for her family's restaurant.

"Tak, tak. Is okay." He let loose a string of words in Polish, but Misha only had a limited vocabulary in the language. Born and raised in Cardinal City, she had never visited the country her parents immigrated from.

"Tata," she said. "English."

A big, loud sigh came down the phone. "You have to come home and talk sense into new chef."

Noticing the teenagers edging closer, she stepped onto the train as its doors opened and took up a place near the door. "We talked about this. I can't keep coming home every time you have a problem. You need to start solving them on your own. Roksana is old enough to have a go. And what about Ciocia Violeta. She's there every day." Her aunt was the feminine influence in her life after her mother passed away, and while Misha attributed much of her laid back attitude to the woman, Ciocia wasn't good with conflict. Roksana was a bit flighty, but despite her youthful face, she was twenty-one and certainly old enough to handle her own battles.

"That's why we hired the new chef, so you no' need to come in all the time."

She was sensing a but.

"But," her father continued. "He is impossible. Doesn't listen to us. We try and try and *try* to explain how to make the kopitka, but he make something fancy and customer no' coming and you have to tell him." A shuffling sound came over the phone as her father must have moved for privacy. When he spoke next, his voice was low and surreptitious. "He make gnocchi, Mishka. Not kopitka. He make Italian food in Polish restaurant."

"Well, that's because they're the same."

He gasped. "You know that's not true!"

It was. "So just tell him it has to be made the way you like or you fire him."

"You no' seen this man. Nobody tells him what to do. He is dangerous, and big like a house."

The vision Misha conjured in her mind was riveting. A giant, dangerous chef? Sign her up for that adventure. Sensing her father needed to rant some more, she let him ramble on. The conversation went round in circles for the short ride to her next place of employment. As she listened to her father, knowing the vent was good for his blood pressure, she idly glanced around the cabin and caught sight of the horny teenagers still watching her, conspiring amongst themselves. Did they follow her, or were they going the same way? Whatever the case, they certainly had their eyes on her.

"Tata," she said. "I have to go."

"You have more yoga classes today?"

Her heart squeezed at her lie. "Yes. I'm very busy tonight, but I can come and see you in the morning. I'll have a chat with your impossible chef and help him see sense."

After a grunt of thanks—which was also unheard of—her father cut the call.

Misha stared at her blank cell as the doors opened. He *never* said thanks. Filip Minksi was a proud man who had suffered from debilitating arthritis most of his adult life. He'd once blurted out in a fit of despair, that the condition made him feel like a burden, so he powered through what he could on his own. This chef must really be escalating things.

Well aware of the trio following her like lost puppies, Misha headed down the short street to where The Kremlin nightclub prepared to open. A few yards from the entrance, where the surly Russian bodyguard manned the door, she quickened her stride and smiled brightly as he ran a big hand over his shaved head. The six-foot-five man had trouble fitting through the doorway with his massive shoulder span, but Yuri was a softy at heart. She'd had nothing but quiet, kind words from him, and he kept the worst of the rabble out with an iron fist.

"I brought a few puppies, Yuri." She slapped his rock hard pec with the back of her hand. "Should we teach them a few tricks?"

He looked down at her with a frown. "They causing you trouble, *lapochka?*"

"Oh, Yuri." She felt her eyes soften. "When you call me sweetheart, I almost think you've changed your mind about you and me."

His brown eyes darkened with unmistakable desire. "No, *lapochka.* When you change *your* mind about more than one night, then I am yours." He raised his brow in question.

"Sorry, big guy. You know I'm all about spreading my wings." She would not be caged.

Not an escort like some other girls in the club, she treated her body like a temple, but she wasn't exactly stingy with her sexual conquests. Pleasure was a gift from the goddess, and she took her happiness wherever and whenever she could, especially when so much of her life at the moment was the opposite.

Although Yuri shrugged, disappointment burned in his eyes before he went back to standing like a soldier, eyeing the boys whose bravado faded fast. "You want me to turn their puny puppy bodies into sausage?"

Misha pivoted and winked at the group. "What do you think boys? Will Yuri turn you into sausages, or will you come back as paying customers to see the show a little later?"

Each boy blushed from head to toe, and the tallest one gave a salute before saying. "Um. We'll come back and pay."

"Yeah, no worries. We'll pay," said the second, and all three walked away.

Yuri grunted. "One of these days, *lapochka*, you will not have me around to keep you safe."

"One of these days, Yuri, I will not be around to keep you entertained." And the little life left in his eyes would turn dull and dead like the rest of Dimitri's soldiers. She gave him a soulful glance and then sidestepped to go inside.

Sweet stale beer. Old cigarette smoke. She wrinkled her nose and walked down the dark hallway leading to the main club area. Establishments like these never had windows, designed to trap you inside without any idea what time of day it was. All the better to con you out of money.

She traveled through the maze to the small backstage dressing room. Lockers were to the right of the door. Racks overflowing with stripper costumes were in front, and on the side walls were mirrors and dressing tables littered with makeup and supplies. She dumped her yoga bag in her locker.

"Namaste, girls," Misha said brightly as she slid onto a stool in front of a mirror with bulbs glowing softly around it. Sweet mother of the sky, her curls were energetic today. Blond frizziness abound.

"Angel," Anastasia greeted Misha using her stage name. Anastasia was a brunette in her early thirties. A skinny smoker with fake breasts and old eyes behind her blue eyeshadow. "How can you be so chirpy this early in the day?"

"Babe," Chyna said to the right as she tugged on her skimpy Cat Woman leotard. The girl looked to be in her teens and it broke Misha's heart every day to see her in there. Catsuit on, she stuck an afro comb in her black hair and began teasing. "Angel just said *afternoon*. How can you think it's early?"

Anastasia huffed and went back to putting on her eyeliner.

Two more girls graced the dressing room: Katarina and Dominika, the twins. Both red-headed Russians hardly spoke a word of English. They stuck to themselves and performed a burlesque duet wearing a soviet furry outfit that ended as a tiny fur bikini—and then nothing.

Misha strolled over to the roster by the costume rack. She was on second and last and had to waitress in between. Yuck… also scheduled to the east section where the Nazi sat. Dimitri put her there more often these days. The Nazi came in a few times a week and treated anyone not blond and blue-eyed like the jam between his slimy toes. Of course, as the only blond, blue-eyed girl, Misha got the full force of his brutal attention. She couldn't tell how many times she'd had to give the man a lap dance, and how many times the bouncer had to stop him touching her with his greasy fingers—he also sucked at tipping—but was never kicked out. Whatever connection he had with Dimitri kept him safe.

Unease bloomed in her stomach. The Nazi's attention had become insistent over the past few weeks. He'd asked multiple times for a private topless lap dance and even tried to entice her out back for a full service demonstration. Thankfully, the full service wasn't in her Dimitri-approved catalog of expertize, so when she declined, the bouncers backed her up.

"Now, who will I be today…" she murmured to herself as she

scrolled through the clothes rack. Cowgirl, Wonder Woman, French Maid, Fallen Angel… a pang of anxiety wound tight in her chest when she realized it probably wouldn't matter. Dimitri might send word of the outfit he expected her to wear. Collecting herself, she took a few deep breaths. In—*future*. Out—*past*. From the way the girls dragged their feet, she wasn't the only one in need of a pick me up. It was time for their pre-show ritual. Misha spun to face the room and clapped her hands. "Girls, who am I today?"

They put down their tools and swung on their stools to face her. A zip of excitement ran up Misha's spine. This was the part she loved. She plonked her hands on her hips, embodied the character she envisioned, and flamboyantly flourished her hand and tossed her hair. Deliberately obtuse with her actions, she wanted the girls to work for the answer. More flourishes, more shimmies.

"You are the circus person, *da*?" Katarina placed her chin on her knee, a slow red-lipped grin lifting her cheeks.

"*Nyet*." Dominika thwacked her sister with a fluffy Russian hat. "Look at the way she moves hand in front of the breasts. Is too much action for circus lady."

"Ooh. Ooh." Chyna jumped from her stool and stuck her hand in the air. "You're one of those old Flapper girls."

Anastasia stood and waved Chyna down. "Sit down before you hurt yourself, love. She's obviously a clown."

A clown? Eyes widened around the room. They paused. Then burst out laughing. Who would have thought of a clown in a strip club? With tears running from the corners of her eyes, Misha scooped up a feathered fan and fluttered it in front of her. "I'm a Brazilian Samba Dancer. See?" She shimmied her shoulders for effect.

Katarina's deep red eyebrow arched. "You expect us to guess that! Pah. You dreaming, girl."

A loud knock on the dressing room door had them all jolting

with surprise. The door opened to Petyr, one of the bouncers. He stroked his furry mustache, dark eyes roaming the room. "Angel. Boss wants to see you."

"Like, actually see me?" Shock washed through Misha while the girls looked her way with sympathy. Nobody came back from seeing the boss without big news. The last time Dimitri saw her in person was two months ago when he'd casually apprised her that the terms of their agreement had changed. She was no longer just a waitress at the club. She was a dancer, and if she wanted her family protection to remain, she wouldn't complain.

That knot of anxiety in her chest came back.

three

MISHA MINSKI

TWO MINUTES LATER, Misha trailed Petyr into the cold dungeon—the basement level—and shivered. She hated going down there because she had to pass all the private rooms that nobody was supposed to know about: the illegal gambling rooms, the sex rooms, the… she wasn't even sure what was in some of them from the sounds that came through the doors. She could have sworn she heard a goat bleat one night. Ew. There were money-counting rooms, storage rooms, and perhaps drug-sorting rooms, but she had the suspicion most of that was done off site. Either way, it was none of her business.

She was there to pay her debt and keep her family safe.

Petyr knocked on the door with a gold plaque that said *Boss*. When they entered, he left Misha and closed the door behind, locking her inside with the Russian mobster who had once been her high school friend.

She gasped, heart leaping into her throat at the sight of Dimitri pummeling a stranger in the guest chair. Seeing her enter, he held out his finger, then resumed his beating. Trying not to show fear—she should know better by now—she avoided the blood bath in front of

26

her and stood to the side. *Stiffen your spine, pretend you're a proper lady.* A Duchess wouldn't be afraid. She'd cast her aloof gaze over the rest of the room, anywhere but at the grizzly, uncouth sight. The gold caught her attention first. From the set of gold-knuckles on display on his desk, to the trimming on the enormous Anaconda tank filling the wall behind Dimitri's desk, to the gold-winking gun strapped under his arm holster. It was all designed to intimidate, whether you were a business man, one of his lackeys, or someone like her.

Misha winced as she heard a bone crunch and forced her eyes somewhere else: the snake behind his desk. Wrapped around a massive tree limb, the beastie stared back with hungry eyes. Rumor had it Dimitri fed the snake bodies of his enemies. Seeing the size of the tank, the jaw, and the man slumped and groaning in the chair, Misha believed it.

Dimitri was a full head shorter than Misha and had the body of a jockey, but what he lacked in size, he made up in psychopathy. He plucked a napkin from his vest pocket and wiped his red stained hands. "Apologies you had to see that, Misha, but it is what it is."

"And what is it, Dimitri?"

He gave her a solid look. Misha knew that look. Often she'd seen it just before a person was turned into a squealing pulp of a mess like the man wriggling on the chair, struggling to hold on. It was a flat look, empty. It was a look that hid a brain firing at a thousand miles per hour, trying to work out if she was still the friend worried about his day, like she was in high school, or if he had successfully moved himself into the feared category. Definitely the second, but she would never tell him that.

"It's what happens when people don't do as they're told," he eventually said.

"Message received, loud and clear."

"Has it, Misha? Has it been received? Because people are talking."

He stepped over the bloody body to get back to his desk. He unclipped his golden gun and placed it inside a drawer. "They are saying I let you get away with too much." He retrieved a fresh handkerchief from the same drawer and wiped the splattered blood from his boyish face. "They say I am getting soft."

Her blood turned to stone.

"Do you think I am getting soft, Misha?" he asked as he wiped, spreading the cloth around his jaw.

"No, Dimitri, I don't."

"So why do you allow your family to hire a man to protect them? From me."

What? Hire a man? For a moment, guilt pricked her heart, and she felt terrible for neglecting her family over the past few weeks, but... she'd needed a break, damn it. "I-uh... I didn't know."

He stared at her again with those busy empty eyes, and then he poured Scotch into two glasses with an elaborate sigh. "Misha, it's good to see you. Please sit."

"Yes, it has been a few weeks."

When she didn't move to climb over the moaning man, he gave a pointed look at the vacant chair next to the grotesquely filled one.

"Um." The man was really injured. Oh God, maybe he was going to end up snake food. "Shouldn't someone..."

Dimitri pressed a button on his desktop intercom. "Please remove Mr. Douglas. I am done with him for now."

Two-seconds later, the door opened to Petyr's stern face. He flicked a glance at Misha, then dragged Mr. Douglas out. His body had gone floppy.

Misha sat down on the maroon leather chair with wooden handles and tried not to wince at the cold seeping through her yoga pants. Was it just the temperature, or was it blood?

When Dimitri leaned back in his chair, eyes like two beads of black coal, she knew she wouldn't like what happened next. He liked to play games, to make her do weird things, just because he could. She'd learned a long time ago, that it was safest to just do as she was told.

He sucked his teeth, eyes narrowed. "You will wear the devil outfit tonight, I think. It is appropriate, no?"

She nodded briefly and kept her eyes downcast. When he said nothing else, she lifted her gaze. He'd turned on the two CCTV monitors on his desk and occupied himself with the footage of his club opening. He removed a ledger book from his second drawer and opened it. Occasionally he would flick his eyes to the screens, and then back to the book, no doubt sizing up who owed him what. It was a few minutes before he spoke again.

"You have not had a drink, Misha. It is rude."

She eyed the glass. Okay. It was this game. The "Puppet" game. Wear what I tell you, drink what I tell you, do what I tell you... A trickle of fear lifted into her gullet and she pushed it down with a sip of Scotch. Then she put the glass down. *There. You got what you wanted.*

His eyes flashed with pleasure and then went back to his screens. "You say you knew nothing of the man your parents hired. When was the last time you spoke with your family?"

"Um." Her mouth went dry as she lied. "It's been a few weeks."

"You know this man put two of my men in the hospital."

"No. I didn't know."

Dimitri steepled his fingers as he studied her. "This man is working in your family restaurant, and he refuses to pay us protection money."

Could he be speaking about the chef? Had her father found a solution to their "protection" problem without consulting her? She guessed she shouldn't really be surprised. He knew nothing of her arrangement with Dimitri, and that's the way she wanted to keep it. Her family were innocent to the dark reality of this world.

"I'm sorry, this is the first I'm hearing of it."

"I want to believe you, Misha, but I know how close you are with your family. Tell me how you do not know about this new development?"

"I've been living in my city apartment and focusing on—" she wanted to say yoga, but somehow, letting him know about that part of her life meant the last vestige of her identity would belong to him. "Here. I've been working here and they know nothing about it."

Thump!

Misha jumped as he slammed his hand on the desk, rattling the gold-plated brass knuckles and Scotch glasses.

"Friends do not lie to each other."

"I swear, I knew nothing!"

"Well, you see, we now have a problem. I have hospital bills to cover, and you are already behind in your payments. I look weak. Soft. I am not a soft man."

She bit her lip, knowing she'd regret the next words. "Perhaps your protection services are no longer required."

Although hope flared momentarily, it was stamped down by the simple flicker of darkness in Dimitri's eyes.

"*Nyet*, Misha. We have been keeping our end of the bargain. There is no trouble at your restaurant when you make payment. But even your job here cannot keep up with the new debt."

"I don't know what else to tell you. I'm giving you everything I earn. I—" a lump formed in her throat. She needed her yoga studio. She would not give it up. It paid for the rent on her city apartment and it kept her sane. She finally had a life outside her family duties. Giving that up would be like giving away her identity.

"Now, Misha, don't be sad." Dimitri's eyes dulled, but still, she had the sense it was all an act—better than the one she put on stage every night.

She felt like she was drowning. This was never going to end. He'd always find something else to hold over her. It was hard to believe she ever thought he was a friend. Once he saved her a spot in the cafeteria line, now he extorted money from her. What had happened?

"Perhaps we can make another arrangement," he said.

Bile rose in the back of her throat. She knew what he was going to say.

He sat back in his chair, never taking his eyes from her. "You will increase your services at the club. There are customers who ask for you, but because of my trust in our arrangement, in our friendship, I have kept them away from you. This can no longer continue. It is well known how you like to play around with all the men in your own time, why not make it official and earn your keep?"

Revulsion burned in her throat. He thought she was a whore. A man stays strategically single, dates a lot, and he's called a legend. A woman? Totally unfair.

As if she'd been dismissed, he went back to inspecting the ledger book. "I will give you until the end of your shift to think about it."

What the hell was her other option?

As if hearing her thoughts he glanced up and added, "If you decide not to expand your services, then you will need to pay your debt."

"How much are we talking?"

He turned the book and pointed at a figure scrawled in blue ink.

Her heart stopped beating. *Forty-five thousand dollars.*

She couldn't afford that. So, it was either sell her body or… she glanced at his snake flicking its forked tongue and then back at Dimitri's straight face.

"You know I always look out for you, like a *siostra*. Since school I have had your back because you had mine."

Misha wanted to laugh in his face. His protection was more like obsession. Having a thick accent and being a little scrawny back then, he hadn't been a popular kid. Plus, his know-it-all attitude and weird affinity with snakes and crawly things hadn't done him much good. When no one sat with him, or spoke with him, Misha would always make the time to be nice. She felt sorry for him. He wasn't quite right in the head, but when her father's restaurant had first been attacked a few years ago, and Dimitri came around saying he could stop it— she'd felt it was her only option. At first he only expected a free meal or two, but then the attacks on the restaurant escalated, and he wanted more money. Working at his bar was the start, then the dancing, now… it would never end.

She plastered on the smile she wore every night on stage.

"End of shift, Misha," he reminded her. "I will have your answer. And don't forget"—he met her gaze—"devil."

A curt nod, and then she was out of there. On her way back to the dressing room, she swiped a bottle of vodka from behind the bar and took a few deep swigs. Tonight, she was going to be the very embodiment of her devil costume. Tonight she was going to be someone else. It was the only way to keep smiling.

four

WYATT LAZARUS

IT WAS pitch black when Wyatt woke in his borrowed bed. His lids snapped open as he lay there, all senses straining because something was off. The wind knocked the windows from the outside. He pushed his sixth sense out to feel for the sin of wrath, but his sin wasn't like envy or greed—wrath mainly reared its ugly head when shit got real. He sensed nothing but the breeze, his heartbeat, and his ragged breath.

Then he registered the temperature. Hot, but it wasn't a hot night. It was *he* who felt sweaty. Feverish. His skin prickled and warmed as though he'd come down with the flu. Maybe that was why he woke… but he never got sick. None of his siblings did. They were born with resilient immune systems and regenerating cells that healed exponentially, making recovery time short.

So why was he awake?

He held his breath, slowed his heart and listened.

Seconds ticked by.

Then a woman's moan hit his ears and everything went on red alert.

What the actual fuck?

A shuffle. Something dropped.

"Where's the goddamn light?" she hissed through the dark.

Wyatt tensed. Either he was having a weird dream, or there was a woman in the room with him. Two thunks reverberated on the cheap floating floorboards. Boots? Sliding and scuffling followed. Why would a female be searching his room, and—another soft thud as something fell to the floor—*Christ*, she was getting undressed!

Who would be getting undressed? Must be the daughter who used to live there. *There* being the semi-detached apartment above their suburban home garage. It was only one room, a bathroom and a tiny kitchenette. One bed. Sliding doors opened onto the garage roof that doubled as a balcony with external steps leading down to ground level.

It had to be her. What was her name, again?

Movement as his bed dipped and another moan, as though she wasn't feeling too good.

He swallowed, mouth dry.

"Ahh," she sighed, landing ungracefully, face first onto the pillow beside him, sending a waft of feminine perfume and alcohol into his lungs. "Home at last."

She's drunk.

Her hand arced out, perhaps to stroke the sheet beside her, but hit his ribs instead. She patted around to test the odd shape her bed had taken. Her soft palm hit his face, his hair... down his naked chest. Wyatt winced and froze, holding his breath as if it would turn him invisible.

What should he say? He couldn't say anything! He couldn't speak. She was going to freak.

But she didn't. She made an appreciative sound while her hand headed south, bumping low over the ridges of his abdomen, slick with sweat.

An electric shock sparked between them and they both jackknifed up.

Fifteen years of martial arts and combat training had him springing to land deftly on his feet, while she stumbled and grabbed her head with a pained groan.

"Stop spinning, room," she muttered.

He turned his side-lamp on but, when his thumb went to depress the switch, he pushed right through it. The damned thing crumbled in his hand like a cookie. *Shit.*

She switched her lamp on and the room illuminated.

Wyatt lost all train of thought as his eyes locked onto her body—pure, lush feminine curves, toned in all the right places—naked except for a dark crop-top and panties. It was the kind of body men would give their left nut to see in the flesh. Blond hair stuck up in a disarray of curls around her head. Wide blue eyes blinked but, where he expected fear, he found desire burning back at him.

Aw, hell no.

He scrambled back, hands out, and shook his head. He wanted none of this. No fucking way. He didn't care how cute she looked, or how many of his atoms were clambering to touch and taste her like— he shook his head to dispel his derailing thoughts. What the hell was wrong with him? *No.*

"I like this dream," she purred and seductively crawled over the mattress toward him.

He refused to speak, and she made a girly growl of appreciation that shot straight to his groin like an aphrodisiac. He thickened immediately, and she noticed. She licked her lips, eyeing him at the crotch. When he didn't move, she glanced up, confused. "You're so quiet... like a *koteczek*. Come to Misksha..." She couldn't say that last word properly and repeated it a few times, then she broke out laughing. "Miscop. Mishko. Mizzzz." She giggled again. "I'll get it right at some point. *Koteczek,* come to Misha."

She tripped over her knees, collapsed and rolled off the bed, calling out for her *koteczek* to come out and play. He didn't know what the fuck she rambled about, only that he'd better take control of the situation. The last thing he needed was for her father to think he took advantage of her, especially when they were already disagreeing about most other things.

He should kick her drunk ass out. Surely there was room for her at the main house. It would teach her a lesson for turning up unannounced. But Vooyek would be pissed. He was a good man. Alek was a good kid. In fact, the entire family was decent, even that chatty older sister. He shouldn't give a shit about the way they ran the restaurant. He should just fix Betty and get the hell out of there, but he couldn't help inserting his expertize, especially when it came to meal prep. For Christ's sake, they used instant potato in their kopitka. There was no way in hell, he'd serve that in his restaurant. He'd skin any chef alive if they tried that shit with him. *Seriously, fucking Betty Crocker instant potatoes.* If it was his—

It's not your restaurant, an insidious voice clipped from the back of his mind. *You're only there to earn enough dough to fix Betty, and then you're out.*

He growled at himself.

"Ooh *koteczek* has a growl." Still on the floor, she rolled to her knees then rested her head on the mattress, as if it was too heavy to keep upright. She muffled half-heartedly into the bed: "Like a tiger. Rwoarr!"

When she quieted, and her breathing evened, Wyatt gently helped her back onto the bed and settled her on pillows where she promptly tunneled into, moaning about the delicious smell he'd left behind. When he put the blanket over her, she kicked it off until she was bare. He tried one more time, but after she dislodged the blanket again, he left it and went to stand on the other side of the room until he figured out what the hell he was going to do.

But instead, all he could do was watch her, mesmerized. He stood there for minutes, perhaps hours with the awareness of her presence tingling down his skin. As he stared, conflicting emotions encircled him. Eerily at peace but incredibly aroused at the same time. Every inch of skin felt hot and clammy to touch, not to mention the fucking shame boner that wouldn't go away. This was wrong.

Light from the lamp made her skin sparkle with glitter. Curious woman. With her every breath, new parts of her body came to his attention. Delicate collarbone. Firm thighs and calves. Breasts swelling over her barely there top. She had the kind of body you worked for. Not muscular, but trim, taut and voluptuous at the same time. This woman wasn't a slacker, by any means. She worked hard, and from the sound of her drunken talk earlier, she played hard. The thought sent an unruly thrill through him, shattering the calm, and with each passing second, his heart rate picked up, his breathing escalated. He was stuck—enraptured.

Traitorous fingers twitched to touch her. When he held his palms in front of his face, the sight of his Yin-Yang tattoo on his left inner wrist had the wild beating of his heart stumbling to a halt. He blinked and rubbed his eyes. He rubbed his thumb over the ink, but it was still there, equal parts black and white for the first time in years. Completely in balance.

Bullshit. Fucking bullshit.

It was a coincidence, nothing more.

But the room began to spin as the truth punched him hard. Why else would he feel feverish? Sweat still prickled his scalp, and he itched all over. It was a biological response. There was only one reason for this… she was his mate.

No.

Sara had been.

The fiancée who'd betrayed him, not this drunken woman in his bed. But the tattoo was never perfectly balanced with Sara. It was close, but not perfect.

All the anger and self-loathing he'd felt over the past few months came flooding to the surface, threatening to choke him. It filled his veins with napalm. It trembled through his muscles. It tightened his face until he tasted blood on his tongue.

This Misha wasn't his soulmate, the one who would bring inner harmony to his turmoil, because if she was, then he'd had no right to be angry at his brother. No right to run from his family. Every ounce of righteousness he'd thrown up as protection was unfounded.

No.

With an almighty roar of defiance, Wyatt stormed to the bed and tipped the mattress, rolling Misha effortlessly to the ground. She landed with a thud on the other side. Before she had a chance to rouse and respond, he threw open the door and left in only his boxer shorts, breaking into a barefoot run down the suburban street dusted with dawn. It wasn't until he was halfway down the road that he noticed the broken door knob crumbling in his hand.

five

MISHA MINSKI

WHEN THE ALARM sounded for Misha to wake up, she found herself lying on the floor next to her bed with drool dampening the blanket she used as a pillow.

"Wow," she mumbled through a cotton mouth. "Must have been drunker than I thought."

Yep. She could still smell the alcohol on her breath. Gross. But with the ultimatum Dimitri gave, she didn't blame herself. She'd snuck out after shift, avoiding answering him. Groaning, she wanted nothing more than to roll over and go back to sleep and that happy dream of that perfect specimen of a man, but she'd promised her father she'd see to the new chef, and she always kept her promises. She dragged herself up and went to the sliding door at the balcony. Pulling the glass door aside, she sucked in the fresh restorative morning air, let the coolness invigorate her, and completed her sun salutations.

Tilting her head toward the warmth of the sun, she greeted the morning and paid respect to Lakshmi—goddess of good fortune. No matter how bad her day was, or how bad her life was, she always knew that a moment in the sun was enough to make her remember how small she was in the grand scheme of things, and how little control she had over the world.

With each inhale she brought the future, and with each exhale, she banished the past. Soon the cloud from her brain ebbed, and she stretched all the kinks and toxins out of her body, well, almost. She still had a monster version of bad breath.

When she went into the bathroom, she noticed things. Suspicious things. Her clothes were strewn around from the night before—normal—but there were other things, man things. Men's shavers. Men's cologne. She took a whiff, eyes fluttering as the scent drove into her lungs. Sweet, woody and zesty. Goodness, it curled her toes. How did they make that stuff so delectable? The bedside lamp was broken, as was the door handle. A single pair of worn men's jeans and a black T-shirt hung in the closet.

Someone had been staying at her place.

It's not your place anymore. You moved to the city.

Right. Right. She had to get used to things changing if she was serious about separating herself from her family. The closer she was to them, the more likely they'd learn about her secret job.

Flashes of her arrival the previous night hit her behind the eyes. A man was in her bed with her—a chesty, half naked, total Adonis. Had that been real? For a moment, she considered, but then dismissed it. Probably pent up with unfulfilled sexual frustration. She hadn't had a one-night stand in weeks!

But the man things…

And all of her spare clothes were gone. Must have been shifted to the main house.

"Alrighty, then." Feeling more clear headed, Misha followed the smell of butter cooked mushrooms to the main house and entered through the rear porch. The old wooden door creaked and slammed after she entered the kitchen. Her grandparents sat at the round table playing cards. "Babcia. Dziadzio. Who's winning?"

"Who always wins." Her grandfather tipped his bifocals down to peer at her over the top. "Your babcia."

Completely ego free, Babcia licked her finger, and drew another card from the center pile. "Good answer."

"You want some mushrooms?" Ciocia asked from the old vintage stove. She wiped her forehead with the back of her hand.

"Sure, sounds good." Misha glanced around. "Tata here? Or Roka? I need to borrow clothes before heading in to see this infamous chef."

A squeal came from the hallway, followed by thudding footsteps down the wooden hallway. "About time you came."

Roksana entered the kitchen with Alek immediately after her. Both siblings began to speak profusely—Roka with her voice, Alek with his hands.

"Whoa! Just let me get dressed and have something to eat first."

Roksana dragged her into the living room. "You sit there while I get you some clothes. Then we'll talk. Alek"—Roksana signed as she spoke to their brother—"you go and get the food."

What was going on? Suspicion coated her insides as she sat down in her father's old chair. But she had to admit, it was nice receiving attention. She leaned back, eyes running around the room. Two sofas faced a small television on an Elm coffee table in the corner. Tassels dangled from the fabric light-shade hanging from the center of the ceiling. So many memories in that room. Glancing at the doorway that led to the bedrooms, Misha could picture the ghost of herself, standing there when she had been a young girl. Toddler on one hip, a bottle in her hand, Roksana crying for her mama from her room. Her father had been sitting in the same chair Misha now sat in, his gnarled hands slipping on a vodka glass as he sobbed to himself. *"I was good to her. Not like other man. Why she leave me..."*

"Misha!"

"Yeah?" She jolted out of the past. Roksana had been saying something. Alek walked up from behind with a plate of food.

"Here are your clothes." Her sister shoved jeans and a tank in her hands. "And, like I was saying about the chef, you need to be prepared before you head in."

Thirty minutes later, Misha had come to the conclusion that: One, this chef was an extremely grumpy man who spent all their money on luxury food items, and played loud angry music (her father's complaints); Two, he never spoke—had something wrong with his voice—but was a badass who could cook the shit out of Bigos and Gołąbki (Alek's input); Three, he had something to hide. His energy was dark, and he never told them his name so they all referred to him as *chef* (Ciocia Violetta); Oh, and four, he was a babe (Roksana's input of course).

Armed and prepared with information, she was on her way to the restaurant in her father's borrowed car shortly after. He would follow with Ciocia which would give her a few minutes to speak with the new chef alone.

Steam still billowed from the sewer grates as she pulled the car into the lot of the food center. A thumping bass vibrated through the walls as she approached the back entrance. When she opened the heavy steel door and pushed inside the kitchen, the hard-rock riffs almost blew her eardrums away. Wow. Tata wasn't kidding when he said the chef liked to listen to loud music.

Frosted light filtered through the high windows to garnish the stainless steel appliances with ambience. It softened the hard edges of the tiny room. Fresh groceries and supplies were half-sorted on the bench that divided the room. On one side were the ovens, on the other, the cool room and larder. Down the end of the room were the sinks and dishwashers. But no chef.

Her father had told her the chef's motorcycle was broken, and he usually walked the few blocks to the restaurant, so she wondered how he'd managed to get to and from the markets with the groceries. And where had he been if not at her little room over the garage? When did he get time to change into his uniform? Maybe he stayed with a girl-friend, or maybe he caught a cab. Catching a cab to the farmer's market was dedication. Most other chefs had just turned up to do their job, and that was it. Some of them rarely did that! Dedication or not, the music was a little on the angry side, so she could see why it bothered her aunt and father. Roksana and Alek, on the other hand, didn't have a problem with it.

Pulling out her phone, she selected an upbeat song and synced via bluetooth to the internal system. She was feeling rather nostalgic today, always did when entering this place fraught with so many memories—good and bad.

Within seconds, the soft notes of a song from her childhood began to play.

Misha inhaled deeply and let the dill and vinegar scent infuse with her memories, taking her back to her childhood, playing in her grandparents' vegetable garden and greenhouse. She closed her eyes. The music dimmed until she virtually stood in her memory. White tiger moths and ladybirds flitted past the chamomile flowers. Her mother kneeled in the cucumber patch, snapping off the early shoots for pickling, handing her the too-large cucumbers to eat on the spot. She could almost taste the fresh flavor and feel the juice running down her chin.

A loud bang made her jump, and she opened her eyes. Two deep blue eyes glowered from beneath dark furrowed brows. A straight nose led down to lips twisted in an almost cruel snarl. Dark scruff that, perhaps, would have been shaved if he'd returned home that morning. His sharp jaw accentuated incredible cheekbones. Across the bench, wearing a black muscle shirt and a backwards ball cap was the man from her dreams.

"Wow. You're real," she exclaimed. He'd truly been in her bed last night, and she'd truly ran her fingers down his sexy front... wait... had he also truly upended her from the bed?

Ooh. *Game on.* Her lips curved as a devious response entered her mind. This was going to be fun. Her elevated mood only served to lower his. He collected his phone from the bench, pointed it toward the bluetooth speaker and re-synced, knocking her song from the playlist.

AC/DC came on with *Danger*. He turned his back on her and returned to unpacking his groceries as if she didn't exist.

"Open hostility." Her grin widened, practically buzzing with excitement. "You know"—she moved to stand in front of him—"I can speak in song too."

She pointed her phone at the speaker and synced. Taylor Swift's *Shake it Off* blasted on. She punch-danced around the bench, a dare in her eyes, loving every minute of it. Take that grumpy pants!

"Haters gonna hate." She winked, then cruised back around the bench and helped herself to an apple. She tucked it into her mouth and collected the remainder of the fruit into her arms, shaking her rump all the way to the cold room, pretending she didn't care what he did next, but inside, anticipation made her body sing like the song. *Please play with me, sexy koteczek.*

When another hardcore AC/DC beat came on, she almost dropped her apple in delight. He was playing! She finished packing away the items in her hands, and then went to lean her hip on the doorjamb, chewing her apple, eying him with the awareness of a battle opponent. He could be a warrior with that physique. Hard muscles bulged in his arms and rolled in his back as he shifted a heavy fish out of his basket. Nah, he was probably a softy at heart, like Yuri.

The chef knew she watched, but acted as though he didn't.

And when the throaty lead singer sang the title of his song, she laughed: *If you want blood, you've got it.*

"Well played, good sir, well played." Maybe he wasn't so uptight, after all. Or… maybe he was. For some reason, that made her even more excited. Excited and hot. She fanned her face and considered continuing the game, but decided watching him was more interesting. They were running out of time before the rest of the family turned up. She waited patiently until the song ended and then turned the music off completely.

He was in the middle of filleting the fish with an extremely sharp knife. Blood ran down his long, capable fingers. Obviously she'd picked the best time to shut the music down. He met her eyes with a steely gaze.

"I'm Misha," she said, all playfulness gone. "Your boss's daughter."

In response, he pulled entrails out of the fish and slopped them into a waiting container.

She almost gagged. Gross.

"Tata asked that I go over a few ground rules with you regarding the menu."

More entrails slopped.

"You're causing quite the stir in the kitchen, and some customers aren't happy with your menu changes."

He stopped completely, made a cocky eyebrow arch and disparaging shake of his head. She could almost hear his thoughts, *Nobody dares to be unhappy with my menu… I do what I want.* In her thoughts he also sounded like a young Sean Connery.

But customers were complaining, and they were leaving. Their traditional, home-style Polish comfort food was becoming too upmarket... too posh, and the patrons were preferring to cook at home. She sighed and bit her lip, wondering how to approach this. She'd underestimated how difficult it would be to speak with someone who couldn't speak back. At least with Alek, he could hand-sign.

"Can you use sign-language?" she asked. "I feel like there's only one side to this conversation."

He went back to his task.

"Guess that's a no?"

She'd just have to show him by, well, showing him. Misha spotted the unopened packets of instant potato under the bench. To get there, she'd have to squeeze by him in the space barely wide enough for one person. Uncertain, her gaze landed on him again, but he completely ignored her. Should she squeeze past him, or take the long way around?

Biting the bullet, she headed toward the gap between him and the stove. Somehow, he predicted her intention and used his body to block her, slamming his fish-gut hand on the bench to cage her in. Suddenly she had a face full of pec muscles twitching in irritation. When she looked up, all she could see was the raw, angry scar running across his neck from ear to ear. *Savage.* One thing was for sure, he certainly wasn't your normal chef. With that powerful physique and dangerous glint in his eyes, he was something else entirely.

Her mind urged her to caution. What if he was like Dimitri?

He lifted his hands to push her away from the instant potatoes, but caught sight of the blood on his fingers, as though he'd forgotten. He huffed and went to the wet area to wash. Misha took the opportunity to collect the big bag of instant potato and made room for herself on the far end of the bench to roll out dough.

"So," she said, collecting the flour. "I'm just going to make the kopitka the way the family likes it made, then you can take a few pointers and—what? Why are you looking at me like that? Do I have something in my teeth?"

He'd come to stand next to her, incredulous hands on hips.

She rubbed her teeth with a finger.

Nope. All clean.

So why was he, oh dear... *he's coming at me like a Mac truck.* Misha tensed.

The chef grabbed the instant potato, perhaps intending to throw them out, but Misha still latched onto the plastic packet. Suddenly they were in a tug of war. He gave a flick of his wrist—that was all it took—and his powerful grip ripped the packet in two, spraying white powder-like flakes all over the countertop, down his front, down her front, onto the floor... everywhere.

Surprise plastered his handsome face.

She blinked as flakes landed on her lashes and then laughed. "And here I was thinking we were done with the snow months ago."

A frustrated sound ripped from him and he thumped the stainless bench, hard. A fist-sized dent caved the metal surface. *Whoa.* For a minute, she froze. That dent was unnaturally big. Strong. He was strong. She should be scared, but... somehow she wasn't. He wasn't Dimitri. The chef had felt embarrassed over touching her with bloody hands whereas Dimitri reveled in it.

"Wow," she breathed. "What have you been eating for breakfast?" That was one decent dent. She rubbed her hand over it. Her father won't be happy.

A choked sound came from the chef and when she looked up to catch his eyes, something vulnerable and raw stared back at her. He breathed hard, nostrils flaring, chest lifting. It looked as though he was doing everything in his power not to lose his shit.

Just as she opened her mouth to speak, he shoved the impossibly heavy kitchen bench out of the way and made a break for the exit.

That was so not normal. The bench had needed five men to install, and he swatted it out of the way like a pesky insect.

"Wait." She ran after him. "Chef."

WHEN MISHA BROKE through the back door and into the waste area, it was empty. She walked around to the front lot and found him leaning against the restaurant wall, hands on his knees, breathing in deep gasps. He caught sight of her and straightened, running a hand over his head, pulling his cap off to reveal jet black hair.

"It's okay," she said, walking slowly. Instinct told her to treat him like a wounded wild animal. *Caution*. "Whatever that was, I'm not going to tell anyone. You can trust me."

Maybe *that* was why he worked there anonymously. It was clear he came from a fancy restaurant. The way he'd filleted that fish with dexterity was not a skill learned in a prison café. He'd moved about the kitchen with complete confidence, as though he'd been in charge of one once. This man had secrets.

He tracked her movement as she approached. It was hard not to be intimidated by him. Biceps bulged, jaw flexed, eyes pierced. The man was two-hundred and something pounds of cut, lethal muscle. Alek had told her what he did to Dimitri's men. Alek had also acted

49

out the violent act with vigor, like a hero-struck teenager, punching the air and pretending it was his opponent.

"What's your name?" she asked, but the chef stayed tight lipped. "Don't want to tell me?"

He shook his head.

"Are you running from the police?"

Another shake.

"But you are running from someone." She stepped closer. Almost there. A yard away. A glance down at the old wound on his neck and he flinched. There was something about the way he got nervous when she looked at it, something more than usual.

"You running from the person who did that?" she blurted, pointing.

His gaze zipped to her so fast that she knew she was on the right track. Wow. The dude had baggage. Who was she to judge someone on their past? Actions were what counted.

Standing there, staring at each other, she didn't know what to do but try to lighten the mood. "Hey. Turn that frown upside down."

That earned her an eye roll. She smiled and shuffled closer. Within touching distance, now.

"No use crying over spilled potato flakes, right?" She tried for another laugh.

He deadpanned, but his eyes began to dance.

"Are there any clichés that will make you laugh?" she asked. "How about I use my posh accent? That always diffuses a tough situation. *Yes, dah-ling. What say we forget about all this nonsense and head inside for a cup of tea?*"

A horrified expression came over his face.

"Am I really that bad?"

This time, his lip twitched.

Damn him, he was doing this on purpose, trying *not* to smile.

Drawn to him like a devil to a flame, she stepped closer, into his personal space. She needed to see that smile, wanted to obliterate the pain in his eyes, and to give him something else to look forward to. Before she could help herself, a sigh escaped her lips, and she touched his scruffy jaw. It was only meant to be a swipe, to remove the caught potato flakes, but the instant she made contact, the heat of his skin seared her nerves, catching fire down her arm.

All at once she was consumed with him, his scent—woody and citrus—his heat, his rugged exterior. He must have felt the same charge between them because he leaned into her hand, now cupping his face, and released a jagged breath. She knew then and there that this dark, mysterious man was going to be her next big mistake, her next one-night stand. A moment with him between the sheets would probably be the most passion she'd seen in her entire life. One night's memories would keep her fire fueled for years to come. The very idea had her heart hammering in her chest.

His lashes lowered, gaze stuck on her tongue flicking out to wet her lips.

She leaned in. He leaned in. Heat bounced between them. Dopamine hit her bloodstream. *Yes. Kiss me now.*

Suddenly, her back slammed against the wall. It all happened so fast. One minute, she was in front of him and he was against the wall. The next, he caged her in, darkness and frustration simmering in his eyes, accusing her. With his hips pinning her to the wall, his enormous hand wrapped around her throat, and eyes flaring with defiance as if to say, *Is this what you want?*

She should be afraid. She should be peeing her pants. But she wasn't. Regret flooded his blue eyes as they darted down to where he touched her. He let go. Eyes filled with something softer, almost yearning, flickered back to her face and he lifted his fingers, hesitated, then drew back.

He wanted her. He was trying *not* to want her, and that was... what was that? Some kind of warning? *Stay away, because I'll only hurt you...*

But he didn't. He'd pulled back with regret.

With the braveness of a deer staring into the eyes of a wolf, she pushed forward until her lips touched his, and he let her. He tasted better than he smelled. Human-made aphrodisiac ran down her tongue, tingling through her body and hitting her between the legs.

Fingers speared into her hair and pulled, exposing her neck to him. She gasped, feeling every bit the prey. For a second, she feared he would run away. Turmoil roiled in his every movement, every twitch of muscle, every stilted breath.

Misha never wanted anything more than another kiss from this man. It was almost primal. Almost irrational.

"This doesn't have to mean anything," she rasped. "It's not like we're getting married or anything. Just one—"

His mouth slammed onto hers, demanding entrance with his tongue. When she welcomed him, he dominated with an unquenchable thirst. Teeth clashed. Sparks of pain shattered her scalp, harsh pressure at her mouth. She whimpered, almost at her limits of pleasure and pain. Rough. Insistent. Desperate.

She liked it all.

It made her feel alive, wanted.

They were skirting the edge of pleasure, intoxicated with the taste of each other. Then just as quickly as they came together, he pulled them apart. He must have seen something in her face, perhaps in the way her lips had swollen. He looked in dismay as his finger came back from her mouth with a tiny red stain. Blood.

He paced away.

"It's fine," she called. "I'm fine. Just... maybe ease off a little next time."

The sound of car tires crunching snapped both their heads around.

A stone of dread landed in the pit of Misha's stomach as she recognized the vehicle and its occupants. Dimitri and his closest guards.

"Shit." She scrubbed her face. "Can you go back inside? I'll deal with this."

She didn't want to deal with it. She wanted to tell the chef he was the cause of her new problem, maybe make him pay for the mess he'd created... but it was hers in the first place. Dimitri was only interested because of her connection with him from high school. She had a responsibility to either fork up for the hospital fees, or pay with her body. A shudder ripped through her and the chef noticed.

Confusion flittered across his features.

"Look, seriously," Misha added. "I know what you did to the last men to collect payment from us, but it only caused more trouble. I'll deal with this. Please. It's better to give him what he wants." The desperation must have leaked through her tone, because he hesitated. "Please," she begged again and gave him a gentle nudge toward the kitchen door. "I've got this."

But she didn't want to, because there was only one reason Dimitri would be there this time of the morning. Probably a good thing they were interrupted, because very soon, Misha's life wasn't going to be her own.

seven

WYATT LAZARUS

WYATT STOOD inside the Pierogi Palace. With the kitchen door cracked open, he could see where Misha argued with a short dark-haired man wearing a suit.

Trust me, she'd said before she'd forced him back inside. He was thankful because the words were the wake-up call he needed to put things into perspective. He'd never trust another woman while he had breath left in his lungs. He would do well to remember that.

Kissing her was a mistake. He should never have allowed it to get that far. He'd only thought if he was a little rough, he'd scare her away. But when she'd said, *It's not like we're getting married*—and teased!—her words challenged him. They'd provoked some kind of arcane rebellion, an instinct to prove her wrong. To show her that it would be more with him. Much more.

Fucked. He was seriously fucked in the head. He knew that now, and there was nothing a bullshit tattoo or mystical fated mate could change about that.

He reminded himself to tread carefully. He knew nothing about her. Who would be attracted to someone as violent as him? *Sara.* A

54

liar who used him, blindsided him, and who made him believe there was more to him than his birthright.

He should have known better.

Shouting outside made him peek through the crack in the door, watching, assessing. The sense of wrath fluctuated, making his gut twinge. It wasn't Misha's, no... he further opened his awareness and checked. She was still frustratingly free from the sin. It was the short man who stood next to her. Pure, uncut and lethal. Wyatt had never felt wrath so potently before. The sin practically pumped life in the man's system. Ingrained in his blood so deep that Wyatt could only deduce the anger was long suffering... and aimed at Misha.

It piqued Wyatt's curiosity. He stayed put, wiping his wet hands on the towel he'd slung over his shoulder.

Wyatt studied the man harder. All over him, gold glittered in the morning sun. He wore more bling than a goddamn jewelry store. Tailored suit. Slicked hair. Short. Standing with an air of self-impor-tance, as if he thought the world should kiss his glossy boots. Who did he think he was, the fucking president?

Sounds behind Wyatt had him turning. The Minksi family made a commotion as they arrived in the dining room beyond the kitchen. Must have come through the front entrance. *Still afraid of me.*

He scanned the disarray in the room. The kitchen was a white powdered mess, and the fish entrails were still out.

Roksana glided in, saw the mess, did a one-eighty, pirouetting perfectly before heading back out. Probably to blab about the mess to her father. She was a ballerina with a personality similar to his youngest sister, Sloan. An irreverent chatterbox. A wave of melan-choly washed over him. He didn't know whether Sloan was still an obscene talker, or if she had finally caved to the whims of sloth. He missed her cheeky smile and impractical jokes—even when they were directed at him.

Alek poked his head into the kitchen and gave Wyatt a quick wave before ducking back out. Relief washed over him. Thank fuck it was Sunday, and the boy was in to provide a buffer between Vooyek and the demanding Polish women. Despite Alek's disability, he was easy to get along with—he even signed "*Yes, Chef*" when Wyatt gave him instructions. When the two of them were in the kitchen, it was peaceful… quiet, almost. No sounds except the chop of a knife, the stir of a pot, and the hiss of the frying pan.

Vooyek cooked on occasion, but his arthritis worsened as he aged, and he preferred to stick to the dining room with his sister and daughter, making nice with the patrons.

"What happened in here?" Roksana dared to enter the messy room again. She skirted the bench to where Wyatt stood. For some reason, she wasn't as afraid of him like her father and aunt were. Too young perhaps. Too naïve. Too prideful. That kind of self-worth only came from the irrefutable knowledge you were good at something. Better than most. She must be a good ballerina. In fact, Wyatt remembered her father arguing with her to get to rehearsal once or twice. At her age, she probably danced professionally.

Wyatt collected a broom, intending to clean, but Roksana stopped at the cracked open exit and stood frozen, staring through.

"What is *he* doing here?" she hissed, face paling as she checked her wrist watch. "It's not even nine on a Sunday. He usually sends his goons to collect payment."

Instincts honed over a lifetime perked up. *This was the man who ran the show?* The reason behind sending those Bratva henchmen? The reason Alek suffered a mild concussion. Anger speared him so suddenly, that he had to lean on the broom for support. He shouldn't care so much about this family, but it was becoming impossible to ignore their plight.

He should have accepted Vooyek's offer for free board instead of insisting he pay his way. If he had, he would have the money to cover the part he'd ordered for Betty, and be gone already.

Wyatt's gaze traveled to the exit. Why would Misha think she could deal with the Bratva on her own?

Trust me.

Maybe she was one of them.

He went to stand next to Roksana and watched through the crack. The speaking on Misha's part had ceased, and she was nodding sullenly, like a naughty child being schooled.

Roksana clicked her tongue. "That man, I swear."

Wyatt nudged her shoulder to get her attention, then pointed out the door. *What about him?*

"They went to school together," Roksana explained. "He was a weirdo she was nice to—because she felt sorry for him, mind you—which only served to make him obsessed with her. But it was never sexual, which was even weirder, you know? It's like the serial killer type obsessed. Doesn't make sense." Roksana's eyes flared dramatically at Wyatt. "And after we had the attacks on the restaurant, he shows up all psychopath in shining armor with his protection proposal, and it's not healthy, you know? And, like, he's got a short man complex. His eyes are black. They're like—*oof!*"

The door opened, shoving Roksana to the side, narrowly missing Wyatt. He stepped back to allow room for Misha to slot inside.

"What are you doing standing near the door?" Misha barked at Roksana. "Get inside. I don't want him to see you."

"What? He's seen me before. It's not like—"

"Get inside!" Misha pushed her sister further in and checked over her shoulder, but it was too late. The man caught sight of Roksana, gave her a pointed look, and then smiled his shark smile at Misha.

Even Wyatt caught the veiled threat, and the disgusting gold spark in his mouth.

Misha slammed the door. She closed her eyes and leaned against the solid surface, as though relieved to have something tangible between her and the man she left. A deep breath and she mumbled, "Inhale the future, exhale the past." When she opened her eyes, a smile grew but didn't reach her eyes. "Be a *dah*-ling, Roksana. Go start setting up the tables and earn your allowance. Money doesn't grow on trees, you know. Chop-chop."

"Jeez, fine." Roksana sulked and turned to leave, giving Wyatt an eye roll as she passed. "When Duchess Misha is out, you know she's pissed. Good luck."

Instead of turning on Wyatt, Misha took the broom from him and headed to the white mess on the floor, sweeping a pile, muttering in a posh English accent about the quality of the help these days.

What was wrong with this woman? Christ, he needed to get out of there, but he hated loose ends. He stalked up to her, frowned, and then vehemently pointed outside. *What the hell was that?*

She ignored him and continued to sweep, so he took the broom from her. It crushed into splinters in his hands. Two broom halves clattered to the ground, and the sound was deafening.

Aghast, he stared at his hand. Fine saw dust lay on his fingertips as though he'd ground the wood with his powerful grip. While he came to terms with this new, sudden power, the weight of Misha's stare burned into him. Panic welled and his vision turned dark at the edges. First the ceramic lamp had crushed beneath his touch—then he'd ripped the wooden doorknob clear off. The fist sized dent in the bench... Now this?

He'd threatened to crush her throat outside. The reality of it floored him, and she knew. She knew his strength, and yet she wasn't making a comment. Suspicion narrowed his eyes. Probably filing away the information to sell to the highest bidder. He tensed and then forced himself to relax.

"You know, meditation would probably help with that, darling," she said mildly and went to collect the dustpan and brush. "And, I get what you're trying to ask me, but I'm not responding on purpose. You don't need to know what went on out there. No offense, but it's none of your business, just like all that"—she waved at his hands—"is none of my business... unless..." A goofy smile curved up her face. She glanced over her shoulder to make sure no one else was in the room with them, then seductively leaned into him. "Tell you what, I hate calling you *Chef.* Tell me your real name, and maybe I'll tell you what happened out there. Deal?"

Infernal girl turned everything into a game. After everything he put her through outside, after seeing the violence he was capable of, she still teased him.

Once again, that arcane instinct rushed to the surface, wanting to prove her wrong. It was clear she didn't think he'd tell her his name, she already went back to sweeping. Already ignoring him.

He took the broken broom handle and whacked it near her hand, barely escaping her fingers. Her gaze shot to his, sparkling with life. He used his pointer finger to write a W in the spilled potato flakes on the counter top. She watched avidly, making cooing sounds of encouragement as the letter took shape, and as his finger moved to start the Y, he froze.

Why did he care what happened to her outside?

That man was a short-assed dick, but like she'd said, none of his business.

He swiped the W away. With all the self-control he could muster, he carefully retrieved the dustpan gently from her grip. It still felt like a forceful snatch, but at least he didn't break it. Continuing the sweeping, he only lasted a few seconds with the pressure of her watchful gaze on him, and then the dustpan broke.

His only conclusion was that it was her fault. Her presence did things to him, made his blood boil in frustration, in… lust.

Misha attempted to remove a towel from his chopping board, so he stabbed his knife, pinning the fabric to the surface. She'd squealed and jumped, but still no angry retort. The woman had the patience of a Zen master.

Alek walked in at that moment, as though he'd been watching at the door, waiting for an opening. He signed a greeting to Wyatt and continued to help with the meal prep.

Because he knew it would annoy Her Royal Duchess-Self, Wyatt spent the rest of the morning being obtuse.

If she addressed him as anything other than Chef, he ignored her. If she replied to his requests with "*Yes, Chef*" then he rewarded her with a few minutes of attention about the kopitka, but then went back to doing things his way. It annoyed the living daylights out of her, and he was pleased to see the Duchess re-emerged once or twice.

After lunch, Roksana came in and leaned on the kitchen bench with her elbows, head on her palms, watching Wyatt with a secretive smile.

"Ooh, is this a staring competition?" Misha joined her to stare at Wyatt. "You know I'll win."

It's only a competition if he played, and Wyatt ignored both of them. He considered stabbing something nearby, but managed to squash that urge and continued with cleanup. After a few minutes, Roksana said, "Someone is here to see you, *Chef*."

He looked up. *Bullshit.*

No one knew he was there.

But she had a dreamy look on her face. With each of her following words, Wyatt's tension worsened. "He's totally buff, like you. He's got all this cute, sexy messy hair. And—" She peeked at

Misha. "He's got tatts all over him. Totes badass. Maybe he's a biker dude or something. Maybe Chef was in a gang."

That persistent little—he bit the curse off, because he felt no anger toward Evan anymore. Only guilt and shame occupied that space. If it weren't for his little brother's persistence, Wyatt and their entire family would still have that Syndicate mole living in their house… in his fucking bed.

"Ooh." Misha turned to Roksana. "Do tell."

"He said he's Chef's brother."

"No shit!"

"He asked for Wyatt Lazarus. Said Wyatt's got black hair, an attitude, and thinks he's scarier than he really is. Sounds a lot like you, Chef… or should I say, Wyatt."

Wyatt shrugged and shook his head. *Just act like you don't know who it is. Eventually, they'll go away.*

Too late. Recognition plastered Misha's face. "You're right. They do look similar."

She raced out the front. Wyatt could hear her squeal of excitement filter back into the kitchen.

Wait. *They looked similar?* How the hell would she know? Did she know Evan?

Buried feelings rushed to the surface. Even after all these months, jealousy and denial still burned in his blood. He knew it was ridiculous. Evan had never had an affair with Sara. It had been all lies. So why was his gut churning with the same torn up emotions?

Wyatt tried to resist heading out into the restaurant, but his curiosity got the better of him. He dumped the rag, untied his apron, and went out.

eight

WYATT LAZARUS

DECORATED with red walls and elm hardwood trim, the dining room stretched long and narrow through the small commercial block. White table cloths, more wood paneling on the walls, brown leather sofas near the rear. Simple orange flower arrangements scattered everywhere. The smell of cedar and spice permeated the air. It was like Fall vomited in the room. And there, at the back, sitting on a dinky round table for two, was his youngest brother. Same overgrown haircut, a few more scribbles inked on his used-to-be-blank left arm, looking smug and so sure of himself.

He should be. He was the first to find his soul mate and unlock his powers. The little fucker could electrocute Wyatt where he stood.

Things had been strained between them for years and when Wyatt had learned all the bullshit Evan had been peddling about Sara was true, the strain had pulled tighter. Wyatt hated being wrong. When he'd left the family a few months ago, he had good intentions. He'd wanted to be a better brother—the one he used to be, the one who stood up for Evan when he was bullied in the playground as children, the one who growled away the monsters under the bed—but anger and pride had swallowed him whole.

Something clicked inside Wyatt. He wasn't sure if it happened because of his proximity to the woman now speaking with Evan, or if it was just time for him to accept... but he'd never be able to outrun his demons, he knew that now. His family would never let him get far.

Misha stood next to the table, hip cocked to the side, talking with an animated expression on her face. Her infectious enthusiasm made him want to feel the same excitement. Wyatt wondered if she did anything boring. Life in her orbit would be fun.

He strode up to the table.

Evan took his eyes from Misha and watched him approach.

Just as well.

What did that mean? He checked himself. Was he... protective of Misha's body? Did he care that another man stared at her?

"Wyatt." Evan stood as he approached.

Misha cut herself short, jaw clicking closed when she caught the tension between the two brothers. Then she grinned and slapped Wyatt on the chest. "You never told me you had a brother, you old dawg. Why weren't you at the opening of Hell?" Totally enjoying the flummoxed look on Wyatt's face, she went back to Evan and continued speaking. "So, after the day I've had, I *really* need to go out tonight, blow off some steam, you know? I actually have a night off work. Do you know if Grace is working?"

"Um." Evan darted a glance at Wyatt. "Yeah. She's in surgery."

"Bummer. What about Lilo?"

"Why don't you call her?" Evan gave her his cell phone.

What the fuck? Evan's girl and Griffin's girl knew Misha.

"Great idea," Misha said. "Calling from your cell. I can pretend I'm a kidnapper or something and she'll totally freak!"

"No, don't do that!" Panic lit up Evan's eyes. "She really will freak. More than you know."

So… from Evan's reaction, and Misha's lack of understanding of her prank's potential consequences, Misha knew nothing about Evan being Envy. If she did, she'd know pulling a stunt like that with their family wouldn't go down well.

"Oh, you're such a party-pooper. I can see how you two are related now." She smirked. "Okay, well, you guys obviously need to talk, so I'll leave you to it. I'll call Lilo from my phone." She handed Evan's cell back to him and left.

Wyatt watched her saunter away, waggling her hips as though she knew he watched. When he turned back to Evan, his brother's eyes were laced with humor.

"You and Misha Minski, hey? Lilo's going to be stoked."

Cut the bullshit, is what Wyatt would have said. *Why are you here?* Instead, he stared, unsure what to do. Actually nervous.

"Okay. So." Evan averted his gaze. "I know you want to be left alone, but we can't humor you for much longer. We need you back, and I see we're just in time."

Wyatt frowned. *In time for what?*

Evan had no clue what Wyatt was thinking. Feeling frustrated and seriously considering learning more sign language from Alek, Wyatt caved and picked up Evan's phone to type his question out, but the damned thing crushed in his hands like sand.

Fuck. Not here. Not now.

"Shit," Evan breathed, awed. "Did you just Hulk-smash my phone?"

Hadn't meant to, honestly.

When Evan reached for the steak knife next to his plate, Wyatt tensed. Maybe he wasn't over the whole accusing him of being in love with his fiancée thing. But if he wanted to stab him, sure, why the fuck not? Wyatt could take it. Maybe it would cut out a little of the guilt weighing him down.

Evan took Wyatt's wrist in one hand, took note of his balanced Yin-Yang tattoo.

"I knew it," Evan said, waving the knife in the direction Misha went. "It's her, isn't it?"

Wyatt frowned and shrugged.

"Don't know what I'm talking about? How about the phone?"

Wyatt blinked.

"How about this?" Evan stabbed Wyatt through the hand with the steak knife.

Damn. He shut his eyes to ride out the pain. He guessed he deserved that after the way he'd treated Evan over the past few years. Wyatt expected more violence, but… no. There was no wrath emanating from him. It was…

Evan laughed, eyes wide with mirth as he looked down at Wyatt's palm. "You fucking broke the knife, bro."

What?

Wyatt tugged his hand from his brother. His flesh was a little pink where the knife had hit, but otherwise picture perfect. Evan huffed another laugh and threw the broken knife at Wyatt. It bounced off his chest and slid to the table.

"Look what your skin did to my knife."

Wyatt darted a worried glance around. A few patrons scowled at him but, thankfully, the dining room was virtually empty now lunch was over. An old woman sat in the corner playing suduko, and a family of four paid for their meal at the cash register. The two young children pretended to be ninjas between their parents' legs, and the parents couldn't be happier. For a moment, Wyatt forgot about Evan's outburst and got caught on the happy family. Rosy cheeks. Chubby hands. Laughter. Not a care in the world.

Not for someone like him.

He turned back to Evan and made a waving down motion with his hand. *Keep it down.*

Evan snorted, still laughing.

Wyatt stood, but Evan stopped him. "Wait. Wait, I'm sorry. Hell" —he scrubbed his face—"It wasn't meant to go like this. Fuck, I had a speech rehearsed and everything."

You did?

Wyatt eased himself back into the chair.

"Yeah, I was going to come in and ask how you've been, maybe shoot the shit for a bit, ease into it, you know? But the truth is, we miss you, bro. It's not right that you're not home. I mean, I can see what might be tempting you to stay, but... When are you coming back?"

Wyatt's heart clenched. He stood, crossed to the serving counter and retrieved a pen and notebook, then went back to Evan.

How did you find me? He wrote and turned the pad to Evan.

"You serious?" Evan fidgeted in his seat, then lowered his voice. "You left a trail of bodies across the country. Weren't exactly incognito."

Nah. That's not it.

"Fine. I had a few dreams, okay?"

Dreams?

Part of the reason Evan knew Sara had been lying to them was that he dreamed seeing her in another life. At the time it was a crazy idea. Sara was dead, or so they'd thought.

"How's your throat?" Evan asked.

How the fuck do you think it is? he wanted to say. Instead, he shrugged.

"Can you speak?"

Wyatt shook his head.

"Have you tried?"

A pause, then… another shake.

Evan pulled out a folded piece of paper from his jeans pocket. He unfolded it and peeled a few sheets apart to reveal a group of sketches. On the top of the pile was a picture of Wyatt in the Pierogi Palace kitchen. Alek was there, and so was Roksana. Even Vooyek in the corner.

And there it was, staring Wyatt in the face—black and white evidence of how he'd been so wrong about Evan. His psychic dreams were obviously real, there was no denying it.

I'm a dickhead.

Evan tapped the kitchen picture. "I drew that a few months ago. We thought to give you space, but then last night I drew this." He pulled out a sheet from underneath the sketch. This drawing had a completely different tone. Dark, scratchy lines that covered the entire page. It took a while for Wyatt to understand. When it came to him, his blood cooled. That wasn't right. Fuck, no.

"Fire. Here," Evan said in a hushed voice, eyes darting around the dining room. "Had to warn you."

When? Wyatt wrote on his notepad.

"Don't know. But if you can put a time on the picture in the kitchen, and I drew that a few months ago—it might give you an idea of the time frame between sketch and eventuality. Then again, nothing about these dreams are predicable. It might not mean anything at all. Plus, there's this…" Evan's voice trailed off as he pulled out yet another sketch.

Wyatt wasn't sure he wanted to look, but forced himself. The picture was of a tall woman with long white hair talking to a man who looked remarkably like the golden man in the suit. They stood together in a what looked like a nightclub, Misha was in the background. It was all connected.

"The Syndicate is involved." Evan stabbed the white-haired woman.

Wyatt's finger trailed her familiar face. She was the one who'd shot Sara, cleaning up the Syndicate's mess, execution style. Wyatt's heart clenched. Sara had confessed everything in her final moments. She'd wanted forgiveness. She'd told Wyatt she'd held back vital information from the Syndicate. As far as he could tell, they knew nothing about their powers being triggered by a person embodying their sin's opposing virtue, and in a twisted way, they had Sara to thank for that. That was months ago. Who knew what the enemy knew about them now?

Wyatt looked wistfully out the window. All he needed to do was stop fucking around with excuses, get his bike fixed and piss off. No pressure, no expectations, no regrets. No fucking Syndicate dominating his world.

"I know what you're thinking, and you should stay," Evan said, tone somber. "You've got the chance for something good here, Wyatt. Don't throw it away."

Wyatt scrunched up the papers. If Misha was involved with the Syndicate, he wanted nothing to do with her.

"I'm serious, bro. You haven't been around, but both Griff and I are fucking sitting sweet. I'm in love, he's in love. I know it sounds sappy, but we can go out every night and be who we're meant to be. Hell, it feels fucking amazing. Liberating. We've never been happier. You can have it too if you just stop and think about it for a minute."

He unfolded the paper he'd scrunched and wrote on the back. *You just said M is involved with the Syndicate.*

"What? No. That's not... shit, I'm fucking this all up again, aren't I?" Evan slipped out another piece of paper from between the scrunched lot. "See here?"

It was a sketch of Misha being threatened by the golden man, his hand around her throat. Such a brutal picture, so similar to how he'd attacked her only hours ago.

"She needs your help, Wyatt."

Wyatt wasn't ready for this. Too much had happened today. He needed to get out, clear his head.

As he walked out the front door, he caught Evan's shouted words over his shoulder. "A Lazarus never quits."

Too bad he already had.

nine

DIMITRI

STILL COATED in a layer of fury, Dimitri entered his office and stood before the snake terrarium. The mesmerizing flick of the forked tongue calmed his mind.

Misha was becoming harder to handle, and she was a threat to everything he'd built since high school. Her performance that morning was the last and final straw.

Filthy whore defied me, again.

He roared and swiped the contents of his desk to the floor.

Their meeting hadn't gone as planned. His staff noticed her disregard for his orders and rules. She was his weakness, and for what? His insistent need to savor his revenge? Her incessantly bubbly outlook on life threw his ridged rules back in his face. *Enough!*

If she didn't come up with the money her family owed by the end of the week—no, a week was too soft—in forty-eight hours. Yes, that was more like it.

Dimitri picked up his fallen intercom from the floor and buzzed his assistant.

"Notify Misha Minski the terms of our arrangement have

changed. She now has forty-eight hours to pay her debt. Make sure she understands."

Without waiting for a response from his man, he let go of the intercom button. Initially, he'd sought to keep Misha's defiance between the two of them. That was why he'd attended her in person. But after she claimed her family was not responsible for his men's medical bills, he was done with her. The way she put their needs before his made him sick. No filthy Minksi whore would put anyone before him. Restitution was required—*nyet*, demanded!

He pushed his intercom button. "Send someone in to clean this *gryaznyy* mess."

A knock at the door almost immediately.

"*Voydite*." Dimitri smoothed his hair and sat down at his desk.

But it wasn't his assistant who came in. It was someone else.

A masked woman dressed in white leather entered the room like she owned it. Dimitri reached for the drawer that held his pistol, but before his fingers closed around the handle, she was on him. His hands were shoved to his lap and pinned ruthlessly by her knee. Razor sharp nails stroked his neck in warning—one push, one wrong twitch, and he was done. Long white hair floated around her head, still moving from her lightning fast approach. Two soulless eyes blinked at him from beyond the bird mask and she cocked her head, studying him.

"I sense despair in you," she said, words cold as ice. "It is dripping like blood from your pores."

He bucked in resistance. "The only thing I despair is you."

"*Nyet*." She mocked him and it only served to kindle his fury. "You are sad because your people are losing faith in their fearless leader. Your followers are leaving—starting their own businesses and stealing from you. Your play thing is playing back. Your *family* does not want you."

He growled. "How did you get past my guards, Falcon?"

Beneath the mask, her eyes narrowed and turned hard. Clearly not a fan of the name she had been given by the masses, but there was no other way to address her. She was an enforcer for an organization Dimitri knew little about, except they had deep pockets. A loan shark, perhaps, but Dimitri sensed there was more. With her money, he was able to build The Kremlin and finance his rise to the top of the Bratva in Cardinal City. All she wanted in return was a cut of the takings. It seemed negligent at first, but lately, she'd been asking for more favors. Sending his men to the Pierogi Palace to collect extra protection payments had been her idea and look where that had ended.

Her delicate jaw tightened, and she pushed off to stand before him, finger stroking the coiled white leather bullwhip attached to her hip.

A warm trickle ran from the stinging prick under his chin.

Ignore it. Don't show weakness.

"What do you want?" he asked. "Money? Our debt has been paid."

Her pink lips curved in a rare smile. "No. I don't want your money."

Falcon leaned toward the snake terrarium and tapped the glass with her white pointed nail, then she trailed a groove in the glass, sending a spine-grating shriek into the air. Her nail cut as though it was made of diamond.

"We have a gift," she said, still fascinated by the animal in the tank.

"Gifts always come with a price."

She turned to him, still smiling, and it was terrifying. "I can give you hope. I can help you win respect."

"Why would you do this?"

She shrugged. "I can give you soldiers. I can give you money. I can give you power."

"Why?" he asked again. He was no fool.

"Your club is looking very nice, Dimitri. I see our first arrangement has paid off. Did we ask for much in return?"

He shook his head.

Falcon opened the door to his office, and a stream of men came in —each wearing a floor length white robe and plastic masks over their faces—slits for eyes and mouths. Two men held a black case between them. They took it to the floor and dumped it with a loud thud. When they opened the lid, cash, gold and all the riches Dimitri ever dreamed of were inside.

"We ask for nothing in return… except chaos."

THE MINUTE MISHA stepped into her small apartment, after a long day's work at the Palace, she headed for the shower. She'd left a message with Lilo and a few other friends with an invitation to go out that night. She needed to dance. She needed to party. She needed to forget about the demands Dimitri made…. and the two burning blue eyes of brooding silence that watched her all day from across the kitchen. Wyatt's presence still felt tangible to her, so when the knock came at her door, only minutes after she'd stepped in the shower, her mind naturally went to him. Maybe he'd changed his mind about a little rumpy-pumpy, after all.

She turned off the faucet, pulled the floral curtain back and shouted, "I'll be there in a minute."

Wrapping a towel around her head, she quickly dried her body in record time. The knock became demanding, and she had to rush putting on her jeans and blouse. "I'm coming!" *Sheesh*. The chef must want her bad.

Misha grinned at her reflection, pinched her cheeks and then jogged to the door.

As her hand wrapped around the old porcelain knob, a spear of wrongness crashed through her. She'd never told Wyatt where she lived. But her warning didn't travel through her nervous system fast enough. Too late, she opened the door.

"*Lapochka.*" Yuri's big frame dominated the hallway. He pushed her back with a hand to her shoulder. "We talk inside."

"Yuri?" Misha stepped back, adrenaline already surging through her veins. He wasn't changing his mind, was he? It all seemed so wrong, all—Misha's mind halted when two other men followed Yuri inside.

Two of Dimitri's enforcers. Petyr and Nikoli entered and shut the door behind them. Each stood to a side of the door, hands clasped in front, waiting like soldiers.

"What's going on?" Her voice trembled, and she didn't realize she'd been back peddling until her butt hit her small dining table, rocking it on its legs. "How did you know where I live?"

Emotion flickered in Yuri's eyes and time slowed. It was the same emotion Misha had seen swamping Wyatt's after he'd realized he'd made her bleed. *Regret.*

"No." Misha put out her hand. "Whatever you were sent here to do, just no."

"I'm sorry, *lapochka*. But you made a fool of Dimitri. He wants you to know he is serious about the ultimatum."

"Okay. Okay, I get it. Pay up in two days. I get it."

But that look wouldn't go away. That look deepened, and as he came toward her, cracking his knuckles, she had the feeling this macabre dance would be the only one she'd see for days.

IN HER FATHER'S borrowed car, Misha drove from the Pierogi Palace to her family home in Weston Park. She'd only intended to borrow the car for the Sunday night out, but... plans changed. It had been two days since Dimitri's men delivered his ultimatum—pay up in forty-eight hours, or else.

Those men had actually beaten her! *Yuri. Nikoli.* Men from the club. Kicked her in the ribs, punched her in the arms. She thought they were her friends. Guess she was sorely mistaken. Ha! Her own joke made her giggle like a mad woman, then winced at her sore ribs.

God, what a start to the week... and the end of her life.

She should be sad about it, but she'd always known life was precious, short and fleeting. Her mother had died in childbirth. Something so natural, yet, so sudden. It was the biggest lesson she'd learned about the tragic brevity of the world.

While her bruises were still visible, Misha had to cancel her Monday and Tuesday yoga classes. She'd avoided her family, avoided the five million missed calls and text messages from Lilo, avoided the restaurant, and avoided *him.* That damned chef with his damned gruff attitude and his cute as hell surly lips. He was all she thought of for the two days. Goddamn it, she wanted to see him crack a smile. Would it kill him to break a damned smile?

No, it wouldn't. But it would bring a small piece of happiness to the shit storm she'd been living over the past few days. When Dimitri had driven into the parking lot that Sunday morning, he had threatened to make Roksana work at the club if Misha didn't increase her services offered. She'd told him she'd find the cash to pay the debt, just out of spite. Then that damned bastard changed his agreement from a few weeks to a few days.

Two days to fork over forty-thousand dollars! She could still hear Yuri's voice, thickly accented, as he gave the final warning while she lay on her apartment floor, still shielding her face. *"People know you declined Dimitri's offer for extra services. They know you agreed to make payment in cash. No changing now or he looks weak. Forty-eight hours, Misha. You pay or—"*

"*Or what?*" *she braved.*

A heavy sigh. A breathy resigned, lapochka, *then: "Or we make you pay."*

The resounding click of the door as they'd left still echoed. It was the hollow sound of her fate, a fate she now accepted, after trying everything to fight against. *Benedict Cumberbatch!* The best way to protect her family now was to wipe the debt with her life. Surely that's what he meant. They couldn't force her to prostitute herself. If she refused, what could they do? Kill her.

"Benedict Cumberbatch!"

She repetitively shouted the same words until the tension drained from her body. The actor's name was such a silly curse word that it never failed to make her feel better. She carried on shouting until she burst out laughing, and then finally, drained of emotion and teary-eyed, she turned the corner of the street to her childhood family home.

In less than an hour, her time was up.

Less than an hour to do one last thing to make her smile... and maybe, just maybe, she'd make someone else smile too.

Pulling into the family driveway, she was surprised to see a figure in her way. She slammed on the brakes, stopping in time for the car's bumper to narrowly miss hitting Wyatt and his prized vintage motor-cycle. He barely blinked at her sudden entrance, while she... she barely drew breath. Dressed in that pair of worn jeans and a black T-shirt she'd seen hanging in her—*his*—closet, he looked so damned sexy that her mouth watered. She wasn't sure how long he'd been out there, tinkering with his bike, but sweat dampened his shirt so it clung lovingly to his sinewy muscles.

Two unfathomable blue eyes locked onto her. Heat arrowed down her spine, pooling between her legs making her squirm with need. Goodness, she was going to jump his bones. Right then. He had no idea what was going to hit him.

Benedict-fucking-Cumberbatch, here I come.

Climbing out of the car, she put on a straight face and stalked up to him, forcing herself to take it slow, to savor the experience. Plenty of time for passion later.

Wyatt went back to turning the wrench, ratchet, or whatever that tool was in his big masculine hands. *My goodness.* She fanned her face. This is what locking yourself in your home for two days did. She was ravenous for him. Dark hair dropped into his eyes as he dipped his head to check his handy work. She needed some popcorn so she could park her ass and just stare.

"You quit," she stated, voice husky and already thick with her desire. "You quit without finishing what you started."

He responded with an *I-don't-owe-you-anything* arch of his eyebrow and stood up, never taking his eyes from his machine. He tested the part he'd just installed, pulling tightly to ensure it was secure. The muscles in his arms went taut, rolling and tensing as if to tease her, to show her all that she was going to lose. All that strength, all that man and sex, gone after today.

Wyatt had stormed out that Sunday afternoon and, curious, Misha had questioned Evan. He'd only said that his brother needed time. He'd also said she looked good together with Wyatt, and he wished them all the best. For a minute, she'd stood there dumbfounded, and then she'd caught onto his meaning. He meant good together, as in a relationship. Like him and Grace, or Lilo and Griffin.

"There's something he needs that only you have. Don't give up on him, Misha," Evan had said.

Naturally, she'd run back to her apartment in the city like a scared little girl and planned to go out clubbing all night. She didn't do relationships, and the predicament she was in was the perfect reason why. But this wasn't a relationship. This was one last night of pleasure before she was pushing up daisies. She could relieve her aching body. He could do the same. Then they could go their separate ways.

"You're going to ignore me?" Misha stepped closer. His silence only encouraged her. "C'mon, *koteczek*. Time to play one last game before you go."

She hoisted his duffel bag over her shoulder and headed to the steps leading up to the apartment over the garage. Without waiting to see if he followed, she took them two at a time until she burst through the front door.

She had his bag. He couldn't leave without it, *so there*.

Jumping onto the bed, she scooted the bag behind her, and waited. She supposed she could spend her last few minutes trying desperately to find another solution to the Dimtiri problem. She'd even considered imploring Wyatt for help. He had crazy mad strength and skills. He'd put those two in the hospital, after all. Alek had said he didn't even break a sweat. But no man was a match for Dimitri's resources.

Anastasia had phoned her after she heard about Misha's beating. She'd warned her that coming back to the club wouldn't be the same. Dimitri had new blood—freaky white robed and masked soldiers—who were in and out of the club, leaving pure white, returning splattered in blood. Something was going on. Dimitri was flexing his metaphoric Bratva muscles. No one was safe.

When the sound of heavy boots pounded the steps, Misha almost squealed in excitement. She wanted this release so badly, she *needed* it. Her nipples were already hardening beneath her tiny crop-top. She didn't want to spend her last hours crying over her situation. She was going out with a bang... or two.

When he crested the doorway with anger filled eyes, she hesitated. *Maybe this is a bad idea.*

He pounced, fingers encircling her ankles, dragging her toward him on the bed. She bumped down the coverlet, reveling in the sensation of the smooth fabric on her already sensitized body. She nimbly twisted out of his hold and scrambled back to the end of the bed, turning toward him at the last moment with a challenge in her eyes.

He lunged, but she kicked him back with a foot to his chest. It was like kicking a brick wall. But he yielded. He retreated to stand at the foot of the bed and gaze down at her, nostrils flaring, jaw clenching, pupils dilating.

Yes, Wyatt. Get excited.

His fists flexed at his side, as though he were testing his strength. Maybe he worried he'd hurt her.

"I assure you, I can take whatever you dish out." It wouldn't be any worse than what she'd suffered already.

Those sapphire eyes narrowed darkly, hotly, landing heavily on her lips. Oh, he definitely considered. To give him a nudge in the right direction, she licked her lips seductively.

"Come and get me," she teased.

eleven

WYATT LAZARUS

MISHA SAT AGAINST THE HEADBOARD, eyes round and bright, blond ringlets wild and free. She wore knee-length gray yoga pants and a tight crop top that barely contained her generous breasts. So fucking beautiful, Wyatt couldn't move his eyes away.

He was hard the moment she'd stolen his bag and run off. Now he was agonized. Zippers and erections weren't a good combination.

Grinning, her eyes roamed down his body to where he strained. Hot desire washed over her features, and, *hell*, it made his cock twitch with want. But the damned thing was, while his body wanted —*needed*—to take her with a crippling desperation, his heart screamed for him to leave. Get on his bike, hit the road, and never come back. Fuck this bullshit. Fuck being led by his cock into more heartache.

Time to play one last game before you go.

Her teasing words resounded in his memory, reasoning with him. This woman was different. She only wanted one night. One time. But with each instinct telling him to take her, to fuck her until they both ached, there was another voice saying she would hurt him, just like Sara.

Misha purred like a cat and made a kissy face at him. "What are you waiting for?"

He launched across the bed. It collapsed under his strength and she squealed.

Shit. He broke the bed. Face hovering inches over hers, he looked into her expectant eyes. Even if this was a one-off, he wouldn't be responsible for damaging her... perhaps worse. He could actually kill her with his disregard. He was trained better than that. Until he got a hold on his ability, he had to be careful.

He never got a chance to try because Misha's swift fingers unbuttoned his fly, springing him free. Before he formed a coherent thought, her cold hand wrapped around his shaft, shooting waves of pleasure through him. Unbidden, he groaned, and she responded with her own.

"That's right," she murmured. "This is for me. I want it. Give it to me."

Fuck, the way she moaned in appreciation, the way she moved her hands, gliding along his length. His vision blurred, his balls tingled. Everything went—

No.

He pushed away and sat back on his haunches. Her cheeks were stained pink, and she glared at him with defiance, but he'd made up his mind. He got off the bed and zipped himself up, clearing his throat.

"Bullshit," she said. "We're not done."

She mustn't understand the danger she toyed with.

"Wyatt. Get here, now."

He could crush her.

Gathering his patience, he stood at the glass sliding doors and distracted himself with the neighborhood scenery. The sun was still up. He still had time to get on his bike and leave, maybe make the next town before dark.

A rustling sound behind him.

"Wyatt," she growled. "Look at me."

The husky timbre of her voice had him turning involuntarily.

Naked.

Completely naked, lying on the bed he'd slept in for the past few weeks, stroking the sheets enticingly. Soft, silky skin. Round breasts, pink nipples. His mouth went dry. She flirted with death, and it stoked every fire in his body. He was there in an instant, yanking her by the shoulders, crushing their lips together, kissing with retribution, teeth knocking. *You want a taste of death? You want to kiss away your life?*

Fingers into his hair, pulling until tiny sparks of pain shot through his scalp. He was afraid to hurt her, but she was stronger than he realized. Demanding. Surprises around every corner... and he... and he liked them. When he thrust his tongue into her mouth and hit the slick sensation of her own thrusting back, a groan ripped from his raw throat. Her taste made him heady.

With a gasp, she shoved him hard, and squirmed away, eyes lighting like fireworks.

Already undone, he reached for her, wanting, and she shot him a cheeky grin, evading his grasp, giggling. "Come and get it, *Chef*."

A game. Always a fucking game.

He lunged.

She kicked out—foot hitting his chest—keeping him at a distance while she impaled him with lust-drenched eyes.

"Fuck, you make me so hot, Wyatt. Take your clothes off," she demanded. "I want to see that incredible body. Make me hotter."

She was insane. Obstinate. Naughty. Fun.

Part of him wanted to wrench her foot away, the other part—the hard part—shouted for him to do as he was told. He'd never met a woman who could match his stubbornness full on. But wasn't that what he always wanted? A woman who called bullshit on his unmoving and strident tendencies? Shame not to see this through.

One night.

He reached over his shoulders, gripped his shirt and pulled it off. She slowly removed her foot to make way for the shirt. That woman had the core strength of an athlete. The knowledge of the positions he could move her into jerked his cock with sweet anticipation.

"Now your jeans." A throaty challenge.

He pushed them down and stepped out.

Misha's eyes grew laden as she took him in. How they glowed with promise as they dipped to his arousal. He liked the way she licked her lips, liked the way she desired him.

This is just one time, he reminded himself. *One time.*

And then he would be out of there.

If she wanted to flirt with danger, fine. He'd be the bastard she wanted. He'd fuck her hard.

Before he knew what was happening, she jumped onto him, straddling his waist. They careened back into the wall, crashing, shaking the foundations. She laughed.

The crazy woman was having fun.

Gripping her thighs for support, mouths clashed and tongues dueled. He didn't know what they were trying to get from each other, but it was raw, passionate, and desperate. If they didn't have each other, right then, the world would fall apart.

He hated it.

This woman was doing things to his mind. Fucked up things he couldn't control. They knocked around the room, pushing and pulling at each other until he couldn't stand it and threw her on the bed in a rage. She landed on her back, breasts bouncing.

Fuck, he wanted to talk—to say *something*. His inability was driving him mad, but he didn't trust his throat. Hadn't had the balls to speak since the event. What if he was broken? What if he wasn't...

Screw it. He had nothing worth saying, anyway.

Instead, he reached down, flipped her until she lay on her front, and then lifted her by the hips until her core positioned directly before his cock.

But he didn't thrust. He stared at her, one hand caressing her perfect ass, the other fisting his length, squeezing tight, straining against the urge to pound into her so hard, he would hurt them both. When she leaned her shoulders down, offering up her rear, he lost all resolve. He shoved in.

Blinding ecstasy wrapped around his cock, and he had to fight the bliss. This wasn't why he was doing this. He was going to fuck her, damn it. Fuck her to prove a point. Not—

He groaned helplessly when she writhed, urging him into movement. Drawing out, he slammed back in, and became lost in her feminine gasps of delight and the way his body wanted to fold around her as though if he didn't, he'd lose himself.

This abandon wasn't him. This irrational need wasn't him.

"Yes, Wyatt," she cried, torturing him. "Fuck me."

Fuck you. The words echoed.

He thrust.

Fuck you.

Anger welled.

Fuck *you.* He thrust again.

I hate you. And again.

I hate... And again.

Soon he fell into a punishing rhythm, gripping her hips with locked fingers, shutting his eyes to avoid the blissful sight of her perfect body sweating beneath him. Blond hair bouncing. Head arching back with passion. But she was burned into his retinas, and he couldn't lock out her sounds, her complete and utter surrender, no matter how cruel and hard he pounded. When his climax roared through him with a painful, blinding numbness, he collapsed around her sweaty body.

Still, she held strong on her knees and hands, holding the weight of him.

And he felt sated.

And he shouldn't.

He pushed her away in a fitful shove until she landed face first on the sheets.

Regret punched him hard when he noticed the angry red blotches his fingers had left on her hips, and the forceful disregard of his treatment. Yeah, he was a fucking asshole. What's new?

"*Oh. Em. Gee,*" she shouted into her pillow and gave a muffled scream. He almost thought it was from pain, that he'd taken it too far —but she rolled onto her back, grinning from ear to ear, laughing and panting. Sweat left a glossy sheen over her skin, and her hand fluttered to her throat as her eyes rolled in her afterglow and she moaned, pressing her thighs together. "Fuck. Wyatt, that was *hot.*"

What just happened?

He stumbled back.

He wasn't even sure if she finished. Yes, she did. She must have. There was a point where she screamed his name into the mattress, and then she went all soft and pliant. Surely that was—*oh God.* He scrubbed his face. Not once in his life had he'd been so consumed with passion that he couldn't remember if he'd made his woman come. He hadn't even used protection. For once, he was grateful that he and his siblings were sterile.

Wait. *His woman?* He'd just called her his woman.

Get out. Now.

Where were his jeans? Frantically, he searched the room.

Holy shit, the room.

"Wow," Misha said, leaning casually on her elbow, head in hand, casting an amused glance around. "You know the sex was good when you need to redecorate."

They'd all but destroyed it. There was a crack in the wall. The light fitting had crashed and lay on the floor. The bed was destroyed. The headboard splintered in half. *Fuck.*

Wyatt fished around in his duffel bag and took out a wad of rolled cash. He'd made a withdrawal from the bank earlier that day. His family knew where he was, so there was no point trying to remain incognito. When he worked at Heaven, he'd been too busy creating luxurious dishes the world had never seen to spend his hard earned cash, so had plenty in the bank. The first thing he did was purchase that motorcycle part he'd been waiting on, the rest he'd shoved in his wallet for later use.

Misha's gaze narrowed on the cash roll with distaste. "What is that?"

Apparently something so disgusting she felt the need to gawp at it.

He counted it out. *Two thousand dollars.*

"Jeez, Wyatt. That's offensive. I didn't do this for money." She shot him a sly look. "I did this for your goddamn Adonis body. *Jeez.* Wait... unless you happen to have another Forty-three thousand or so dollars in there. No? Well, it was worth a try."

Forty-three thousand dollars. That was an oddly precise amount.

He frowned and pointed at all the damage. *The money was for that, idiot,* he mouthed.

She slapped his money away. "Don't call me an idiot, idiot."

Shock radiated through him. He caught her by the wrist and held her captive. She'd said "idiot" as though she knew what he mouthed, as though…

Do you understand me? he mouthed.

"Yes, a little. I took Alek to lip reading classes when he was younger. Those hearing aids don't do shit, and he was too shy to go on his own, so I went with him. It was fun. I can't hold a conversation or anything, but I catch the gist of it."

She twisted her wrist out of his hand. When she moved, Wyatt caught sight of a bruise coloring her jaw.

His stomach plummeted. He didn't… The red blotches he'd left on her hips flashed before his eyes. Had he actually hurt her? He touched her gently, and she dropped her gaze, bashful. With a finger under her chin, he lifted until their eyes locked.

Was that me? he mouthed and pointed at the purple bruise.

"Go slow, I'm out of practice."

He asked again.

"No, it wasn't you." She pushed him away, and just like that, the mood darkened. "The others weren't you either. Oh wait"—she squirmed, feeling out her body—"My hips *are* a little sore, but it's a good sore, if you know what I mean. And that other place." She winked at him. "Do you really want to know how that feels?"

But he wasn't listening to her joke. His mind was caught on the word *others*.

Others with their hands on her.

Rage consumed him. Fuck any man who touched her. He trembled with the need to wring someone's neck. The thought of another man with his dick in her, hurting her.

Just like you? a dark voice mocked.

Forcing the emotion down, he made himself assess her other bruises with a cool head. She never said they were from another man in the bedroom. Even if they were, who gave a fuck. *One time, remember?* Others could mean anything. And now that he wasn't blinded with his irrational need to bed her, he saw clearly. Her smooth, gorgeous body was marred all over. He didn't know which bruise to focus on first. He searched her body, lifting her arms. There —he tested her ribs and she hissed. She was hurt.

He had to know. He pointed at the ribs and her worst injuries, then pointed at himself. But even as he went through the motions, he knew it wasn't his fault. The discoloration was old, yellowing, and when she shook her head, it was confirmed.

If not me, then who? Why?

He waited patiently while she read his lips. When her gaze clashed with his again, she hesitated.

"It doesn't matter," she said, drawing away and squeezing into her pants. "Nothing can be done now."

She dressed with little regard for him until she turned suddenly, tugging on her joggers. "Well, that was fun, Wyatt. Good luck with your journey. Safe travels and all that."

While he stood there stunned, from somewhere in the room, the sound of Snoop Dog's *Drop it Like it's Hot* came on. Misha hunted around until she found her cell hidden between the headboard and the wall. "Oh, there it is." She picked it out, dusted it off and answered. "Hello?"

Dismissed, just like that.

Wyatt wasn't sure what he expected, but it wasn't that. He tugged on his jeans and shirt, shaking his head to himself. He couldn't believe it. Dismissed. What the fuck did he care? He didn't. So why was he arguing with himself?

"Calm down, Roka. What's happened?" Misha gave Wyatt an eye roll, then swiftly, her expression turned grave. "Slow down. I can't underst—What? A Fire?"

Fire?

The room closed in around Wyatt. No. It can't be. That's exactly what Evan warned him about.

"Have you called the Fire Department?" Misha sat on the edge of the bed. Her leg bobbed frantically. "Okay, okay. Where's Tata? And Alek? Shit. I'll be right there."

She cut the call as Wyatt tugged on his last boot.

"Look," she said, eyes wide and glassy with unshed tears. "I have to go. I'm sorry to just leave like this, but you understand, right?"

Wait a god-dammed minute. Wyatt stopped her as she tried to leave.

What was that all about? he mouthed.

She frowned at his lips and shook her head. "I didn't catch that. You spoke too fast." Her face screwed up and for a minute, Wyatt thought she'd cry. She covered her face with her hand, so he couldn't see. "I can't believe he did that. Dimitri, you fucking asshole. It was supposed to be me."

He pulled her hands away and dipped so she could see his face. *It will be okay. I'm coming with you.*

"It was supposed to be me first, Wyatt. Not them. I can't be the one left picking up the pieces again."

He'd never seen such pain in her eyes. This bright, bubbly woman was terrified and trembling.

He gave her shoulder a squeeze for comfort, then dragged her out the door. When they got to the bottom of the steps, he straddled his bike and handed her his only helmet.

"You don't need to do this," she said. "I get it. You're on your way out. I'm sure they're fine. They'll be fine."

But from the way she bit her lip, he didn't think so. He wouldn't leave her like this.

Put the damned helmet on, woman. Whether she read his lips or not, she slid the helmet over her head and climbed on behind him.

That new part better work. He stomped on the kickstarter and the engine roared to life. *Thank Christ.* He revved the engine loudly and drove out. As they hurtled down the road, all he could think was this was his fault. He should have listened to Evan instead of running. If he had listened, he'd be at the restaurant. Whoever set the fire—this Dimitri bastard—he'd better hope to God he hadn't hurt anyone, and if he did, he'd rue the fucking day he'd ever messed with the Minski family.

twelve

MISHA MINSKI

MISHA CLUNG TO Wyatt as they shot through suburban streets on his motorcycle. Through every turn, dip and hill, he controlled the machine expertly. If she wasn't so panicked, she might find it fun, but all she could think was that Dimitri should have come after her, not her family.

She should have known better. If Dimitri wanted to make a quick point, he resorted to violence, but if someone really did him wrong, the psychological game he played was far worse than a direct assault. She'd seen him turn a footballer into a sniveling pile of mess in high school. The quarterback had relentlessly bullied Dimitri, going as far as shoving Dimitri's head down a toilet because he knew he was afraid of water. Misha had felt sorry for Dimitri and consoled him, told him that karma would get that footballer back one day.

He hadn't known what karma was, but Misha had been learning about it from Ciocia since she was a young girl: *No need to get angry about it, Misha. Angry people only end up with the life deserving of an angry person. Karma will sort them out.* But when Misha tried to explain the laws of karma to Dimitri, he took away the wrong lesson.

Misha learned firsthand how Dimitri dished out his own twisted karma. He'd discovered the footballer was afraid of snakes and filled his locker with them… only thing was, they were poisonous. The footballer was bitten and spent weeks in hospital, missing out on playing in the finals, and missing out on the scholarship he needed to get into college. You'd think that was enough to satisfy Dimitri's thirst for revenge, but it wasn't. Years later, that footballer ended up committing himself to a psychiatric asylum because he'd kept seeing imaginary snakes. Dimitri confessed to Misha that he still taunted the man—that he would plant the snakes and then take them away.

Dimitri was a psychopath; Misha had known it for a while, but he'd always left her alone after she did what he wanted. She thought he would get over the mysterious grudge he'd developed for Misha, or at the very least, he would get bored.

How wrong she'd been.

They could smell the smoke from a street away and by the time they pulled into the parking lot of the cultural food center, black smoke was everywhere. Sirens wailed in the distance, but it was too late. The Pierogi Palace was going up in torrid flames.

Wyatt skidded to a halt. Business owners and patrons had spilled into the lot, all panicking. Some were on their cells, others tried to spray down their restaurants with water from hoses in an effort to stop the flames spreading. When Misha pulled her helmet off, the roar and crackling of the fire was deafening. She choked on the fumes.

Roksana, Ciocia and her father all stood too close to the burning building. Other staff members were far across the lot. Something was wrong. Her father tried to go back inside, shouting incomprehensible Polish, but they held him back. Where was her brother? Alek worked in the kitchen after school. What time was it? She searched the lot frantically.

Not there.

Fucking not there!

She ran to her family, covering her mouth with her hand. "Where's Alek?"

Roksana turned to her, tears in her eyes. "He didn't hear the alarm! He's in there. God, Misha. He's going to die, isn't he?" She flew into Misha's arms and sobbed.

Wyatt touched her shoulder. His eyes were hard as stone as he mouthed something… something like, *ask her where Alek was seen last.*

"Roka." Misha pulled her sister away. "Where was Alek when you last saw him?"

"Um. I don't know. I think the kitchen," she sobbed. "He'd just arrived from school. Usually he dumps his bag in the office, then starts on the evening prep. God, I hope he's hauled up in the cool room or something. Please God."

Wyatt's looming presence was next to her one minute, then gone —moving—a dark shadow swallowed by the burning building.

Wyatt!

But maybe he was okay. He was different, Misha knew that. He wasn't normal. The things he could do with his strength. He wouldn't go in there without knowing he'd be safe, would he?

Bright blue and red flashing lights bounced off the black billowing smoke, and sirens cut short, truncating ominously. The Fire Brigade had arrived. Within seconds, they disembarked and firemen spilled out of the truck. One came over.

"You need to get back, ma'am. Sir. Please—" he ushered them toward the rest of the watching crowd.

"My brother's in there!" Roksana cried.

"Someone is in there?" the fireman replied.

"Yes, but Wyatt's gone back in to get him."

94

"Two people?" The fireman shouted at a few of his crew, barked orders, and that was all Misha had time to see before they were all forced back.

An explosion burst the front windows of the restaurant, shattering glass into the lot with a ground shaking *boom*.

Roksana screamed. They all ducked and covered their heads as flying pieces of debris and glass soared over head.

When she thought it was safe, Misha turned to the restaurant and caught the silhouette of a figure climbing out of the window. She held her breath. Could it be?

It was!

Covered in a tablecloth and slung over Wyatt's shoulder, Alek's gangly teenager body dangled in his clutches. She almost couldn't look, but had to see Wyatt's eyes. He returned her gaze with devastation.

No.

No, no, no.

Misha burst into tears.

Please don't let him be dead. Not her dear, sweet Alek.

Firemen surrounded Wyatt as he placed Alek gently on the asphalt. Her brother was covered in soot, possibly burned—how badly, she couldn't tell. Along with the rest of her family, Misha broke free from the crowd and raced to him.

"Alek," she shouted, even though he couldn't hear her.

"Ma'am, you need to step back. Make room for the paramedics." A fireman's big hands blocked her. Over his shoulder Misha could see the paramedics unpacking their kits from the ambulance while the firemen battled the blaze. It was Wyatt who calmly and swiftly took control of the situation.

He checked Alek's vitals. He must have sensed something, something good, because he sat back and his shoulders relaxed. He turned, scanning for Misha. When their eyes clashed, he gave a curt nod.

He's okay.

"That's my brother!" she shouted, resisting the fireman still pushing at her. "That's my brother. He's deaf. He needs to see me."

In the end, she broke through and landed heavily on her knees next to Alek as he opened his puffy eyes.

"You okay?" She signed with her hands as she spoke the words.

Poor kid. There was so much going on in his sight. He'd be freaking.

Brow furrowing, her brother nodded hesitantly. His wide-eyed gaze shot around the lot, and Misha could see wetness pooling in them. She tapped him on the shoulder and signed some soothing words as she spoke them.

Misha looked up at her father, who also had tears in his eyes. "He's okay, Tata. He's going to be okay."

"That's up to us to decide," said a male paramedic crouching down. "Sir, are you injured? Can you tell me how you're feeling?"

Misha translated the paramedic's words to sign language, in case Alek was too frazzled to read lips. "I'm right here, Alek. Right here."

Alek gave her a nod. It was the, *I can do it on my own, sis* nod. She stood back, wiped her stinging eyes and hugged her father. In fact, she hugged them all tightly. How could she ever think that this shit with Dimitri would end with her life? It would never end unless she did something about it.

Standing back with an arm around her sobbing father, they watched the Pierogi Palace burn. Her parents had started it after they'd married. Both her mother and father met a few years after their immigration, but had been together since. They'd grown up there. Now it was gone. It was like a memory of Hannah Minksi being wiped from the face of the earth.

Misha overheard two firemen speaking behind her.

"Tell you what, lucky that kid had a wet blanket over him, otherwise he'd have burned alive."

Another responded: "Don't know how the other dude got out unharmed."

"Fucked if I know. Where is he? Ask him."

"Nah, already looked. He's gone."

Misha searched the parking lot, now filling with police questioning bystanders. Wyatt wasn't there. Disappointment made her soul heavy. He was gone. With nothing left to do, she stood with her family and watched the Fire Department shoot water at the only source of income their family had.

Well… it wasn't their only source.

thirteen

WYATT LAZARUS

BY THE TIME the Minski family returned home that evening, Wyatt had tidied the apartment to the best of his ability. Using rusty tools he'd found in the garage, he reinforced the bed and set it back to its original height. The light fixture that fell was in working order, and he re-connected it to the ceiling. After a good Hoover, the only thing out of place was the crack in the wall and the broken doorknob. He'd make a trip to the hardware store tomorrow to fix that.

Showered and dressed, he sat at the edge of his bed, staring at the contacts screen on his smart-phone. Thumbing through the list, he hovered over the names of his family. First there were his adoptive parents, Mary and Flint. Parker, his eldest brother and leader of the Deadly Seven. His other siblings made up the rest of the seven: Liza, Tony, Sloan, Griffin, Evan.

Seven.

Once there were eight.

But that was long ago and something they rarely spoke about.

Being only five years old at the time, he didn't remember much except the lab they were born into, the tiny room they grew up in, and their kind and loving eldest sister, Despair. Evan hadn't yet been born, and seven of them were squeezed into the living quarters, raised by nuns, experimented on, and surveyed through two-way glass by sick scientists. Their biological mother was the lead geneticist who perhaps felt because she grew them in her womb that she had the right to change their DNA and mix it with other things. Repulsive, unnamed things now swimming in Wyatt's blood and making him invulnerable to things like fire and knives.

He laughed at the irony. *Invulnerable.* Where was this power when Sara had slit his throat, ruining his culinary career and his life?

Wyatt studied his phone as Evan's name scrolled by. Evan had been nothing but honest with Wyatt. He'd warned that Sara was a liar, that she worked for the enemy, but Wyatt had been so eager to have a fiancée, to lead a normal life not born from a lab, that he'd made himself believe Sara was the *one* for him. That he could have a family, a career, and children of his own, despite his Yin-Yang tattoo never holding its balanced shape.

His fucking Frankenstein mother programmed their DNA to recognize a person who embodied their exact opposite, someone to balance the sin they were destined to fight, and to make life livable. It all seemed so ridiculous, so outrageous, that none of them had a choice in who they would be with for the rest of their lives. Wyatt had rebelled, heart and soul.

But the heart was the most selfish muscle of all, and the mind was easily fooled.

There was no denying what he was, no escaping it. Mary knew that. It was why she sent all seven of them around the world to learn the art of war for years on end, and why she constantly told them stories of the fabled *one* they would meet one day.

He snapped his gaze to the door as it opened.

Misha stepped in and the breath caught in Wyatt's throat. She looked like an angel underneath the light of the newly fixed globe. Her blond ringlets glowed in a tumbling up-do and, despite the soot on her shoulders, she had a rosy complexion and a genuine smile on her face.

"You're still here." She cast her gaze over the room. "And you cleaned. Wow. You cook and clean. You're hired!" She laughed, then fizzled out, no doubt thinking of her family business now a charred skeleton.

Despite all this, Wyatt sensed no wrath in her. How could she not be furious? She'd said the fire was caused by someone called Dimitri, who he guessed was the gold-bling man she'd argued with. Probably the one she owed money to.

You're not angry at the man who did that to you today? he asked, but she had trouble following his lips, so he typed the message on his cell and showed it to her.

"No," she said simply. "I'm upset, yes, but I don't have room in my life to waste emotions on an asshole like him. Karma will come for him one day."

Do you need money? he asked.

"All the money in the world won't be enough to get rid of him. Anyway, I didn't come here to talk about that. I came to invite you to have a meal with us." She grinned. "We're frying up some pierogi."

He hesitated.

She might not be angry, but he certainly was. Shame and guilt were coming in a close second. If he'd not run from his new powers, from his destiny, that restaurant might still be standing.

Seeing his reticence, she came over and sat next to him, sighing. "Yeah, this is new for me too."

New for her?

She dipped her head and blushed. "I mean, it's the first time I've invited someone I've been... um, intimate with, to my family home."

She scratched her head. "Normally there is no second date. Not that this is a date. God." She scrubbed her face. "The family want to thank you, and Alek's asking about you. Do you want to come, or not?"

No. He shook his head and went back to his phone, not sure what he was doing with himself, but not that.

After putting up with his cold shoulder, she went to the door. "Well, if you change your mind, you know where to find us."

And then she was gone.

Wyatt wasn't sure how long he sat there feeling sorry for himself, and then he heard the sound of music coming from the main house. Modern music and the mouthwatering smell of dinner cooking. Butter, onions…

Then the song's chorus hit—*Welcome to my house*—and he almost smiled. She was back to her music games, enticing him over, and what was he doing? Stewing in his misery. Fuck, he was a moody bastard. All he needed was to play some Celine Dion, eat ice-cream and shed some motherfucking tears in the shower. Was he going to miss out on life because of his inability to admit failure? Maybe Evan was right and Misha was it for him. Maybe this woman would make his life perfect.

Would that be so bad?

There had been no ulterior motive with her invitation. It was simply a thank you for your help.

He went to the door and looked down at the house, studying the family through a window. Misha's aunt was in the kitchen doing the frying. Roksana tried to taste something from the pan, but got her fingers whacked with a wooden spoon. She pirouetted out of the view, laughing. Vooyek walked to a table only partly seen in the background. A tall bottle of vodka sat in front of a series of empty crystal shot glasses, waiting to be filled. Celebrating, or commiserating? With the music in the background, he guessed the former, which made him curious. Why celebrate after losing your livelihood?

There were more people sitting at the table. More family Misha wanted Wyatt to meet.

She'd never had a boyfriend over for a meal, or a lover, or anyone she was intimate with. This was new territory for her too. That thought bounced around in Wyatt's head until warmth spread from his chest. He was her first.

It felt good.

He supposed he could eat.

WYATT LAZARUS

WYATT LET himself in the back door of the Minski family home. The smell of fried onions and bacon made his mouth water. The next smell he noticed was oiled cedar. Just like the restaurant, there was a lot of wood in the home. Furniture, wall art, paneling. Macrame textile wall hangings. Potted plants and knick-knacks. But the house was warm and inviting, so he wouldn't change a thing.

Damn, he was turning into a soft-cock.

The closer he got to the kitchen, the stronger the sounds of laughter and a television beyond. At the doorframe, he folded his arms and leaned against the jamb. The kitchen was small. The old Smeg fridge, free-standing oven and chrome-plated dining chairs, held a seventies charm. An elderly man and woman played a game of cards at the round table. Their wrinkles were so deep you could hardly see their eyes, but they were creased from smiling. Ciocia Violetta was now at the sink, washing up, humming a happy tune. Pierogi was sizzling in the pan.

Eight plates were laid out on the table. Wyatt counted in his head. Unless there was another person hiding in the house he didn't know about, the eighth plate was for him. That gave him a strange feeling.

Misha walked in holding some cutlery and froze. "You came!"

Her squeal was so loud that her aunt twisted from the sink, eyebrows almost hitting her headscarf. The elderly couple at the table both looked up. Roksana rushed in, shortly followed by her father and brother.

Wyatt waved gingerly.

Misha grinned and the tense mood dispelled. She turned to the table. "*Babcia*, *Dziadzio*, this is Wyatt. *WYATT*." She had to shout so they could hear. "Wyatt, these are my grandparents."

They stared at Wyatt with pale eyes and then nodded. He held out his hand for a shake but both had already gone back to their game, gummy mouths wobbling as if they chewed something.

"*Ye-den, dva, tshih…*" the man said as he counted his cards.

His wife blinked and nudged him. "No. You take too many."

Misha took him by the arm. "Don't mind them, they're almost as blind as they are deaf, but aren't they lovely together? Been playing the same game for fifty years."

He wondered who was winning.

Vooyek pushed passed Misha and took Wyatt's hand in a sturdy, gnarled grip.

"Thank you," he said, blue eyes watering. "For saving my boy's life."

Wyatt patted Vooyek on the shoulder. *It was nothing.*

Perhaps he mouthed the words because Alek was the next to burst in. He touched his fingers to his chin and moved his hand out toward Wyatt. It looked as though he said "thank you" as well.

Wyatt gave Alek a once over. Outwardly he looked fine. The wet blanket had done a good job at protecting the boy's skin as he'd raced them through the burning dining room to escape. No doubt, they'd all wondered why Wyatt didn't have a scorch mark on him, but not one of them had said a word on the matter.

"I'm glad you changed your mind." Misha gave him a lopsided smile. "You're just in time for a celebratory drink. Here, have one." She poured vodka into the waiting line of shot glasses.

His furrowed brow wasn't lost on her, so she added: "You may ask what we have to celebrate?"

He nodded, accepting his glass, careful not to spill on the linoleum floor.

"Well..." She picked up her own glass. "We're all alive. We're all here. And... we have insurance."

"There is always a positive in every negative," Ciocia said beside him, collecting her own glass. "We lost our business, but now there is nothing to protect. We pay protection money to those bastards, but *no more.*" Her last words were said with gusto.

"And my arthritis makes me an old man," Vooyek said with sad eyes. "I cannot run the restaurant forever."

"I have more time to dance!" Roksana lifted her leg and pointed her toe at the ceiling, narrowly missing a jug of water on the kitchen bench. She laughed and made an "Oops face" which had her family rolling their eyes. Although he wasn't allowed a shot glass, Alek sidled up next to Wyatt and watched him like a hawk.

Misha leaned forward and whispered. "I think he wants to be you when he grows up." Then more loudly, "I think we are ready for some good fortune. *Sto lat.*"

"*Sto lat.*" Vooyek shot his vodka back.

Everyone around the table did the same. *Sto lat.*

Then they proceeded to sing a raucous song with the same Polish word repeated again and again. Alek couldn't hear, but joined in with the clapping, thumping on the table, and stamping his feet, checking every few seconds to see if Wyatt watched. He couldn't help but smile at the kid.

The singing lasted another couple of choruses. Perhaps they'd had a few shots before he arrived. It was hard not to be amused. Their behavior made Wyatt think of raucous drunks in an Irish bar. Even Misha's grandparents joined in, clinking their empty glasses together and slamming them on the table to the beat of the song.

When they were done, Misha turned to Wyatt with pink cheeks. "We usually sing it on birthdays to wish good fortune, so we get a bit rowdy, but I think it's valid tonight." Seeing his glass still in his hand, she bade him to drink it. "Bad luck if you don't."

Sto lat, he mouthed and shot it back.

"Great!" Misha exclaimed, taking his glass. "You go and sit in the lounge room and relax, we've got the food covered."

Um, I don't think so.

He was a chef, his place was in the kitchen, but both Ciocia Violetta and Misha ushered him out with Roksana and the other men. When he resisted, Misha added, "If it makes you feel better, you can do the dishes later. But for now, it's almost done. Shoo. Good God, it's like trying to move an elephant. Shoo." She pushed him again.

Wyatt stumbled into the living room where Alek, Vooyek and Roksana had turned off the music and put on a home video. The room was a little musty, but lived in. Comfortable.

Feeling out of place, Wyatt stood at the arched doorway to watch. On screen, a heavily pregnant blond woman was fluttering around an outdoor table, helping two young girls shell beans into a red pot. Every few moments, she would rub her belly and Roksana would rub Alek on the head. There was a male voice in the background of the movie—probably Vooyek on the camera. One of the girls looked around five years old, probably Roksana, and the eldest, was perhaps eight or nine, making that girl a young Misha. Wyatt smiled as the girl chewed on her frizzy ends, then spat out her hair to make room for a bean.

"This is my favorite bit," Roksana murmured from the sofa.

When Wyatt looked back at the screen, the girls screamed, the camera wobbled in a frenzy as something was happening. A bird had tried to peck at Roksana's hand to get to the beans, but Misha had protected her with a broomstick handle, swatting at the cheeky bird until it flew away. Their mother cooed to the girls, and hugged them.

"No need to fear. As long as your sister is here, she will protect you."

The camera panned out to a full-length shot of the wild, young Misha standing proud, holding her broom with dignity.

A sigh next to Wyatt drew his attention. Misha had come from the kitchen. His gaze darted back to where Roksana, her father and Alek were beaming at the screen. Their expressions were the polar opposite of Misha's. Her face was full of something other than happiness—concern, perhaps. Duty. Dread, maybe?

"She died in childbirth," Misha whispered to Wyatt. "We miss her incredibly."

Died in childbirth. So, not long after that video which made the mother's declaration about protection something Misha took seriously, perhaps to the point of getting herself involved with the wrong people. The memory of Misha arguing with Dimitri outside the restaurant came to mind. There were things she wasn't telling the rest of the family, and while they seemed to believe their involvement with that man was done, Misha didn't appear so sure.

She picked up the remote and turned the video off. "Come on guys, Wyatt doesn't want to see soppy old family videos. Let's put on a movie that we all like."

Alek's eyes lit up, and he launched to the DVD collection on a shelf next to the TV, almost tripping over his own feet.

Wyatt snorted. *Who watches DVDs these days?* But just as quickly as the sarcastic thought rose, he stifled it down. There was no place for it there. Instead, he forced himself to sit down on the vacant two-seater sofa and settled in.

Alek pulled out the *Die Hard* DVD and showed it to Wyatt for approval.

Wyatt smirked at the kid, then punched his fist to his heart in a classic gangsta show of solidarity: *A man of my own heart.*

A blush stained Alek's cheeks as he set the disc in the player and they settled in to watch. A few minutes later, Misha came back and handed everyone a plate of food, then lodged herself next to him to eat. When her bare feet shoved underneath his thighs, and stayed there, he arched an eyebrow at her. *Make yourself at home, why don't you.*

"What," she mumbled through a mouthful of food. "I get cold feet."

She promptly ignored him and went back to the movie. As if it weren't a huge deal that her cold feet burned a hole through his jeans. As if she didn't feel the connection of their bodies. As if she didn't know what her touch was doing to him.

When he finished his meal, unable to help himself, he set aside his plate and pulled her feet onto his lap where he warmed them with his palms. The adoring look she cast his way made it worth it.

IT WAS ALMOST midnight when Wyatt got back to his borrowed apartment. He felt more at peace than he had in a long time. Good food, good company, and... he felt good. There was no other way around it. Not once had he accidentally destroyed some-thing with his new power. Alek had even taught Wyatt a few basic sign language movements. He now knew *Thank you, Yes, No, I love you…* That last one was awkward, but Alek had insisted teaching it. In return, Alek had asked Wyatt to teach him some self-defense moves. He wanted to be like John McLain from *Die Hard*. No one in the family had objections, so Wyatt, already a little buzzed from a few more vodka shots, taught Alek how to block an attack.

Still thinking about how well Alek had responded to teaching, Wyatt pulled his shirt and pants off, then got into the bed. Before he shut the light off, he checked his Yin-Yang tattoo, marking its perfect symmetry and balance with an odd sense of pride.

Sara had never given him this sort of peace. With her, it had always been as though he was afraid to mess up. She'd kept their apartment in perfect order—towels lined up, can labels facing the front. There had been a sense that something would always be around the corner, something to mess up the order.

Evan was right. Being around his mate, even just enjoying her company and having her feet shoved under his thighs for warmth, was a soothing experience. He felt replenished and rejuvenated, ready to take on the world.

Wyatt scrubbed his face. He'd just called her his mate. Wow. He didn't even mince words or skirt around it. *Mate.* Like two animals in the wild. Not just any mate, but a fated one. One in billions. *Mate.* He said it a few more times in his head to test it out. Each time he conjured a visual of Misha's heart-shaped face and bright cupid's bow lips. She always had a rosy look about her, bright eyes and a happy vibe. Little pink nose.

Yawning, he drifted.

He almost missed the sound of the door opening until someone came tip-toeing in.

With a profound sense of déjà vu, Wyatt tensed. Was she drunk again?

"Wyatt?" she whispered loudly. "Are you awake?"

He turned the bedside lamp on, careful not to crush it.

She stood before the closed door, still wearing her attire from the day. The same clothes she'd peeled off before they'd—heat flushed his skin as he remembered what an asshole he'd been, rutting her like a wild animal in this very bed. He caught her worried gaze.

What's wrong?

He sat up.

She bit her lip and averted her eyes. "Can I sleep here?"

A lump formed in his throat.

"Just sleep, I swear. I don't want another night on that horrible sofa, plus… I don't want to be alone."

He shifted the duvet on the opposite side of the bed. She climbed in, pulling the cover up to her chin, laying stiffly beside him, staring at the ceiling. He switched off the light, casting the room into darkness.

When he laid down, he found he couldn't sleep. He was hyperaware of her body next to him. Couldn't get the memory of her nakedness from his mind, but he didn't want her to know, so held his breath and flexed his toes. Eventually, the sound of her breathing evened out as she fell asleep, and Wyatt gave himself permission to turn on his side and study her.

Beams of soft moonlight peeked through the gaps in the curtains. It was enough for him to make out her profile. Her lashes were like wings, shadowing her cheeks. Her nose dipped from her forehead and then scooped back out in a perfect arch. There was a little knob at the end that gave her features just enough of a difference to make her a curiosity. Then there were her lips, perpetually rosy, as though she were always flushed from the rush of just being kissed—or fucked.

But what he liked most was her curly hair spread on the pillow. Wild, carefree and… resilient. Happy. Just like her.

With her optimistic outlook on life, her loyalty to her family, her patience and vivaciousness, he was drawn to her. It was as though she was made for him—the warrior of wrath.

No. He frowned. That wasn't right. It was Wyatt who was made for her. She was born naturally, a twist of nature, two lovers coming together. It was he who was made—created—to need someone like her. To protect someone like her. To want her with every fiber in his being. It was he who would break if he lost her.

Raw emotion crushed his chest, soon followed by concern, and a trickling sense of fear. There were things she hadn't told him, or her family. Hiding. Secretive. She didn't fool him. The fire today hadn't relieved her as much as the rest of her family. She was still afraid, and she'd come to him for comfort.

She trusted him.

WYATT LAZARUS

AFTER YEARS OF COMBAT TRAINING, Wyatt had learned to sleep at the edge of consciousness, ready to move within a split-second's notice. So when Misha woke next to him the following morning, he roused. And when she slowly and quietly got out of the bed, trying not to disturb him, he became curious.

Dawn's pinkest hues came through the curtains, so where did she have to be so early?

Sleeping next to her had been painstakingly awkward. With his body so aware of her presence, and his mind slowly coming to terms with her importance to him, all he could think about was touching her. He'd wanted to pull her into his arms and take solace in her warmth, to give in to his baser instincts. But even with his thoughts pushing him toward her, there was a nameless resistance, like a rubber band, and he wasn't strong enough to break it. Regardless, he was smart enough to know when he was getting the brush off. She was trying to sneak out like a thief, meaning; she resisted more than him.

As Misha fumbled for her shoes on the floor next to the bed, Wyatt sat up. His sudden movement caused a little chirp of fear from her mouth. When her mind caught up with her eyes, her hand fluttered to her throat.

"Jeez, Wyatt. You scared me. You're like the waking dead."

He cocked an eyebrow at her shoes. *Leaving so soon?*

"Um." She gulped, tongue running over her bottom lip as her gaze raked down his bare torso. Then, catching herself ogling, she bit down and looked away. "Yeah. Look. I had a great time. Like, *really* great, but this between us, whatever we had yesterday is finished."

Brush off. Loud and clear.

Except... he wouldn't accept it. Yes, he resisted, but he was also drawn to her. She didn't know it yet, but they weren't done.

"I'm not good for you, Wyatt." She tied her unruly bedroom hair into a top knot.

She should wear her hair down. The blond ringlets stuck out, but he supposed it only made her more lively. He wanted to tug on that hair, bring her down to his lips, lower. She blushed when she caught the simmering lust in his gaze and a heatwave of hormones engulfed him so suddenly that he almost lost focus. His skin prickled as his body produced pheromones. His scent became stronger. It was all part of the package his mad scientist mother made of them to help trap a mate.

He couldn't say he was completely averse to the pheromones, not if it got her to change her mind, and that made him an even bigger bastard than he thought.

Misha caught his scent, her jaw dropped and her eyes fluttered closed. She inhaled deeply.

"God, you smell amazing," she groaned. "It's unfair."

She didn't know the half of it.

Wyatt shifted toward her side of the bed, uncaring that his arousal clearly showed through his boxer shorts.

"I'm sorry." She put her palm out. "I'm a one time only kind of girl."

Now *that* was unfair. He pointed at his bed. *You came back to me last night.*

"Yeah, but that was in the same day, and we didn't actually repeat the—you know—so I'm counting it as one time. Please don't push me on this."

Wyatt held his palms out in surrender. Fine. Lifting his hands to rest behind his head, he leaned back on the pillows. It was a pose he knew held maximum visual effect, putting his physique on display. She tried not to gawk, and he loved the heat coloring her cheeks. He would get to the bottom of her resistance. Couldn't be any worse than his, could it?

She looked everywhere *but* him.

He tried clearing his throat, testing the sound. He wanted her attention but didn't want to—how did she say it?—push her on this.

Misha glanced over at his throaty sound. Once he was sure she watched his face, he asked. *What are you doing today?*

She laughed and shook her head. "Okay. Small talk. No problems. I've got yoga classes today. You?"

He shrugged.

"Okay. Great. Thanks for the chat." Misha walked to the door, and every atom in Wyatt screamed for him to not let her go, but he was incapable of stopping her.

Just before she stepped through the door, she tossed a glance over her shoulder. "It was nice knowing you, Wyatt. Thank you for everything you've done for my family."

And then she left.

It was nice knowing you?

What the fuck?

A growl of frustration tore from him, and it sounded clear cut and so precise that he shocked himself. He tensed as he brought his finger to run over the ridge of his scar. Was it possible his vocal cords had regenerated enough to return his voice? Rumor had it they were all created with advanced regeneration abilities. Mary and Flint had seen scientists in the lab play around with jellyfish, salamander and starfish DNA, among other things. The man who'd bankrolled their experiment had wanted to test out their regeneration limits by cutting off a limb, but they had been only children. Hearing the ultimatum of the mad man, Mary had moved her plan forward to extricate them from the lab. The day Evan was born, she'd spirited them all away, except it hadn't gone according to plan. His biological mother had by then realized how wrong the entire experiment was and decided to stay back to burn the place to the ground. Sensing her despair, his eldest sister had run at the last moment to their mother, right when the elevator door was closing. Explosions ripped apart the lab before anyone could retrieve his sister—Daisy. They'd named her Daisy because she'd loved flowers.

None of the seven had tested themselves to see if they could regenerate. Strangely, over the years of their training and combat missions, none of them had lost a limb or even a finger. They were too good at what they were created to do. They'd been shot, stabbed, concussed, knifed across the throat... but the limits of their healing hadn't been pushed quite to the extent of what he'd recently faced. When Grace operated on Wyatt's throat after Sara had sliced it, she hadn't been hopeful he'd regain use of his voice, but there was a chance, she'd said. You never know with the human body.

Did he dare to hope now?

Did it matter?

Wyatt wasn't sure how long he stayed in his room. It wasn't until Alek knocked on his door that he got out of bed. The boy wanted to continue his self-defense training, and with nothing else for Wyatt to do, he obliged. Dressing himself, he joined the kid down in their kitchen for what started as a light breakfast, but ended with Wyatt cooking a gourmet egg-white omelet with French toast and fruit. He couldn't help himself. It had been a while since he'd had a home kitchen all to himself. The only other person awake was Ciocia, who ushered the two of them outside the minute he'd eaten his last spoonful of fruit.

When it was just the two of them on the driveway, he mouthed, "*Do you know where your sister has gone?*"

Alek shrugged.

Yeah, Wyatt never expected him to know, but it was worth the ask.

Right, then. Time to get physical. Wyatt spent the next few hours teaching Alek how to read his telegraphed attacks before he made them. A drop of the shoulder, a twitch to the side… it all helped the boy learn to use his eyes to the best of his ability. Next were heel palm strikes, groin kicks, elbow strikes. The kid's appetite for learning was insatiable. He reciprocated by teaching Wyatt a few more hand signs. It made communication between them easier. At the end of their session, he gathered the courage to ask the kid where his sister taught her yoga classes.

The instant he received the address, Wyatt was like a new man. He had a goal and a purpose: he needed to see her.

He showered, ate a delicious ham and dill pickle sandwich in the kitchen made by Vooyek, then donned his helmet and took off on Betty. The coy looks Misha's family had given him before he left made him realize Alek had told them he'd asked about her whereabouts, and perhaps they'd even registered that she'd stayed in his bed last night. Rather than be embarrassed, Wyatt was more interested that none of them objected, meaning Misha's resistance to him was not from family judgement. It was something else.

sixteen

WYATT LAZARUS

WHEN WYATT ARRIVED at the address Alek had given him, he was surprised to find a decently refurbished warehouse in the city center, just outside the prestigious Quadrant, and not far from his family building—Lazarus House.

The warehouse bricks were a blend of orange and red, with cream rendered features running around the windows. Two enormous topiaries sat on either side of a double glass door that displayed the words *Health Studio* with white stickers. The street was clean and respectable. No homeless people, no rubbish floating around.

It was a nice neighborhood.

Parking Betty in front of the warehouse, Wyatt tugged his helmet off and tucked it under his arm. Sun glinted in his eyes and he squinted, bypassing the two sweaty women chatting in front of the double glass doors. He strode to the door and pulled. It didn't budge.

For a minute he thought he'd pulled instead of pushed, but then a woman spoke in a deep smoker's voice. "Studio is closed, hon."

He turned to find an older woman staring at him as she pushed a strand of bright blue hair behind her ear. Next to her stood a younger woman, also in yoga attire. Her round eyes seemed familiar—he jolted with recognition. It was Lilo, Griffin's girl. The reporter.

He blinked away his shock. She didn't know what he looked like, or who he was. Did she? Even if she did, what did it matter that his family knew he was here? Probably nothing. Evan had already found him working at Misha's family restaurant.

"Are you okay?" Lilo asked, brow furrowing.

Hell, he'd been staring while his brain went into a frenzy.

She kept talking, but Wyatt zoned out as he checked Lilo up and down. She seemed nice. Attractive. Her hair was a mess, and she had mascara smudged at the edge of her eye. The strap holding the mat slung over her shoulder was knotted. She was a disarray, not the kind of girl he thought Griffin would date, but then again, Misha wasn't the kind of woman he pictured himself with.

Wyatt tapped the words on the glass door, hoping his intention was clear.

"It's closed." The blue-haired woman's gaze turned suspicious. She no doubt wondered what a black clad man who rode in on a motorcycle would want with a yoga studio.

Not missing a beat, Lilo caught the tattoo on his wrist as his hand came down from the glass door. Her intelligent eyes darted to the scar on his throat, then back up to his eyes with a gasp.

"So," she said, with an incorrigible smile, "this is going to sound strange, but are you by any chance related to Griffin Lazarus? Because you look so familiar and, my goodness, you both have similar features, and that tatt—*ahem*—I mean you have... you know what? Never mind I asked." She cut herself off when her eyes landed on his tattoo again and she glanced warily at her friend.

She was mindful of their family secret. Wyatt respected that.

Lilo waited for him to answer.

He nodded. Yes, he was related.

Her eyes lit up. "Oh my God, so you must be Wyatt. You're the only brother I haven't met. I'm so excited to meet you. Griff said you were on, um, you were on sabbatical or something—"

Right. Sabbatical.

"—he's going to be so excited you're back." She gasped again. "Oh, and Evan. He's always talking about you. Have you been home yet? Is this a surprise? Should I keep my mouth shut? I don't want to ruin anything. Although, I must admit, I'm pretty terrible about keeping secrets, aren't I, Bev?"

"It's true. She's terrible."

"Unless the secret is super important." Lilo held up her pointer finger. "And then I'm like a vault. So tight, that you could put state secrets in there, I swear."

Wyatt was stunned into silence. She talked. A lot. He blinked back at her, taking it all in.

There was a pang in his chest when he realized he'd missed so much in the months he'd been running. This woman sounded so familiar with his family, more so than him. And apparently, she was good friends with Misha.

He tapped the door decals again.

"Here," Lilo said, whipping out a tiny notebook from her bag. "I always keep a notebook. You know, reporter thing. I work for the Cardinal Copy. Write down what you're asking. It will be easier."

He wrote Misha's name down.

Surprised eyes hit him. "You know Misha?"

He nodded, then wrote: *Do you know where she is?*

Lilo bit her lip. "I'm not supposed to tell anyone, but I guess you're family."

Wyatt's heart clenched.

"She's gone to her other job." Her voice held a conspiratorial tone.

Other job?

Unease prickled the back of his neck.

"If you hurry, you might catch her." Lilo pointed down the road. "She takes the monorail. But please don't tell her I blabbed. She'll have my cojones in a vice. She can be quite…"

Wyatt stopped listening and shoved his helmet back on. He paused. Shit, that was rude. He lifted his visor and pointed down the road, just to confirm.

Lilo nodded. "She left literally seconds before you arrived. I don't know much about the place, except it's in Little Russia."

Wyatt gritted his teeth, nodded his thanks to Lilo and started his engine.

"Is everything okay? Misha told us about the fire," Lilo asked.

He didn't have time to chat. Revving the engine, he snapped his visor down. With one last look at Lilo and her blue-haired friend, he nodded. Yes, Misha would be okay. Especially if he had anything to say about it.

"Tell her to return my calls!" she shouted as he tore down the street, leaving them behind.

Little Russia. Wyatt tried to ignore the dark insecurities creeping into his mind. *She's hiding things from you.* A second job? She's not who you think…

When he arrived near the station, he slowed and parked so he could surveil without distraction. Catching sight of Misha waiting at the station platform, he couldn't move. Instead, he waited until she got on the train, then drove to the station near Little Russia and waited across the street, still on his bike, helmet on, visor down.

Inside the quiet, insulated confines of his helmet, suspicions grew louder.

When Misha walked out from the train platform and onto the street, he waited. He watched. Like a creepy stalker, he tracked her as she moved down the street until she got to a large black door with an enormous bouncer manning the stoop. The guy must be on steroids. Muscles barely fit into his suit. Those kind of muscles made a man slow. He'd be no match for Wyatt, not now, not ever.

When Misha disappeared inside, Wyatt finally looked up at the sign over the doorway. The Kremlin Nightclub. With a growing sense of urgency, he took his helmet off and scanned the rest of the street. He was in a seedy end of town. Bars, nightclubs… strip-clubs… dirty streets, unsavory looking people. As Wyatt left Betty parked on the road side, he caught the eyes of two scrawny, toothless men eyeing her off. Fuck no.

Without a second thought, Wyatt strode up to them and hit one in the chest with his palm. The guy fell back onto his ass. Wyatt used two fingers to point at his own eyes, then back at the men, and at Betty. *Mess with Betty, and I fuck you up.*

"Shit man," said the man still standing, scrambling to get away. "We ain't done nuthin'."

Keep it that way.

Grinding his teeth with pent up frustration, Wyatt went to the bar across the road from the Kremlin, ordered a drink and sat down at a table where he could watch both Betty and the club. As dusk fell, and the bar got rowdier, Wyatt held his position.

What the fuck was that place? Why was Misha working there? Why did she hide it from her family, but not her best friend?

So many questions curdled his mind. He tried to research the place on his cell but the shitty reception wouldn't allow him to open a browser. Wyatt deeply missed his sister Sloan's tech hacking skills at that point. He was sure she'd get more information. All he needed to do was call her. But he didn't.

Wyatt hadn't touched his drink, but smelled like a brewery. At one point, the bar had gotten so crowded that people stood next to him chatting and shouting at each other, spilling beer all over him. It took all his restraint not to smash the faces of some frat boys who'd come staggering into the bar after being kicked out of the club. They were sneering and mooning drunkenly over the best pair of tits and ass they'd ever seen. Apparently one of them had gotten handsy until a white-robed and masked freak had almost chopped his hands off with a "fucking samurai sword".

As the night went on, it was clear most of the clientele in the nightclub were men, and that made every nerve in Wyatt pull tight.

Misha hadn't reappeared.

Still working.

At The Kremlin. Where only men went.

Misha worked in a strip club and, apparently, the Syndicate's foot soldiers were the bouncers.

After the knowledge hit him, he got stuck. He sat there nursing his beer, watching the club until closing time. He wasn't done, though, and there was nowhere else to go that he could continue surveillance without drawing attention. It was either go in, or…

Wyatt left a tip on the bar and left. He checked on Betty's safety and then went down a side alley. Once he was sure no one watched, he skirted a drain pipe and climbed to the roof. The bar was only one story and had a flat roof. There was a sign facing the road. Perfect place to sit under and continue his recon. Fuck, he knew he was skirting stalker territory, but he couldn't deal with the fact she was in there doing God knew what, under the watchful eye of not only the Bratva but the Syndicate too.

Every alarm in his body sounded.

He hardly knew her. Maybe she had no idea who the Syndicate were. Not many people knew because the Syndicate were all about subterfuge, about knocking the legs from under you without you knowing they'd been there. They'd planted Sara in his life for years and he knew nothing until it was too late. He hadn't even known she was Syndicate when she died the first time. He'd mourned that fucking bitch like the love of his life. It still hurt to think about. But it hurt more to think that right up until the end, until she took her last breath, he'd hoped she would somehow make things right.

With Sara, there was a duty. What he felt for Misha wasn't duty. It was raw need. But what if the Syndicate planted her too?

EVERY NIGHT for the next eight days, Wyatt returned to The Kremlin and watched from the roof across the street. Misha arrived like clockwork at four in the afternoon. She left at three in the morning, tired and on her own. She usually wore a jacket leaving, but only her yoga attire arriving. Each night, Wyatt followed her to the train station, making sure she arrived safe—that was what he told himself —because a woman walking on her own in that neighborhood at night wasn't a good thing. What was she thinking?

Did she have a death wish?

Her words from the night of the fire came back to him.

It was supposed to be me first, Wyatt. Not them. I can't be the one left picking up the pieces again.

Perhaps she did want to die.

Sara had wanted to die. She'd made a deal with the Syndicate for them to bring her back as one of their freaky clones. They'd promised her they would fix her heart disease, and so Sara had killed herself in the bomb explosion that tarnished the Deadly Seven's name and caused a rift between Wyatt and Evan. She gave the term suicide bomber a new meaning. Was it really suicide if you came back as a cloned replicate?

Too many of Wyatt's buttons were being pushed with Misha's

circumstances. Why couldn't she be a goddamned teacher in suburbia, or something equally innocent and boring? Something that would have absolutely no ties to an organized criminal group like the Bratva, or the Syndicate.

Because this is the world you live in, dickhead. It was full of unsavory shit and selfish people. It was why Wyatt and his siblings were created.

Every night, after seeing Misha to her city home, Wyatt returned to his borrowed apartment in the burbs, and knew the family had no idea of her second job. With the restaurant gone, she shouldn't be beholden to anyone. There was more to the story, or she was working with them.

On the ninth night, Wyatt knew he couldn't stay in the borrowed apartment any longer. It had grown awkward without his job at the kitchen and worse with every passing day Misha failed to return to the suburban home. She avoided both him and her family. Coupled with the fact that numerous Lazarus family members had been calling him, leaving messages and texting, meant he was due to return to the family fold. Part of him was excited, part was afraid, but for the most part, he knew it was time.

He had to do a few things first.

He handed the Minski family a check to replace the damaged furniture in his room. They tried to refuse him, but he insisted, and when he put his chef-face on, people tended to do as expected. They were sorry to see him go, but he exchanged numbers with Alek and Roksana. He told them to call if they needed anything. Anything at all.

Then Wyatt headed to The Kremlin. This time, he was going as a patron.

seventeen

MISHA MINSKI

IT HAD BEEN JUST over a week since Misha had last seen Wyatt, and despite trying to convince herself that he was no one to her, she couldn't stop thinking about him. Even now, walking to work through the almost fresh air of Cardinal City, she still had the scent of him seared into her memory. It was as though he stood right next to her.

But she didn't do relationships for one simple reason—people leave. Whether it's her or him, inevitably one of them would go first, and the other would be left picking up the pieces of their broken heart. When Misha's mother died suddenly, it had almost destroyed her father. Misha was nine at the time, and she remembered a lot. When it became clear Alek was deaf, her father struggled even more. There were many nights she'd see him crying softly to himself with a glass of vodka slipping in his hands. Without his one true love there to help him raise a family, Misha had picked up the slack. Like her mother had always said, she was the protector of the family, the one they called when the going got tough.

Alek had texted yesterday to say Wyatt continued to stay at the garage apartment. In fact, he'd been teaching Alek self-defense tactics.

Why, was her first thought. Who were they to him?

It had been easy to say goodbye to Wyatt when she knew he was leaving, but knowing he stuck around and helped her baby brother... a tightness in her chest followed her daily.

Yuri guarded the entrance to The Kremlin as usual, and as she'd done each day since her beating, she gave him little acknowledgment beyond eye contact as she entered. This time, Yuri halted her with a meaty hand to the shoulder. Misha tensed and clutched her bag.

"Please, *lapochka,* when will you speak to me?" Yuri asked.

Misha could hear the pain in his voice, but it didn't matter. "I have no words for men who beat me."

"I was only following orders. If it was not me, it would have been someone else who hurt you worse."

"So, I'm to thank you?"

"*Nyet.* But, you see there was no choice."

"You once said that you would be with me if I agreed to more than one night. What if I had agreed and we were together? What then? Would you still have followed orders?"

Yuri grit his teeth, jaw tendons popping. He had no answer.

"See?" Misha continued. "Relationships mess everything up. It's better this way. At least we know where we stand."

Misha didn't want anything to do with any of them, least of all Dimitri, but after he'd texted her the night of the fire, demanding she return to work the following day, she feared for her family's life. Worse—he had threatened to bring Roksana in to replace her if she didn't return.

She knew deep down that Dimitri wanted her, not Roksana. As long as she turned up, did whatever he said, his people would see he had control over her, and he would leave her family alone. Well, that's what she assumed. She hadn't seen Dimitri all week. He'd been too busy running around with his new friends, the white-robed ones with Halloween masks.

An air of excitement, danger and fear that went beyond the usual drugs, sex and violence, was present in the club. It was volatile. Dancers had gone missing. Problem customers had too. It was as though anyone daring to speak out of line just disappeared.

Misha walked deeper into the dark club, hugging her bag to her chest. Dimitri now had an army of soldiers in masks ready to do his dirty bidding. It was obvious even Yuri felt uncomfortable about doing things he never thought he'd do—like assaulting his *lapochka*.

For the staff of The Kremlin, Misha's beating and restaurant destruction had served as a warning. If Dimitri could do that to his one and only friend, then he would do that to anyone. Debtors fearfully fell in line, and Dimitri's influence was growing. All Misha could do was to try to find a positive in the negative, just like her aunt had taught her.

Following that piece of advice was getting harder every day.

When she made it to the dressing room, she rested her palm on the closed door and took a deep breath. Unsure what or who she would find inside today, she hesitated. A few nights ago, Chyna had gone missing. She'd been requested for a private party and never returned. Every night since, Misha prayed she would be in there, applying her cat's eye makeup, teasing her hair with an afro comb. She pressed open the door.

"Namaste, ladies." Misha forced a bright smile on her face as she waltzed in.

The room smelled like soured perfume, spilled alcohol and stale smoke. That lump in Misha's throat expanded. No Chyna.

Anastasia and the Russian twins, Katarina and Dominika were silently applying their costumes. A new skinny girl dabbed blue eyeliner onto the bottom rim of her red, sunken eyelid. When her eyes rolled back, she blinked purposefully in an attempt to focus and gain her wits. *Junkie.* The track marks on the insides of her elbow confirmed. How sad.

"No word on Chyna?" she asked quietly, shoving her bag into her locker.

With cameras and microphones in the room, none of the girls answered, but Anastasia gave a crisp shake of the head. Before she shut the door on her locker, Misha closed her eyes and centered herself.

I have two arms, two legs. I'm healthy. My family is healthy. My family is safe. Inhale the future, exhale the past.

Then she shut the metal door with a loud clang.

"Right, then darlings. Who am I today?" She clapped her hands together. No word from Dimitri meant she got to pick her costume, and that was a positive.

Katarina, the twin with the mole over her lip, turned to Misha and sighed. "I am in no mood for games today."

"Now, now, darling. That's no way to speak. We have a job to do, and a show to put on. Come on. Who am I?"

"You are the Duchess, no?"

"Ding ding ding. Two points to the better looking twin." Misha clapped, laughing. A reluctant smile twitched on Katarina's lips.

Dominika rolled her eyes. "We all know who is better looking because I get more tips."

Then they went round-robin and tried to guess who each girl was going to be. They were subdued, and down, but they liked this game. It was the only way Misha could get them all amped and ready to go out. It hadn't always been like this. Hell, sometimes dancing was fun, and Misha got to keep all of her tips, but lately, it was like working at a funeral parlor.

She spent the next few minutes shimmying into her outfit. A black string bikini with a dental floss thong. A tiny peach colored skirt and matching jacket that barely contained her breasts. She wore a string of pearls around her throat, and black high-heeled pumps. At the last minute, she applied a feather fascinator to her chignon, rounding out the tarty English Duchess look.

Five minutes later, the thump of music vibrated through the walls. The club was open. More women crowded into the room. A few waitresses and dancers Misha had never met before.

As Misha finished her makeup, a knock at the door made everyone still.

The only people who knocked were the men.

Followed by two muscly guards, Dimitri gave the girls a once over. "You are all ready for tonight, *da*?"

Nods all around the room.

Then Dimitri's eyes landed on Misha and her blood froze.

"Everybody, out." He gave a negligent flick of his fingers toward the door.

Scrambling like ants, the room emptied. She watched helplessly as the bouncer shut the door, leaving Misha alone with Dimitri.

But she wouldn't be cowered. Like a proper duchess, Misha folded her hands and rested them on her lap. She held her chin high.

Dimitri adjusted the gold cufflinks on his maroon pin-striped suit. He cut a dashing figure. Dark, slim. Eyes like a shark. He inhaled deeply and sighed. "It pleases me to see you have followed orders."

"I really have no choice, darling."

He squinted at her term of endearment. It was all part of her show, of her carefully constructed persona. Let him think it was meant for him. It was more like armor for herself. If she was the Duchess, then she wasn't herself. And she wasn't afraid.

"Then it will please me more to see you working the VIP room tonight."

Her mouth went dry.

"We have an important guest. He will need much attention." Death shrouded his gaze. "Misha, we have been through much, have we not?"

She inclined her head in agreement.

He casually closed the gap between them and wrapped his cold fingers around her throat. He applied only soft pressure, but the intent was there. He could crush her, and nobody would say a word. Just like Chyna, she would disappear.

"I will not tolerate more dissent from you." Dimitri leaned in until his breath hit her cheek. "You make me look weak in front of my men, and everyone suffers because of it. The next time you refuse me, you will not be so lucky. Your family will not be so lucky. Am I making myself clear?"

It was on the tip of her tongue to threaten him back, to say, stay away from her family. He must have seen the opposition in her eyes because his brightened with fury and he leaned into her, tightening his grip around her throat.

"I lit the fire myself," he taunted. "And I would do it again. I would make you watch this time and listen to their screams."

She choked, her airways blocked. Bastard!

"You and I, Misha. We are intertwined beyond death. There are no lengths I won't go to keep you compliant and in my debt. Remember that next time you seek help to be rid of me."

He let go and stood back, eyeing her curiously as she heaved in deep breaths. She rubbed her throat, wondering why the hell he cared so much about keeping her under his thumb. Was it really all because she reminded him of a time he was weak and fragile?

"So, now we are in agreement, I believe you are up first on the main stage. Then I expect to see you in the VIP room for the remainder of the night, *da?*"

When Dimitri opened the door to leave, Misha caught sight of another woman out there. A woman with long, pale silvery hair. Hauntingly beautiful. And what's worse, she met Misha's eyes briefly as she walked away with Dimitri. Her gaze was almost... knowing. In that moment, Misha was more afraid than she'd ever been in her life.

WYATT LAZARUS

WYATT WALKED UP to the entrance of The Kremlin where a big bouncer stopped him with a palm to the chest. The man was larger than Wyatt, had more bulk. He sized Wyatt up. Probably thought he could take Wyatt. Let him. See what happened.

"You look like man who make trouble." The bouncer had a thick Russian accent. No surprise there but, shit. Wyatt had done his best to look unassuming, and still he got singled out. He'd even bought a new collared Polo shirt that was a color other than black. Coupled with hair gel, fashionable jeans and a fucking sports coat, he looked like a dickhead, but hopefully the kind you didn't look twice at. Attracting attention was not on his agenda. He needed to be armed with the truth before returning to his family. There was no way he'd be stuck in the cold with his dick in his hand again. He had to know everything about her.

Wyatt pulled out a thick roll of cash from his pocket and showed the bouncer.

I'm just here to spend.

Like magic, the bouncer stepped aside and let him in.

Following the deep bass shaking the walls, Wyatt put his hands in his pockets and trailed down the dark dingy corridor. He emerged in a room where a stage with catwalks lined the far wall, complete with poles running to the ceiling and half nude dancers grinding, sweating, and lusting. Mirrors behind the stage doubled the dancers. Stools surrounded the catwalks, half filled with eager men already waving dollar bills and whistling. Topless waitresses served leering men under the glowing lights, oscillating from pink and blue to red and purple. What caught his attention the most was a spiral staircase that led from the end of a catwalk up to a mezzanine level guarded by a bouncer. Must be VIP.

Misha works here. Wyatt let that thought percolate until someone bumped passed him, irked that he stood in the main thoroughfare. *For fuck's sake.* He moved and stood beside red velvet curtains cascading down from the ceiling.

Wyatt knew The Kremlin was a strip-joint, but he wasn't prepared for the burst of emotion squeezing his throat. It wasn't wrath—the only wrath he sensed was further into the bowels of the building where it spiked every so often. No, this feeling was something else… he shook it off. No time to play Dr. Phil on himself. *Look for Misha.* He searched the room for the tall, leggy blond. Found a few, but none were her.

Liza would have a love-hate relationship with this place. Lust would be making her feel queasy, but at the same time she'd be reveling in it. She didn't like to reveal much about her journey with her sin, but Wyatt knew she wasn't as innocent as she wanted the family to believe. He missed her.

Liza was a straight talker, and he respected that. She and Sloan had had his back for the two-year falling-out the family had over Sara's integrity after she'd died the first time. *Died the first time.* He snorted at the ridiculous thought, but strangely, it wasn't as crazy now that he'd seen a man turn into an enraged beast engorged with a greed-serum.

He wondered what Liza would say about this place, and Misha. Wondered what Sloan would say.

Fuck. Wyatt scrubbed his face and exhaled. He owed a lot of people an apology.

The sense of wrath he'd felt earlier approached. Alertness washed over him and, curious, he sought out the source, only to duck behind a group of men when he found it. Dimitri. And he wasn't alone.

A tall, silver-haired lady walked with him. Something about her was both terrifying and familiar at the same time. She had an ethereal quality about her and seemed to glide through the filthy club without getting a stain on her white leather outfit. White… the color of the Syndicate.

It hit him. She was the silver-haired woman who had shot Sara from a distance, executing her. His gaze snapped back to the woman, tracking her movements across the club and out of sight. It was the same woman. *He knew it.*

Rage bubbled in his blood. His fists clenched at his sides. For a chilling moment, all he wanted to do was chase her and put his fist through her chest, to see how she liked being executed. But he couldn't shake the feeling there was something else he should be remembering about her. He filed her away for later investigation. Misha was his priority now.

The music died down and a man came on stage announcing the next dancer for the evening—The Duchess.

Air solidified in his lungs. No fucking way.

What did you expect you idiot? She worked in a strip club.

Misha strode on stage wearing a skimpy skirt suit, heels and a feather in her neatly styled hair—all those incredible curls were flattened. With bright red lipstick on her lips, and thick fake lashes framing her eyes, he was looking at a new woman. Every horny male in the room drooled over her. And she hadn't removed her clothes yet.

Fuck.

He couldn't do this. Couldn't watch her—she took off her jacket. *No, babe. Put it back on.* Nothing but a black string bikini underneath, glued to the curves of her beautiful breasts. Wyatt's mouth went dry. Then her skirt went and she strutted down the stage, perfect taut ass teasing the men closest to her.

He couldn't look.

But he had to. He wanted that body all to himself—needed it. It was selfish, possessive and overbearing, but if Misha was his woman —*she is!*—then he didn't want her body on parade for the world. He wanted her for his eyes only.

But what if she liked it? What if this was her thing?

Christ. He was a mess.

Wyatt scrubbed his face and found a seat toward the back of the room. He parked his ass and tried not to look, tried not to hear the cheers and filthy comments the men made. His leg bounced. What kind of mess had he gotten himself into with her? He forced his fists at his side and relaxed his teeth from clenching lest he crack them from the pressure his jaw exerted. *Don't forget why you're here.*

He had to stay. Had to work out if she was linked to the white-robed fuckers loitering around the shadows, and for that, he needed time alone with her.

The music died down, the lights changed. Her show was done. Thank fuck for that.

Wyatt dared a glance at the stage. Misha walked in nothing but her heels, a tiny thong overflowing with dollar bills, and two black stars covering her nipples. She climbed the spiral staircase like a master and disappeared up the top, onto the mezzanine level.

Wyatt flagged down a passing waitress and pointed at the stairs.

She began to feel him up, palms rubbing brazenly down his chest. Jesus. *Take your hands off me.* It took him two more attempts at removing her hands and pointing up the stairs.

"Oh, honey, that's for the VIPs. You'll do better down here with me. C'mon, what do you say. You want a lap dance?"

He shook his head and pointed up again, insistent.

"You're going to need deep pockets if you want up there."

He drew out his roll of untouched cash. Her eyes lit up like he held Christmas. He peeled two bills and held them out, then played keepy-off. *Take me there, and the money is yours.*

She licked her lips, practically salivating at the two-hundred. "Follow me, sugar."

When they got to the bouncer at the base of the stairs, the woman plucked the money from Wyatt and tucked it into her thong. She whispered something in the bouncer's ear who stared down Wyatt and folded his arms.

The stripper made a "gimme" sign.

Another two-hundred gone. Fine.

Within seconds, Wyatt was up the steps and walking onto the mezzanine level.

Scattered around the darkened area were more metal poles and plush leather seats. Velvet curtains continued the trend from downstairs, and when Wyatt looked up, he caught cameras watching over everything. Under blue lights in the corner, a topless woman collected drinks from the burly man pouring them. Two black doors were at the end of the mezzanine. Wyatt could only assume they led to rooms for other services rendered. One bouncer stood guard. He didn't look like much, and it irritated Wyatt to know it was only him and the barman up there protecting the women from VIPs who most likely believed they had the right to do whatever their status and money allowed.

Misha had her back to him and was casually draped from a pole at a private table seating three business men.

Another stripper worked a pole in front of a group of business men.

He needed to get Misha alone. Up here, there was only one way to do that.

nineteen

MISHA MINSKI

MISHA ARRIVED in the VIP area and scanned the place for the mysterious important guest, but found only two groups of patrons, and one was being seen to by Katarina. Dominika was at the bar collecting drinks, presumably serving the other group.

Thank god the Nazi wasn't there, but maybe that was who Dimitri saved her for. A shudder wracked her body, and she had to disguise it with a lusty shimmy. Seeing the group of awaiting business men without a dancer, Misha went to entertain. The number one rule in this place was not to leave a paying customer wanting. She'd barely said hello when Dominika returned with a tray of drinks and a stony look in her eyes. In other words, *Get away from my clients, girl.*

Sorry. Misha backed away and winked. Guess there was nothing for her to do there but wait. She strode to the bar.

"Wassup, Joe?" she said to the barman. "You mind if I stash my tips here until we finish?"

Chewing on gum, the man winked at her and pulled out an empty glass. "Here you go, hotcakes."

"Thanks." She pulled out the bills lining her thong and leaned over the bar to shove them in the glass. Usually she went back to the dressing room to safely store them in her locker, but tonight… she was hesitant to do anything against Dimitri's wishes. He specifically said to head up to the VIP area and wait for the special client. She'd rather lose all her tips to the thieving that would no doubt occur the moment she turned her back, than to go to her dressing room now.

Someone tapped on her shoulder. It was the VIP bouncer. "Hi, Sam."

He grunted and pointed with his thumb to one of the private rooms. He slapped a load of cash in her hands and then went back to his position, watching over the floor with complete boredom.

A private lap dance, already? She counted the money. Holy goddess… Five hundred. She eyed the patrons. All were present. This was someone new. She gulped. The important customer.

Okay, Misha. Here you go. Become The Duchess.

Five-hundred would cover another week's rent for the studio. Since she'd had to cancel a few classes the previous week, it would be more than welcome.

She closed her eyes, imagined a stuck-up royal woman who took shit from nobody. She didn't even like the word shit. She said defecation. *I own the world. The world falls at my feet. I can handle anything.*

Opening her eyes, she pasted a haughty expression on her face and glided up to Sam.

"This one, darling?" She pointed at the door on the right.

He shook his head and thumbed left.

Right, then.

"How dare you request me," she began, fully in character as she opened the door. "Nobody makes demands of The Duch—"

Her words lodged in her throat.

Wyatt's muscular frame squashed into the single chair in the center of the small room. His large hands were white-knuckled as

139

they gripped the chair arms, and he watched her with a gaze burning so hot she felt it in the air. Dressed in a polo shirt, sports coat and dark jeans—he didn't look quite himself. Even his hair was neatly brushed.

She quickly closed the door and held her hand to the flat surface, breathing deep to calm her nerves. So many thoughts crashed through her mind. *It was Wyatt.* He knew her family. Did that mean they all knew she worked there? What if he was actually there for a lap dance, then why the hell did he look so pissed and confrontational? What the hell was going on? Wait a minute, was Wyatt the special customer?

No. Impossible.

So, how did he know about this job?

The only other person who knew where she worked was Lilo. Shit. Lilo was dating Wyatt's brother. That must be it. Damned Lilo and her blabber mouth.

Keenly aware of the red, steady flash of light from the ceiling camera in her periphery, she pushed down her shock, whirled around and walked up to him, snaking her legs and fingering her pearls seductively. The closer she got, the more uncomfortable he looked. That fever in his eyes melted.

You paid for a lap dance. You get one. At least for the cameras, anyway.

When she reached him, she bent seductively at the hips, pushed her ass out, and placed her palms on his knees, looking deeply into his eyes. He made a valiant effort not to stare at her sticker covered breasts, hanging perilously close to his face. It gave her great pleasure to see she unnerved him, especially when he'd just done the same.

Now the fact was sinking in, she became increasingly irritated he'd chased her down. She hated people from her normal life coming to this club, plus, his presence could piss Dimitri off. He could think she was disobeying him again. If the men he beat up at the restaurant were about, they'd recognize him.

"What are you doing here?" she hissed at Wyatt but did a shimmy for their audience.

He darted a glance to the cameras.

"It's only a visual feed," she explained. "Just to make sure the customers don't get too frisky with the girls. As long as I continue to dance, they won't know what's going on." Misha leaned into him, then rolled and arched her chest, undulating near his face. "What is going on here, Wyatt?"

Her breasts scraped against the rough fabric of his shirt. He hissed and tried to sit back as though burned. His reaction brought another smile to her face. Maybe this was going to be fun, after all.

She climbed on top of him and he flinched back. You'd think he was actually disgusted with her—oh, nope, there it was—the hard press of his arousal at the center of her core. She laughed softly. He was into it, he just pretended not to be. When his body heat brought the scent of spiced citrus, she went weak.

"You know," she whispered close to his ear. "I would have done this for free."

The chair groaned under his grip. He let go as the armrests began to crack.

"You should really come to one of my classes. I can help you with that. Meditation does wonders for self-control."

Uncertainty crossed his expression in a wave.

She trailed a finger down his cheek to his strong jaw. God, she loved the look of him. So serious and intense and so much fun to play with. He stiffened under her touch, muscles turning rock hard. She trailed down the vein in his neck, traced his shoulder over the jacket, his bicep, then found the vein over his wrist until she ran down that big powerful hand of his. His hand would completely cover her face.

He could crush her without a second thought, just like the chair. The danger of toying with him gave her a thrill, and suddenly her movements turned sultry, heavy, and full of promise.

She whispered huskily, "Don't feel bad, darling. It happens to the best of us."

He gripped her tightly by the shoulders and held her at arm's length.

What are you doing here? he mouthed the words.

"I work here, silly."

She tried grinding on him, but his eyes sparked with something *not* desire. Rage. And then he began to talk with no sound, so fast she could only stop and stare, trying to catch the words on his lips.

"Whoa. Hold up, buddy." He spoke too fast, but she got the gist of it. She climbed from his lap and stood in front of him, with her back to the camera, adjusting the feather fascinator on her head. "You don't get to judge me for this, Wyatt. You don't know me well enough. It was the only way I could protect my family. Not all of us have the strength of ten big muscly men. Dimitri threatened to bring Roksana in if I didn't continue to work here."

Tears burned the back of her eyelids and she had to take a moment. Dimitri had threatened worse.

How dare Wyatt... She took a breath, swallowed and shook off the insult. In a flash, she was The Duchess again and had it together. Like nothing had happened, she began to slowly sway, getting back into the rhythm of the jazz music. She still had a job to do, and her shift had barely started.

Suddenly, she found herself against a wall, wedged by a man with furious eyes.

Are you working for them?

"Working for who? Dimitri? You already know that."

No. He shoved her and it hurt. *The Syndicate.* At least she thought he mouthed that, but it didn't make sense.

"You're hurting me, Wyatt."

But he wouldn't ease off. The ferocity of his gaze told her there was more to his behavior, that there was an untold story behind those demanding blue orbs of pain. But his grip on her shoulders wouldn't relax.

"Wyatt. You're holding me too tight. Please let go."

As though it were the hardest thing to do, he peeled his fingers from her shoulders. Ouch. His fingers were made from stone. She rubbed her shoulders, crossing her chest, covering her nudity.

I'm sorry, he signed, looking genuinely apologetic.

Whoever this Syndicate was, they'd done a number on him.

"Wyatt, I don't know who the Syndicate is, if that's what you said. I'm just trying to keep these people away from my family. 'These' meaning the ones in this very building."

Something passed behind his eyes—a revelation perhaps—because he shrugged out of his jacket and slung it around her shoulders, enshrouding her in the enormous thing. It was warm, and despite her common sense, she wanted to wrap it tighter, but any minute someone would knock on the door and warn her to keep dancing.

"I should be working," she mumbled.

He shook his head vehemently. *Not here.* With the efficiency of a physician, he briskly put her hands through the sleeves and buttoned her up, but then heat flared in his eyes. He arched an eyebrow, pointed at her breasts and then tapped his chest a few times. *Mine.*

She snorted. Possessive much? She was about to say that the only person her breasts belonged to was herself, but then she picked up on something. His actions had looked suspiciously like sign language. "Has Alek been teaching you to sign?"

He made a fist, lifted it and made the action like he was knocking on a door. *Yes.*

She didn't know what to say. She knew he taught Alek self-defense moves, but she wasn't aware Alek instructed him in return. A warmth spread through her, still speechless.

Before either of them could speak, Wyatt tensed and titled his head as though listening to some far off sound. All she could hear was the music and her galloping heart. And, come to think of it, why hadn't the bouncer come in yet? Surely they'd seen Wyatt accost her. Touching was against the rules.

Wyatt spun toward the door and shoved her behind him in a protective move. Someone was coming.

DIMITRI

STRIDING down the hall to his office, Dimitri couldn't contain the buzz of anticipation rising in his blood. Falcon had been right. Misha had served as bait for the man who'd put Dimitri's men in the hospital. How she'd known was beyond him. He'd placed men to watch her family, and she hadn't returned home for the entire week. He'd been hesitant the man would turn up at all. Dimitri pushed open his office door and was surprised to find Falcon sitting behind his desk, in his chair, casually cleaning her nails with the sharp end of a dagger, white boots resting on his glossy desk.

How dare she sit at his desk.

Her flat gaze hit his expectantly and her brows lifted. "Well?"

"It is as you predicted," he said through clenched teeth. "Security just notified me he is sequestered in one of the private rooms with the girl."

"Good." She stood up and tugged on the bottom of her leather jacket. "Then you should have no trouble with the second part of our agreement."

"How did you know?"

"Know what?"

"That he would come here."

Falcon shrugged. "The same way I knew when you were at your lowest. Men are predictable when they despair. They go after hope as if it were gold. She is what he hopes for, what he craves. He stays with her family, even though she is not there. He wants her."

"And me? What do I want?" He tensed, waiting to see how much she really knew about his fears and motivations.

"Power. Revenge."

"I want the girl alive."

"I don't care what you do to the girl." Falcon skirted the desk and headed for the door, stopping as her hand wrapped around the knob. "It is him we want."

"But I want the man dead." Nobody got away with embarrassing him. He wanted people to know that whether it was the next day, or a few weeks away, he would retaliate for any slight against him.

Falcon stiffened, eyes turning hard. Dimitri thought she'd deny his request, but in the end, she lifted her shoulders. "I don't care what happens to him. Just bring me a sample of his blood."

She walked down the hall and disappeared into the club, no doubt heading for the exit. She'd acquiesced to his demands too easily, and for what? A single drop of the man's blood?

He should stop asking questions. What business was it of his? He got what he wanted from her: soldiers, drugs, weapons. It was only a matter of time before every man, woman and child in Cardinal City feared his name.

twenty-one
WYATT LAZARUS

WYATT GAVE the two men blocking their escape a once-over. Bratva. He could tell from the recognizable tattoos coursing up and down the sides of their necks. Wyatt could take them. A quick knockout each, little fuss, and then he would get out of there with Misha. He'd have to get downstairs, contend with the Syndicate Faithful, and perhaps a few more security personnel. Easy.

Misha poked her head out from behind the protection of his body. "Um. Is this because he touched me? Because we're all good now. Just a misunderstanding, right, Wyatt?"

"*Nyet*," the first guard replied. A scar ran down one side of his face to pucker his lip.

I know you. Wyatt shot him daggers. He was the Russian who'd tried to extort money from Vooyek—the one who'd instigated this entire thing. Without him and the friend he'd put in the hospital, Wyatt would never have stayed or met Misha.

"So, what's going on?" Misha asked. "I have work to do, you can't—"

The door opened, and Dimitri strode in. Five-foot three of suave, slick, sinner. His wrath watered Wyatt's eyes. The scathing glance he sent Wyatt's way would probably shrivel a lesser man's balls. Fuck him and the gold loafers he walked in on. Wyatt's brother Tony would have a field day with this dude's misplaced fashion sense. A quick pang of longing for their banter after every mission speared through Wyatt.

Dimitri turned to Scar-face. "Is this the man?"

"*Da.*"

"Okay, then." Dimitri drew a pistol from his concealed holster. He made a show of checking the rounds, then pulled a suppressor from his pocket and screwed it onto the gun's muzzle. "When this is done," he said to his men, "you leave the body in here until after closing. No one outside this room will know of this betrayal, *da*?"

The men nodded.

Dimitri turned his aim on Wyatt.

"Just a minute." Misha stepped from behind Wyatt, despite his attempt to keep her there.

She stood directly in front of Wyatt and put her hands on her hips. Wyatt's heart almost burst from his chest.

"Exactly who is betraying who, darling?" Misha said.

Shit. This wasn't the time to play Duchess. Wyatt caught Misha's hand and the strangest thing happened when they made skin contact —all the wrath in the room winked out of existence. The sickening crawl in his gut just… disappeared. When Wyatt let go of her, the sin came oozing back in. She was the one. Without a doubt.

"You want me to spell it out for you?" Dimitri said with scorn. "He put my men in the hospital. There is still a price to pay."

"But. But you said I owed you for that." Misha's voice tightened, losing her accent. "It's why I work here. It's why you burned down my family restaurant. How can you say there is still a price to pay! It's been paid."

"You argue with me again!" Dimitri shouted, anger trembling through him. The sense of wrath flared so intensely, Wyatt felt the echoing burn in his gut. Wyatt needed to get back in front of Misha, but he didn't want to draw attention. Inch by inch, he edged himself from behind her back.

Instead of getting angry, Misha just shook her head. "You got some bad karma coming your way, Dimitri. I swear to God. One of these days…"

Her calm demeanor only outraged Dimitri further. "I will shoot him in front of you. Will you like that? We only need his blood. He doesn't need to be alive. I will shoot that fucking *svo-lach*."

A glutton for punishment, Misha said, "What, are you a vampire now? You drink blood, Dimitri?"

The two guards exchanged curious glances.

But with Wyatt, a cold realization was settling in. Dimitri wanted Wyatt's blood. With all the white-robed Faithful milling about, Dimitri was as good as Syndicate. And if they wanted his blood, then… they knew Wyatt had developed powers. When Evan met Grace, Sara had been crazed about getting a sample of Evan's blood. She'd said Evan's DNA had unlocked… that the Syndicate needed it to repair their failed replicates—the clones using the same genetic modification as the Seven. Wyatt's biological mother had been very crafty with her lab experiment. She'd made sure no one else could get their hands on the full research because she'd hid the correct sequence under a layer of DNA junk in their blood.

Apparently, after meeting your mate, that junk code dissipated, revealing the right sequence.

Misha was telling the truth—she had no ties to the Syndicate. She had no clue why Dimitri wanted his blood. She was innocent. Nothing like Sara.

He had to make a choice, and he had to make it stick. No more pussy-footing around. It was either go back to the scared little man he was, running from his problems, running from himself, or he had to trust this woman.

"Step aside, Misha." Dimitri gritted his teeth and steadied his aim to prove a point. "Or do I need to remind you what will happen? I will make your family pay. I will make them scream in agony, and I will make you watch."

"I feel sorry for you, Dimitri. You're still that scared little boy trying to prove he's not." Misha reached for Wyatt at her side, trying once again to get in front of him.

Those words were Dimitri's trigger. He put his hand on Misha's shoulder. And that was Wyatt's trigger.

Nobody fucking touched her.

Wyatt gripped Dimitri's hand and squeezed, watching pupils contract in pain, listening as bones crushed in his powerful grip. And still he squeezed.

The thing was, every man liked to think he was invincible, but when pain hit—it paralyzed.

"You fucking bastard," Dimitri screamed, spittle flying from his mouth, injured hand hanging limply. With his good hand, he aimed the pistol. He fired.

A sting at his chest made Wyatt look down at the burned hole in his shirt.

A breath.

Another.

The pain receded. Misha trembled behind him.

"What the fuck?" The stunned guards gaped at Wyatt, and his completely unwounded chest.

The fallen compressed bullet still rolled on the thin carpeted floor. All eyes watched until it hit the lap dance chair.

Wyatt rubbed his chest. No wound. *Bullet proof.* A slow grin spread over his face.

Fear flickered in the eyes of all three opponents. Dimitri was the first to snap out of it. He made to shoot, but Wyatt stepped forward, took hold of the gun, and squeezed. Metal crushed in his fist. He dropped the useless weapon to the floor and kicked it to the side.

Cradling his wounded hand, Dimitri scrambled back.

Wyatt waved for Misha to get out. He'd take care of these idiots.

"*No.* Stop her!" Dimitri shouted, but Misha slipped past Wyatt and slammed open the door, running into the VIP area.

One of the guards lunged after her, but Wyatt hauled his ass back. He held him airborne, watching the man's legs kick underneath him. Scar-face fired. The bullet stung his bicep but bounced off. He threw the kicking guard into Scar-face. Both went down in a tumble of limbs.

There was no suppressor on Scar-face's gun, and the explosion had ricocheted through the nightclub. Screams of panic soon rose above the beat of the music. The track skipped with the thudding stampede of patrons running. Dimitri's eyes went wide with fear.

"No!" Dimitri shouted, panicked. "No shooting."

Wyatt dragged the cowering mess onto the mezzanine. He hoisted Dimitri up until he balanced against the railing, overlooking the club floor below.

The man's wrath seared until all Wyatt could think was to end him —*cut off the pain, delete the sin.* He was made to eliminate sin and, God, he wanted to do it. He wanted to spill entrails and watch them create art on the floor below. Two-weeks-ago-Wyatt might have done just that.

The Wyatt of today? He looked to the side and clashed eyes with Misha, a step or two down the staircase. He didn't know what he expected, but mortification wasn't it. She was as pale as a ghost, and when he stepped toward her, dragging Dimitri with him, she stepped away.

He didn't want her afraid of him. He didn't want her repulsed. Wyatt dropped Dimitri, and he slumped to the floor.

"You better kill me," Dimitri spat out. "Because I will destroy you for this. I will make you—"

Wyatt shoved a boot in Dimitri's face, shutting him up.

For too long he stared at the man, passed out at his feet. It was Misha's soft voice that snapped him out of his daze. "Wyatt, we have to hurry!" And she headed down the stairs.

twenty-two

MISHA MINSKI

LIKE INSECTS COMING out of the woodwork, Dimitri's security and white-robed soldiers appeared from the shadows. Misha raced down the spiral stairs, but Wyatt had somehow landed at the bottom before her. When his boots thudded onto the stage, she realized he must have jumped.

He'd landed without a scratch on him. *What on earth was he?* Before she had time to ponder, he dragged her through the club, shoving furniture and innocent bystanders between the lunging white-robed warriors and security. Women screamed. Men shouted. Guns went off and she ducked.

Wyatt gathered her in his arms and cradled her against him. Carrying her, he used his shoulder as a battering ram, pushing through anything and anyone in his way. Moments later, they burst into the cold night air, but they didn't stop. They jolted and jostled as he ran, bumping along as his boots pounded the pavement.

He ran so fast.

Afraid for her life, she cowered into his chest, clutching onto his shirt.

Oh fuck, oh fuck.

They stopped. He eased her to her feet, and she opened her eyes, dazed to be nowhere near the club but a dark alley. Breathing hard, he reached into his pocket and threw something at a homeless man sitting by a black motorcycle. The man caught it. Cash. It was cash.

Why did Wyatt throw him cash?

The hobo produced a black motorcycle helmet. Wyatt caught it with ease and handed it to Misha. When she did nothing but blink at it. He tugged it over her head.

After a furtive glance down the dark street, he picked up Misha and straddled her onto his vintage motorcycle. He climbed on behind her and motioned for her to rest her feet on the crash bars in front.

"Shouldn't I be at the back?" She was trembling so much, her voice barely worked.

He tapped his chest and made a gun symbol.

Oh right. He was bullet proof—fucking hell, he was bulletproof! —and their pursuers might shoot them from behind. *Oh, God.* Hurrying, she did what he said. Wyatt started the engine. The beast roared to life. A quick turn of the throttle and they were off, hurtling through the alley like a bat out of hell.

On and on they drove, ducking and weaving through city side streets and alleys. She wasn't sure how long they went, but after a while, her heartbeat slowed, and she became acutely aware that while her back leaned against the very warm and secure feeling of a strong man, her ass cheeks froze against the seat of the bike. She wore nothing under Wyatt's sports coat but her thong, stickers, and a pearl necklace. God, if her father saw her—

Her heart squeezed painfully. *Her family!*

She tapped Wyatt frantically. "Stop. Stop!"

He steered the bike down a street lined with retail stores. Apart from a few homeless people, it was deserted. The second they came to a halt, she was off, tugging her helmet free.

"We have to go home. He'll kill them!"

Wyatt took his cell from his pocket and fired off a text message. Almost immediately, it buzzed back, and Misha had never seen him look so relieved in the time she'd known him.

"What are you doing?" she asked, but he held up his finger and typed again.

Misha paced the pavement. *Just focus on your breathing. In. Out.*

Wyatt motioned her over as his phone began to vibrate. Someone was calling. He held the phone to her and shook it with intention.

"You want me to answer it?"

His jaw clenched, but he nodded.

"Okay." She hit the answer button. "Hello?"

"Misha!" Lilo's panicked voice came through. "Oh my God, are you okay?"

"Yeah, I think so." But her voice trembled with confusion. Why was Lilo calling her? Why would Wyatt call her for help?

"Thank goodness," Lilo gushed. "Wyatt said you'd been shot at? First the fire, now this? Why didn't you tell me about the danger you were in?" The phone muffled as though she covered the handset, and Misha could hear insistent voices in the background. When she came back on, Lilo sounded calm and in control. "Okay. Sorry. You've been through a lot. I'll keep calm. Griff said to tell you he's arranging for your family to take a surprise vacation. Somewhere not too far away. Evan's on his way now to pick them up and take them there. Parker and Liza are going to investigate the club."

Misha's legs collapsed underneath her, and she had to lean on the motorbike for support. Her head felt too heavy for her head. "Thank you," she whispered, tears stinging her eyes. "Thank you."

"Don't thank us, it's all on Wyatt. If he didn't text, we wouldn't know."

She gulped. "Yeah, I get it. I should have confided in you. I don't normally keep secrets from you."

"It's okay. I've been keeping a doozy from you."

Misha's gaze shot to where Wyatt watched her intensely, arms folded. An overwhelming sense of helplessness came over her. What the hell was going on?

"Lilo?" she asked, voice small.

"Yeah, girl?"

"What is he?"

"Um." Lilo's voice softened. "I think I'd better let him explain that."

"You won't tell me?"

"Not unless he says it's okay. I'm sorry. I know this goes against the girl-code, but it's not my secret to tell."

"Is he CIA? James Bond?"

"Misha…"

"Alien?" she hissed.

"You're going to be okay. You can trust him. But gosh, girl, I wish you had told me about Dimitri. I could have helped you. You don't have to carry the burden of this on your own. But I guess, I'm one to talk. I never told you about my father, and the kidnapping until after the fact. But—no more secrets okay?"

Misha's face crumpled and she nodded, but couldn't answer through the lump in her throat. The call ended and Wyatt gently took the phone from her tight grip. He typed up something and showed it to her.

We need to get somewhere safe.

Goodness, she was on the run. She couldn't go home. They knew where she lived. They knew where her family lived. But perhaps…

"My studio might be safe. I don't think they know about that place. I don't think."

I can take you to my place, or a hotel, he typed.

He had a place?

For some reason, that unsettled her. He hid so many things from her, yet he knew every dark secret about her.

She pulled the coat tight. "I have spare clothes at the studio. Is it... is it okay if we go there?"

After a moment, he nodded, and helped her back on the motorcycle. A few minutes later, they were parking at the front of her studio. She'd hidden a spare key under a potted plant, which Wyatt disapproved of greatly, but it allowed them entrance. After she disabled the alarm, Misha walked through the lobby and into her studio.

"Um," she whispered, dashing a glance around the darkened room. Gloss hardwood lined the floors and mirrors on the walls meant if she turned the lights on, they'd be exposed. "We'll have to head down the back to the office in the dark. It's kind of around the bend, so we should be safe there."

Wyatt loitered after her, looking uncomfortable. God, she was the one who felt like a fish out of water. The way he'd handled himself at the club, he was in his element.

Definitely Secret Service. Maybe Homeland. Military of some sort.

She opened her office door and ushered him inside. "In here," she whispered.

The window-free office space was small, but not tiny. Rolled up spare yoga mats and floor cushions were stacked next to her computer desk. The beautiful Ficus plant and her Himalayan salt candles brought some much needed positive ions into the space. Misha retrieved her locker key from the desk drawer and pulled out the desk chair for Wyatt.

"You can stay here while I change in the locker room." She suddenly felt self-conscious.

In the end, she took a scalding hot shower to calm her nerves. When she was done, she dressed in a pair of soft flowing yoga pants and an oversized slouch top that tended to fall off one shoulder. Returning to the office, she found Wyatt standing guard at the doorway, surveying across the vast studio to look through the street-side windows. He cut a menacing figure in the dark with his arms folded, face stern and gaze focused. That gel he'd applied in his hair had loosened on the ride over.

"Sorry," she said. "I needed a shower. You can have one too, if you like, but I'm afraid I don't have any spare clothes here in your size."

He gave the barest shake of his head and then returned to his watchful guard.

Alrighty, then.

Misha unrolled yoga mats and laid them on the empty floor space behind her desk. She dropped a few floor cushions down and flopped down, testing the spring of her makeshift bed. Not bad.

"Think of it like camping," she told herself. Ooh. That gave her an idea.

She retrieved some pine incense sticks from her desk drawer and lit them up. Soon, if she closed her eyes, she smelled forest. Much better. She laid down, but still wasn't comfortable. Lifting her heels, she shuffled her butt and pressed both lifted legs and ass to the wall. With her feet in the air, she took deep restorative breaths and tilted her head back to view Wyatt upside down. "Okay, I'm ready."

He'd been watching her keenly during her ministrations.

She patted the floor beside her. "Come on. Sitting like this is extremely calming. All the blood rushes back to your brain."

He pointed out to the street, shaking his head.

Keeping watch. Got it.

Lowering her legs, she rolled to her stomach and propped her chin on her hand. Framed by the blue moonlight, his tall muscular silhouette wasn't so scary. Maybe not alien after all.

"I'm sorry," she said.

His gaze snapped to hers, dark brows drawing together.

"For everything. For Dimitri. From the fire stopping you from leaving the other day. I guess you wanted something simple when you took the job at the Palace, but instead, you got our mess."

Wyatt shook his head and then rotated his fist around his chest in a clockwise motion.

I'm sorry, he signed, and then tapped himself for effect. *It's my fault. They're after me.*

"Dimitri has been harassing me since we were kids, so unless you've known him longer, I'd say I win."

It's not a game.

Misha sighed and shifted to her back, staring at the blank white ceiling. She should put some star stickers up there. She'd rather be looking at the sky.

"Do you think we're safe?" When silence answered her, she looked at him. "He has an army, Wyatt. How can we beat that?"

I have the Deadly Seven.

She laughed. "I'm sorry, I must have mixed up your words. It sounded like you said you have the Deadly Seven."

His cold stare was her answer.

Sitting upright like a catapult, Misha pulled a cushion to her chest and hugged. That would make so much sense. "Are you serious?"

He nodded gravely and showed her his wrist tattoo.

"I don't know what that means."

His eyes flashed with frustration and he hit the doorframe, making the earth move beneath them.

"Whoa. Chill, Bill." She scrambled to her desk. Opening a drawer, she pulled out a notebook and pen. "Here. Writing it down always makes me feel better. We can even burn it later if you prefer. I did that once when I found a college boyfriend cheated on me. Wrote all these nasty, untrue things, but it made me feel better and then I burned it. It's very cathartic."

Stubbornly, he leaned against the doorjamb for a few more minutes before easing into the office where he sat cross-legged on the mat next to her. His long legs barely fit in the small space, but he made it work. Squinting at the page in the dark, he pulled his phone out to turn on the light.

"Wait." Misha hopped up and went to another drawer. "I have a better idea."

Collecting some candles she had in storage, she set them on her desk and lit them. Soft light bloomed, casting his features into chiseled relief. Yeah, he was a babe. She couldn't deny it. Another night with him would be incredible. But while she was waxing poetic about his handsomeness, he was scowling at the light the candles made.

Misha kicked the office door so it shut half-way. "I think we're out of the way enough that it can't be seen from the street. Plus, it really is like we're camping now. Much better."

When Misha settled next to him, his expression filled with judgment.

"Don't look at me like that." Misha folded her arms, scowling. "I know we've just gone through something pretty serious, but I'm not irreverent. I'm not dumb, and I'm not facetious. I just prefer to take my joys where I can get them, no matter how small they might be. If anything, a night like tonight just proved that. We can't spend our short lives wallowing in misery or fear."

The moment she said the words, she regretted them. They'd come out harsher than intended and, to be honest, she knew the lecture was aimed at herself, because deep down, she *was* all those things.

He paled at her proximity, and she shimmied back to give him space. It must have been what he needed because he dipped his head, staring at the blank paper for long minutes. Then he began to write. He filled a page with his words, and a second page, and a third. Anticipation and curiosity licked up her bones. When he was done, he stood and gruffly handed her the notebook, then walked out of the office and went to stand near the entrance.

He'd put an entire studio's worth of distance between them.

"Okay, then," she whispered, almost too afraid to read his words.

Knowing he trusted her with his innermost thoughts, she sat down, got comfortable, and read.

Misha… he wrote. I *don't know how to start, but I guess beginning with my creation is a good place.*

He wrote that thirty-two years ago, he was made in a lab and genetically modified to be an ultimate soldier. He could sense the sin of wrath in every living person and was physically driven to stop the worst of sin—it was a compulsion built into him and his siblings. Stop the sin or feel sick with it.

Sometimes I want to kill people where they stand, just to stop the feeling.

Clutching the letter to her chest, her heart ached. Imagine having a pain inside you, and the only way to get rid of it was killing someone. She couldn't imagine how hard that would have been to resist.

But she read on.

He wrote that he was stronger, faster, and could regenerate and heal at a paranormal rate. Together with his brothers and sisters, they made up the Deadly Seven. Except, when Misha met him, he'd been on the run… hiding from his duty, hiding from his past. In denial.

Then he proceeded to enlighten Misha about the fanatical organization that bankrolled the experiment that created him. The Syndicate was an organization with deep pockets. They wanted his brothers and sisters to destroy half the world, remove all sinners, no matter if sinners could redeem themselves or not, no matter if they were a child or a mistake.

When Wyatt's adoptive mother rescued them from the lab, tragically, they lost their biological mother and one sister—Despair, or Daisy as they'd named her afterwards.

Wyatt believed the Syndicate were behind the attack on Misha and him at the club. They wanted his blood because, through meeting someone—a fated mate that held no wrath and embodied his sin's opposing virtue, he had unlocked his true potential. It's why he was now bulletproof.

Now they want an army of soldiers like me.

A lump formed in Misha's throat and she put the paper down. He couldn't make this shit up. He must be telling the truth, as whacky as it sounded, she knew the Deadly Seven existed. She knew some of them had developed special powers. It was all over the news. Lilo had a lady boner for writing about them at her newspaper.

Misha went back to reading and almost wished she hadn't. Wyatt's next confession was that he'd recently been betrayed by his now dead fiancée. Reading this part of the story almost broke her heart. His fiancée had pretended to love him for years, even went as far as drastically training her psyche to feel less wrath so she appeared to be his perfect match—all so she could gather biological samples without his knowledge, and to turn it over to The Syndicate. She was the one who had sliced his throat and left him for dead, all because she'd wanted his brother's unlocked DNA. But Wyatt wasn't angry about it anymore, because all those horrible events eventually brought him to Misha.

You're my true mate, Misha. You made me bulletproof.

Just through touching her, the sensation of his sin ebbed away. She brought an equilibrium to his soul. She brought peace and purpose. She'd healed him without even trying. He believed Misha was *the one* for him.

Misha looked to the door where he had left and teared up. No one had ever written to her like this before. He'd poured out his vulnerable heart and basically proclaimed his undying love. They'd only just met!

Having the guts to lay out everything like that was incredibly brave.

It scared her. It scared her so much that she tore the pages into tiny pieces—to protect his secret, she told herself—and then she tucked herself into the cushions, rolled to her side and stared into the dark studio, hoping he wouldn't come back, not yet.

She wasn't brave. She was evasive and frivolous. She jiggled her breasts and ass for a living at night and was a self-proclaimed yogi bear during the day. Her father often joked and called her his little butterfly, but she knew the truth underlying his endearment. She was not what a hero like Wyatt needed, and once he realized that, he wouldn't stick around.

twenty-three

WYATT LAZARUS

TWENTY MINUTES after Wyatt handed his story to Misha, she hadn't called out or come to him. Forty minutes later, still no word. An hour had gone by and, still, he'd not heard a peep.

Finally, he couldn't stand it any longer and left his post. He returned to the office and found Misha asleep, his heart sank. And when he found his letter ripped to shreds in the wastebasket, a bitterness entered his mouth. That was it. That was all he had to give, and it wasn't enough for her. She'd thrown it out.

Numb, he went back to stand near the entrance and watched the dark street outside for signs of life.

He wasn't sure what he expected from Misha. He guessed, a part of him thought since he'd come to terms with her importance to him, she would too. But why should she? They'd only known each other for a few weeks and most of that time was spent apart. He had a biological urge to produce pheromones around her, not the other way around. It wasn't like he gave her instant calm just by being there. No shit, she was a drug for him. When she touched him, the grimy sense of wrath ebbed away like an ocean.

He scrubbed his stubble, thinking. It was too much for her. He'd revealed too much, too soon, but after all the secrets in his past relationship, he didn't want to start a new one with lies. You couldn't dump a secret like his and expect a normal person to shrug it off. Not only had he confessed his true crime fighting-identity, but his deepest pain, and what she meant to him. Hell, he never did anything in halves. He was surprised she hadn't run for the hills.

All out on the table now.

I'm such a dickhead.

Sara had taunted him before slicing his throat. She'd said she picked him out of the Seven because he was the dumbest, most gullible. Maybe she was right, but he was also stubborn and helpless to leave Misha now. Like it or not, she was carved into his life. Accepting that notion was liberating. He just had to convince her he was worth it.

Wyatt didn't sleep. At first, he was concerned with maintaining watch, ensuring no one had followed them from the club. Staying at the studio had gone against his better judgement, but he found he was fast becoming powerless to say no to Misha. When the soft light of dawn unfurled through the windows, he moved from his spot near the studio entrance and found Misha awake and tidying the office.

"Morning," she chirped as she tied a string around a green rubber mat.

Momentarily stunned, he did nothing but stand there and stare. He expected some resistance or awkwardness from her, but there was none. What the hell was going on?

While he waited for the other shoe to drop, he admired how pretty she was after waking. This was the second time he'd seen her in the morning, and her vibrancy was no less diminished. Her blond hair had taken a life of its own, and his fingers twitched to touch.

Was it just him, because of his connection with her? Or did the whole world see her this way?

"So," Misha said, finishing her packing. "I was thinking that I really need to go to my happy place and do some salutations. It's the best way to start a morning and, to be honest, if we top it off with some meditation, you'll probably find it really helps with your"—she screwed up her face and made a mincing motion with her hands—"you know, your squashing things."

He knew how to meditate. He didn't need another teacher—had one for almost a decade of combat and martial arts training. Once, he'd spent the day with other novitiates learning to balance on a wooden pole with one foot. They'd had to balance on top of that pole for an entire day, remain calm with their heart rate under control, while being pelted with pebbles continuously, all without falling off. He'd been the last remaining novitiate balancing on the pole.

Meditation was not his problem. He was fine.

Wyatt put his hands on his hips and paced away, but like a magnet, his gaze drew back to Misha and her infectious grin.

"So, what do you say?" She beamed. "Up for a little resistance training? It's the least I can do to say thank you for your help."

If it meant spending more time with her, then he'd do it. He may be quick to react, he may be hot headed, but his stubbornness could have its benefits. Quitting wasn't really his thing, he'd do well to remember that.

A pang in his chest at the memory of Evan staunching the blood flowing from Wyatt's neck. His consciousness had faded in and out, but the sound of Evan's strained voice still carried to him. *"A Lazarus never quits."* It was the family mantra Wyatt had started in high school. Get kicked down, get back up again. Get hurt, or bullied, keep on trucking. But Wyatt had quit after Sara, and he was ashamed of it.

He nodded to Misha. *Let's go.*

"Excellent. Here take this roll." She handed him a yoga mat and did a little happy dance. "We'll get some coffee on the way and, you'll see, everything will make sense after."

He doubted that, but fine. *Lead the way, Duchess.*

He hesitated outside the studio. They should probably head straight to his apartment, it was safer that way, but he'd not seen a peep of pursuit all night. After the injuries he'd given Dimitri, it was likely he'd not come after them immediately.

"Please." Misha implored with her eyes. "I really need coffee."

Wyatt sighed. Once again, he found himself powerless against her wishes. They were most likely safe for now, and he was fine functioning without sleep. He motioned for Misha to lead the way. Twenty minutes later and they'd passed three cafés. The clouds brewed with promised rain, and Wyatt was beginning to think she took him on a wild goose chase until she stopped out the front of a little brew house on the east-side of the Quadrant.

The shop was nothing but a customer service counter in a wall. Behind the counter were two beach-bum looking men, a cappuccino machine and a manual slow-drip coffee brewer.

"Hi Brian," Misha said, grinning at the barista who wore a slouchy beanie.

The man looked up from cleaning his machine, and when his eyes beheld Misha, they sparkled. "Wassup, sunshine?"

Misha turned to Wyatt. "These guys make the best coffee in the city. Well worth the extra long detour."

He'd believe it after he drank it.

"Ah, a non-believer," Brian said before turning to his friend stocking the small fridge behind them. "We have a non-believer, bro."

The smaller man had long dreadlocks. "We love non-believers."

Misha's grin widened, and they all shared knowing glances with each other, as if Wyatt's mind was about to get blown by their incredible coffee. But Wyatt knew food. He knew coffee. He knew wine. There was no way this tiny, dinky piece of negligible real estate brewed the best coffee in the city.

The little bastards looked increasingly smug as they prepared two coffees in takeaway cups and then handed them to Misha.

"Best coffee in the city, or it's on the house," claimed the beanie guy.

Wyatt scoffed through his teeth and picked up the cup. He removed the protection cap and took a whiff, letting the aroma infuse his senses. Everything inside him relaxed.

Misha took a sip of her drink. Her eyes fluttered closed, and she moaned sensually, savoring the flavor as if it was sex in a cup.

"So good." She licked her lips, still with her eyes shut.

Wyatt had to agree, and he hadn't even tasted it.

Her eyes popped open, completely oblivious to the three male gazes of appreciation pointed her way. A slow crooked smile curved his lips. She was so eager for his approval on the coffee, he didn't have the heart to let her down.

He hesitated.

"Come on. Try it." She watched him, waiting with tenterhooks.

Over the lip of his cup, their eyes met, and he took a sip. He waited for the inevitable bitterness of burned, overcooked beans, but... the liquid hit his lips and failed to scald. He tipped the cup and let the smooth flavor roll over his tongue. Surprisingly, it sailed over his taste buds. He almost elicited an uncontrollable groan himself.

"How good is it?" Misha exclaimed. "Am I right, or am I right?"

She might be right. The coffee was good.

Misha turned back to the smirking hippies. "Put it on my tab. Oh, and could I please have just a cup of freshly boiled water?"

"For you, sunshine, anything."

Oh, puh-lease. From the way the beanie guy locked eyes with Misha, it was clear he wanted into Misha's pants. An unsettling thought tensed every muscle. What if he'd already been there? She dated a lot. She was beautiful. Jealousy swarmed in Wyatt's bloodstream, and he eyed both guys again, trying to ascertain if they—

Fuck! Hot coffee spilled over his hands. In his anger, he'd squeezed the cup without knowing. He was seemingly invincible, but he still felt every sensation on his skin. For a moment, he wished his new ability made his senses dull to sensation, so scalding burns wouldn't affect him, but then he realized that would make him desensitized to everything.

Stiff chance of that. Not with Misha in his life. Lifting his gaze, he caught her coy smile, and instantly a rush of hot desire speared through him. Yeah, he wanted to feel *everything*.

"This training session couldn't happen soon enough." She eyed the spilled mess. "C'mon, then. Let's go. We're almost there."

Funny how her meditation session had now completely morphed into a training session.

Almost there turned out to be another ten-minute walk and despite wanting to humor her, Wyatt couldn't halt his impatience creeping in. The weather was turning as gloomy as his mood, but Misha continued to find pleasure in the smallest things. She stopped and pointed out a chalk painting on the ground, lamenting on how its impermanence should be celebrated and not overlooked. With the looming weather, its artistic magnificence would soon be forever wiped away. Wasn't that a shame?

When they made it to the park in the heart of the Quadrant, Misha took Wyatt down a hidden path, through some trees, and into an area not traveled by many. They were away from the morning joggers, away from the group fitness classes, and hidden in the thick of trees. As they came to the base of a water tower on metal legs, he wondered what the purpose of their expedition was.

Misha placed her empty cup on the ground. "I'll pick that up on the way back. Here, put your used one there too. We only need this hot water."

She proceeded to climb the ladder with her yoga roll strapped to her back, and the remaining cup balanced on one hand. Not liking her climbing one-handed, Wyatt tried to take the cup from her, but she refused.

"Don't stress. It's not the first time I've been up here with something in my hand."

He frowned and climbed after her, watchful in case she slipped and fell. When they crested the tank, he discovered it was flat topped and with a diameter of about three yards. Empty bottles of beer, a newspaper, and some random trash were scattered around.

"Damn kids." Misha peered over the tower and dropped some bottles. It took a few seconds until they thudded to the thick grass at the bottom. They were a long way up—ten yards, perhaps. Enough to seriously injure her if she fell.

"I'll take those to the trash later." Once the top was cleared, she held her hands wide with a satisfied huff. "We're here. What do you think?"

Rotating three-sixty degrees, Wyatt had a full view of the treetops, park and even further out to the lake at the center of it all. The city buildings surrounding them were far enough you couldn't see into any windows, and the sound of traffic was negligible. When a lilac tinged gust of wind blew into his face, he couldn't help but inhale deeply. Incredible.

Misha sighed. "It's great, isn't it? I mean, to find something like this in the center of the city is almost unheard of. I come here any time I need to remind myself the world is bigger than my small problems."

twenty-four

MISHA MINSKI

"HAVE YOU DONE YOGA BEFORE?" Misha asked Wyatt as he unrolled his mat next to her.

He shot her an incredulous look which made her laugh. With that cocky attitude, he'd probably trained with the masters in India.

"Okay." She straightened and faced east. "How about, when was the last time you practiced it?"

Wyatt shrugged evasively, sat on his mat and unlaced his boots.

Boot removal was probably a good idea. The rest of his attire wasn't really conducive to yoga, but the jeans and polo shirt would have to do.

While Misha waited for him, she faced the rising sun, feeling its heat through the clouds. After falling asleep the previous night, her mind and heart had been in all sorts of knots. Her first thought upon waking had been to get out into nature and clear her head. Knowing Wyatt had forgone sleep in order to protect her had instilled a sense of duty. He'd contributed, now it was her turn.

She'd never be as brave as him, both physically and emotionally, but she could teach him this. Right now, it was the only thing she was sure of, so she pushed all of her focus into the moment to avoid the heartbreak she sensed in the future. She let her gaze travel around the green scenery and spent time cataloging each sight. What a great day for a picture memory. She wanted to remember it all. From the tips of the treetops, to the distant ducks quacking, the gentle scent of earth, to the rolling gray clouds.

A masculine throat cleared. Misha turned from the sun to look at Wyatt, and then another kind of heat burned through her. Not only had he removed his clunky boots, but his shirt, and her eyes were rejoicing. He had the kind of body that went beyond Instagram pretty. It was strong, lithe, and deadly. The scar at his throat wasn't the only evidence of old pain. Scattered over his torso were many ghosts. Puckered bullet wounds, deep slashes and shallow scars. Her heart bled for him.

This was a man who put his body on the line to protect people like her. He put his life on the line every day. The notion almost floored her. His job was dangerous. Lethal. Every time he went to work, he might never come back.

And that thought sat too close to home. If she ever decided to be with someone, she wanted to be with them forever. Live together, die together. It was selfish, but it was all her heart could take.

When her eyes lifted to his watchful gaze, the smug male challenge in his expression dissipated. They shared a moment of naked vulnerability, and then Misha snapped her sight to the east.

"Okay," she said in her soft yoga teacher voice. "It's time to begin. Let's bring our feet to the edge of the mat, and dangle our arms to the side, palms to the front. Close your eyes and breathe. Be present. Be aware. In through the nose, out through the mouth. Inhale the future, exhale the past."

She slid a glance sideways to see if Wyatt complied. Standing almost a full head taller, he was the epitome of the mountain pose she was about to instruct. Perhaps she should be facing him for her sun salutations. He certainly had presence. And heat. Look at all that gorgeous heat.

Focus. Back to the pose.

With the patience of a Zen master, Misha led Wyatt through a series of poses, flowing from one form into the other. The lethal man kept up, never once wobbling or breaking hold. Downward Dog, Plank Pose, Upward Facing Dog... it seemed effortless for him. Misha couldn't stop stealing glances at his tight, contorted body, glossy with a sheen of light sweat. Part jealousy, part awe, part feminine appreciation clogged her mind and gave her little respite from her jingling nerves and pumping pulse. After a few sets of salutations, she stopped and collected the cup of hot water.

"Okay. You seem to have that down, so I want to try something else. Hold this."

Lip quirking, he gently took the cup.

Damn. "It was supposed to be boiling hot, but, um... I guess it still might work." She looked in his soul-cutting eyes and lost her train of thought. He watched her so intently, so patiently, it frightened her.

He should be at least slightly pissed. She'd avoided talking about his letter, but he was relaxed, as though he knew something she didn't. Any other man who'd released that number of bottled-up secrets would be more confrontational, maybe even take off. But he was still there. When she noticed a glimmer of amusement in his eyes, she cleared her throat.

"Okay. So, hold the cup. Close your eyes and remember your breathing. I'll try to get you riled up. Wrath is your sin, right?"

He nodded.

"So, I'll try to get you angry, and you need to keep yourself calm. If you fail, you'll squash the cup and the hot water will spill onto your hands. Hopefully, you dislike the hot water enough that you learn to center yourself and avoid using excess strength. Sound good?"

Wyatt's dark eyebrow arched, he popped the lid from the cup, and took a sip. Then he dunked a finger in the liquid.

"Not hot anymore, huh?"

He shook his head.

"Guess I shouldn't have stopped to gawk at the chalk artwork." Disappointment slumped her shoulders. "God, I'm all over the place sometimes. And I was looking forward to harassing you. Bummer. We'll have to think of something else."

Wyatt positioned himself on the mat, standing with the cup in his hands. He shut his eyes and stilled.

What was he doing?

After a minute, he opened one eye and looked at her. He made a wind up sign with his hand.

Telling me to hurry up?

"You want me to harass you anyway?" She couldn't stop the grin forming on her face and the bounce in her step as she went to stand inches from his front. He nodded and she clapped her hands. "Excellent. This will be fun. For me, anyway. For you, I'm going to take you to the cleaners!"

A snort popped out of Wyatt, and then he closed his eyes and waited.

"Okay, okay, let's see. Trash talk." Misha's mind whirled through so many one-liners. Where to start? "Okay. Your yoga was really bad. I mean, like, really bad. It almost looked like you were playing a game of Twister."

His lip twitched, but he held his eyes closed and remained still.

Yeah that sucked. Worst trash talker, ever.

All right, then. *Let's make this harder.*

Misha walked around Wyatt. Her voice turned hard and

venomous. "Your bechamel sauce is disgusting. I didn't want to say anything to you before, but the last time you made it at the restaurant, it was all lumpy and floury. I think it may have curdled. You need to go back to culinary school."

At this, his lip twitch turned into a smirk.

"Damn it, Wyatt." Misha threw up her hands. "It's not supposed to be funny."

He opened both eyes and mouthed to her, *So make me angry.*

It was Misha's blood raising, not his. "Okay, you want me to make you angry? Why don't you talk? Have you tried, or are you too afraid?"

A frown puckered his brow, and she knew she was getting close. Sure, he'd suffered a major trauma that would ruin anyone else, but he wasn't anyone else. A sick feeling churned in her gut. If she wanted to push him, she might have to say some mean things. Things she might regret.

Memories of Wyatt fighting at the club flashed through her mind. His anger had got the best of him. He'd crushed those security guards and nearly sent Dimitri over the balcony to his death.

No. She had to do this. He needed to learn to calm his soul, and if she were to believe his letter, that she was the one person deemed his opposite, then she had to believe she could help him.

Lowering her tone, she stalked around him. "You said in your letter that you were created in a lab. That you all have these crazy regeneration skills, so why can't you talk?"

His frown deepened.

"I think you *can* speak," she accused. "I hear you clear your throat, and there's a solid sound there. I hear Alek clear his throat, and it's different. So if your throat can make a sound, then the only explanation for you not speaking is that you're too afraid to try. Or..." she inspected his reactions and noticed the tension hardening his muscles. "Or, you're lying to me. This whole tortured soul act is a lie. So what is it, Wyatt? You're either a liar, or a scaredy-cat."

His gaze snapped open and pinned her. The cup wobbled in his hands.

"Breathing, Wyatt," she reminded softly, and he darted a glance down to his trembling hands.

Exasperated, he shook his head and shut his eyes. His breathing evened out.

Misha couldn't help the elation hitting her blood stream. She had to make him angrier. See if he came back from more. The perfect thought hit her, and a stone dropped in her stomach, but it would work, and it would kill two birds with one stone.

"I'm not going to be with you, Wyatt. I know you think we've got a connection, but we don't."

He shifted uncomfortably.

Misha stopped pacing and stood in front of him, face to face. Menace poured from him in waves.

"Forget that I've told you I'm only a one time girl, we can't be together because I don't like you that way. You're dangerous, volatile and you run away from your problems. I don't want someone in my life who isn't going to stick around when the going gets tough. I don't want someone who walks away from their family."

It cut, because it was the truth.

"I want someone who can promise me they'll always be there."

A growl of frustration ripped from his throat and he frowned deeply. An aura of danger thickened the air. His muscles twitched and hardened, as though getting ready to pounce. Misha took a step back. For the first time, she wondered what would happen when he lost his cool. A glance over her shoulder revealed she had little breathing room. If he came at her, she'd fall.

Strangely, Wyatt didn't lose his temper. The ticking in his jaw subsided, and the tension dropped from his shoulders. His breathing evened out, and he calmly opened his eyes. What stared back at her was a man with a mission. He lowered the cup gently, placed it on the floor, and then rose to stand before her. Imposing, half-naked, sweaty man was all she could see.

The light danced in his eyes as he clearly struggled with some decision. When he cleared his throat, Misha knew what it was. He was going to attempt to speak.

For her.

Her heart clenched. *No, no, no. Don't do it. Not for me.* Not when she was the one who would run from *him.*

He lowered until his lips rested against the shell of her ear. For three glorious seconds, hot breath tickled her skin, shooting sparks through her system.

"You're the one who's afraid." His voice was raw, raspy and deep, and it sent shivers of desire cascading through her.

"Wyatt, you spoke."

His expression still held a determined quality, a hard set to the mouth, and a razor sharp focus. Aware of every breath, every movement, Misha watched as his hands gently braced her hips.

"You're afraid of being with me. Admit it," he rasped, tugging her closer.

Christ, his voice was sexy. Deep vibrations shimmied through her body, making her weak at the knees. While all her instincts wanted to scream, *say something, speak again*—her mouth said something else. "The cup didn't work. Probably because you're not afraid for it to spill. But… you wouldn't want to hurt me, would you?"

Catching the direction of her thoughts, he released his hold on her.

"No!" She forced his hands back to her hips. "Keep them there.

We're doing this, and you're going to resist your temper. You're going to control your strength."

His eyes darkened. "You didn't answer me."

"And I'm not going to. My feelings don't factor into this situation. We're talking about you. Why did you hide your voice for all these months? What are you afraid of?"

He didn't reply, so she kept pushing.

"You're used to getting what you want. You're used to winning, to being the best. And the fact that someone you trusted took advantage of that, you couldn't stand it. It was better to stay silent. All the better to keep yourself from defending your actions, from leaving your family, from... from apologizing for the hurt you caused. Why speak when you could ignore the fallout instead. Yes, Wyatt, I'm calling you a coward."

His fingers flexed on her hips, and he glowered. He'd retreated back into silence, so maybe she was right. Maybe his lack of voice was all linked to his insecurity, or maybe... he knew he wasn't a coward. She didn't really believe it either, but she was close to riling him. She thought back to the last time he almost lost his temper. She'd called him a liar.

"You know what? I don't know what to believe. One minute you're running, the next you're fighting. Maybe you're not a coward, but you *are* a liar. All this is an act, and you love it. You're just like the woman who betrayed you. You love manipulating and—"

Wrath flared in his expression. In that moment he wanted to hurt her. She could see it in his face. His grip tightened, and the pressure on her hips took on a sharp sting.

"Liar," she whispered. "You're the liar, just like your ex-fiancée."

He squeezed. She winced.

Instantly, he relaxed, surprised. "You want me to hurt you."

"What? That's ridiculous."

He rolled his shoulders smugly, suddenly at peace with his thoughts. "You think that if I do, then you have an easy way out of this."

"There is no this, *koteczek*. I'm just helping you because you helped me."

But instead of answering, he put a heavy palm over her heart. Nothing. He said nothing, but stared at her and felt her heart rate jack-hammering beneath his touch. It was a moment of unrestrained connection that amplified with each gust of wind against their skin. Thunder rolled gently in the distance. She smelled ozone in the air. Misha couldn't tell where her heart ended, and the storm began.

"This is real," he murmured. "Don't run away from it."

A wet blob of rain hit her cheek. Then another. And another.

Before long, the smattering drops came down harder. Misha closed her eyes and raised her face to the sky, letting the sensation of water wash away the tears brimming in her eyes. He was right. She accused him of running, but it had been her excuse her entire life. Don't get too involved, run from love, run from emotional risk because the pain of losing someone wasn't worth it. But... it was more than that.

She didn't believe *she* was worth it. She wasn't worth the pain someone else would feel when they lost her. Better not to get close, not let someone hurt that bad. Better to leave this earth without making a dent in it... but as the thoughts formed in her head, she knew her ideology was full of holes. How could you be in someone's life without love? That pain you felt when they died was a tribute to that love. That pain proved your worth.

Finally understanding her problem somehow... liberated her. She smiled at the beautiful sky, watching the lines of rain slash down. You can't have love without pain, and without any of it, there was nothing.

Wyatt's hand slid to hers and he tugged, directing her to the ladder. He was already a step down, but she resisted. They stared at each other. Water sluiced down his body, running in rivulets that delineated all the hard lines of his torso. Thick black lashes spiked, and his cheeks took on a flushed glow. With his free hand, he pushed back the stringy, jet-black locks from his face. Powerful. Built. So goddamned sexy. How on earth could she pretend to not want him any longer? Without the feelings he evoked in her, she was empty. She was nothing. She didn't want that anymore.

"No," she said. "Let's stay."

He glanced up at the sky. "But it's raining."

"Exactly, silly. We don't run from the rain. We make love in the rain."

twenty-five
WYATT LAZARUS

WITH ONE FOOT on the top ladder rung, and one foot on the water tank, Wyatt looked up at the woman whose hand he held. Rain spilled from the turbulent sky, but it was warm and gentling on his skin. It refreshed, it cleansed, and it wiped the slate clean.

An angel in the flesh, Misha looked down at Wyatt, clearly with impure thoughts radiating from her eyes. Her devious intent hit every male button in his body. It always had. She could entice the worst and best from him with a glance. His eyes trailed down her long neck to where nipples peaked through her wet slouchy shirt.

No, silly. We don't run from the rain. We make love in the rain.

Every bone in his body ached to do that—make love to her, to claim her for his own. This was the opportunity he'd waited for, yet... something stood in the way. She used sex as another wall around her heart, and Wyatt didn't want half of her, he wanted all of her.

Good thing he was built for destroying walls.

He let her guide him back to the top of the tower, and when she lifted her face to the sky and bade him to do the same, he did that too. The water was a joy on his skin and he couldn't remember the last time he did something simply because it made him happy.

Speaking made him happy, but only when he did it for her. It felt intimate. Before he met her, before Sara had sliced his throat, Wyatt had used words to hurl insults, to bully kitchen staff into submission, and to shout his fury at the world. He'd had a voice, but he'd alienated people, made enemies and lost friends. Now, he knew time was a precious commodity—a non-renewable resource—he had to choose his words wisely, because he couldn't take them back.

Wyatt cupped Misha's face between his hands. He forced the raspy sound out of his mouth. "I won't leave you, Misha. Ever."

Her face crumpled. Distance formed behind her eyes.

Don't do it Misha, face this head on.

"You can't control that, Wyatt. You can't make promises like that. Dimitri has armies. He's insane. I've seen him shoot down someone for sneezing on him."

"He can't hurt me. I'm bulletproof."

She hesitated. He already knew she was attracted to him. It wasn't Wyatt who'd propositioned her for sex; she'd come onto him first. So, if it wasn't the attraction, and it wasn't her fear of losing someone she cared for, then… "What's holding you back?"

"I'm not the person you need, Wyatt. You're this amazing, brave man who saves the world, and I'm the kind of person you fuck once, and then cut out of your life."

His heart clenched at her harsh words. She tried to turn her face away, but he held on and forced her to meet his eyes. "You realize that you stepped between me and a gun. Me, who is bulletproof. Only someone completely selfless would do that. Misha, you're not the kind of person you cut from your life, you're the kind you hold on to with both hands."

"What if two hands aren't enough?"

He brushed away the tear on her cheek as it mingled with the rain. "Then I'll hold on to you with everything I have. I'll use my lips"—he kissed hers—"my body"—he enveloped her in his powerful arms, and then he lifted her hand to his chest—"and my heart."

A burst of laughter bubbled through her tears. "Who would have thought my *koteczek* was a poet."

"Only for you."

Her lashes, dripping with water, lifted. The raw emotion staring back almost had him undone. "If I let you in, *koteczek,* I'm not letting you go."

"Good."

Her gasp of surprise confused him. Did she really need more convincing? Fine. He'd convince the fuck out of her.

His lips hovered near hers, but hesitated. He wanted to push her down, tear her clothes from her body and make her his. But he was acutely aware the last time they'd screwed like animals, and he wanted to make this special, to make it last. *Make love in the rain.* She was used to one-night stands, and he was used to betrayal. He wanted to remember every moment with Misha, to sear the sensations into his mind.

Dipping his forehead to hers, he pressed against her. Their hot breaths intermingled through the rain, little white clouds puffed through the air between them, but it wasn't cold. It was nice.

Aching for her, he didn't know where to begin. Her plush lips, taut nipples, tight curves. All of it. He wanted all of it. A groan of anticipation filled the air, and he wasn't sure who it belonged to. It didn't matter that they stood on top of a water tower, drenched in rain, or that the ever present city loomed around them. It was just the two of them in that moment, hearts beating against the other.

She made the first move. Delicate fingertips scraped down his torso, from his chest to his abs, sending slippery pleasure shooting to pool with heat in his groin. Careful not to exert too much force, he traced her jaw to her ear and then to her nape. When her touch tickled inside the waistband of his jeans, he almost jerked into her hand. He studied her reaction to his hardness. Her breathing increased, her pulse fluttered at her neck. She liked it. She liked him. It all felt right.

Misha pulled back, and a rush of cool air came between them. For a moment, he feared she'd turn this into a game, but she lifted her shirt over her head to splash at their feet. Standing before him, half-naked, she trembled. Perfectly round breasts were hard, nipples peaked and straining toward him. Tiny goosebumps rippled over her flesh, but she didn't look cold. She looked flushed with fever.

"This is the first time I've been with anyone more than once," she confided.

"And it will be the last time," he croaked. "Nobody else after me."

It was a demand he didn't have the right to make, but he was making it. So fucking what?

His lips found hers with a gentle touch. It was the kiss he should have given her from the start. Not some hard and fast coupling where he didn't look in her eyes as he fucked her from behind, but the kiss to show how much she was worth. He slid his tongue past her lips, while hers caressed back. Hot, slippery and damned erotic. Deep heat rose in his body. Prickling awareness told him he reacted on a biological level, pumping pheromones from his pores, demanding she become his.

He tugged until her soft front met the hard planes of his chest. "You're mine, Misha."

She moaned into his mouth, submitting. "And you're mine, *koteczek*."

Her words snapped whatever control he had. All the lust and desire he'd leashed since she'd danced for him came roaring to the surface, flooding his senses. He scooped her up and lowered her to the mat. Deepening his kiss, he let his hands roam over her body, learning her, relishing her for the first time. But it wasn't enough, he needed more.

Snarling with impatience, he found the top of her waistband and tugged her pants down. She lifted her hips enough for him to get them over her ass, and then she helped kick them off the rest of the way. He sat back on his heels to study her, bare and pale under the falling sky.

Stunning. So fucking beautiful, and he wanted her with an irrational fury, a fever possessed desire. It had never been like this with Sara—the second her name entered his thoughts, he pushed her away. Done. He was done comparing, done thinking of her.

Misha. Misha his bright bubbling goddess. His infernal drug. The woman who had his heart and didn't like waiting for it. He smiled when she gave a bark of protest at his pause and rose to meet him. Mouth crashing against his, she tore at his jeans with impatient hands, desperate to get into them. The button popped, the zip came down, and she pulled his length out, heavy and hard into her hands.

He groaned, eyes rolling in pleasure as she stroked him.

Misha, Misha.

Then quickly, rashly, he pushed her down and irreverently kicked off his jeans. He kissed down her neck, licking and tasting the water pooling on her skin. From the dip in her collar bone to the valley between her breasts. His fingers found her nipples, and she arched into his calloused touch.

"Wyatt," she begged and thrust into him, her core meeting his erection.

Impatient. So delightfully impatient.

He grinned against her skin, already making his way down her stomach. He cupped her sex, teasing her gently with a finger while he laved around her belly. She whimpered and pushed back. But he made her wait. His turn to play a game. He slid back up her body, letting their wet skin slip and bump together, then he whispered in her ear and told her all the naughty things he would do to her, how he was going to take his time and make her beg for more.

"You talk dirty," she groaned, then gripped him by the shoulders, excitement flaring in her eyes. "Oh my God, please tell me you role play too."

A chuckle rumbled through him and he nuzzled into her. He would do whatever she asked. Fuck, he was falling in love. Maybe he already was. His humor gave way to pure emotion, and he pulled back to stare into her eyes. There was only one thing standing in his way.

"No secrets between us, Misha. Now's your chance. If there's anything you need to tell me, do it now."

twenty-six

MISHA MINSKI

MISHA LAY before the big warrior, naked as the day she was born, and he was worried about secrets between them. They were on top of a water tank in the middle of the city park. Sure, they were far from prying eyes, and it was raining, but there was an element of danger, of arousing urgency. Someone might catch them.

"No, *koteczek*. You know every dark and dirty thing about me." She took his hand and placed it between her legs, urging him to continue.

But he didn't.

He tugged away and pierced her with intense, storm brewing eyes. Then without warning, he gripped her knees and yanked them apart. Misha gasped as rain kissed her intimately. Squirming, her hands rose to find something to latch onto, but found only the edge of the wet rubber mat. It was something, an anchor to steady herself as the first lick of his tongue between her legs set her mind spiraling. She moaned, arching into him.

A strangled sound of satisfaction came from him as he unleashed himself on her. His tongue swirled and twirled and teased. He pushed a finger inside her and pumped. He sucked and devoured with a single-minded ferocity she couldn't resist.

This man is a god. A fucking sex god.

She must have shouted it, because she felt him chuckle against her flesh before resuming his relentless pace. She wouldn't last long at this rate. And to think she only wanted one night with him. She threw her head back with abandon as her body tightened, and then, just as he brought her to the edge of insanity, she propped up on her elbows and looked down at him with the irrational urge to take a picture memory, fearing this is all there would be.

Sensing her movement, he glanced up. "What are you doing?"

"Taking a picture memory. Making sure I don't forget."

His eyes flashed with sexual hunger, and then slowly, torturously, he licked a long stroke down her center before resuming his feast. Her vision blurred with climbing bliss. Seeing her man—dark shock of hair, vibrant blue eyes filled with passion—pleasuring her was the most erotic thing she'd ever witnessed. The sight tipped her over the edge. Her climax crashed through her, screaming with intensity.

When she opened her eyes, he'd risen to his knees between her legs, cock jutting proudly. And goodness, it was great. He was great. Every muscle and tendon in his body pulled taut with need until she could see the shape of him beneath his skin. He was strained. So tense. Afraid.

And she knew why.

The last time they'd come together, he'd hurt her—bruised her—in his passion. God damn it, she'd liked it, but she understood his hesitation. She diffused the situation the only way she knew how, with humor.

"And on the sixth day, God created cocks," she said with an

impish grin and lifted herself to take his erection in her hands. She whispered as she stroked, "Don't overthink it, Wyatt. You won't hurt me. I trust you."

He gripped her nape, brows drawing together. Still hesitant.

"You trust me, don't you?" She stroked him lovingly. "You know I'm telling the truth."

She guided him down until his tip met her entrance. "Do it," she challenged.

Pushing her back to the mat, he eased inside until he was all the way in. He stilled, letting her adjust to his thickness, until she writhed with impatience.

"I'm not letting you go," he murmured, then drew out slowly, and thrust in hard. She slid on the wet mat. "Two hands, Duchess."

It was another joke. She should have laughed, should have gripped the mat for support, but his raw hunger snapped her inhibitions. Like a wild woman, she clawed at him, kissed him, moved with him. She tasted his skin, inhaled his wicked scent, and begged him to go faster and harder. And for a while, they did. Relentless. Unforgiving. Electrifying. She didn't want it to end, but couldn't get enough of the man.

Slowing his pace, he lovingly tended her mouth with soft and gentle but fleeting kisses.

"You're playing with me, *koteczek*," she snarled half-heartedly.

"No," he said gruffly. "I'm loving you."

Misha pushed him off and twisted until she was on top and he laid below. Clearly, he let her. There was no way this big strong hero conceded to anyone—but her. That awareness kept her from moving. They stared at each other, chests shuddering with stilted breaths, hearts beating a staccato rhythm, rain pouring around them, adding to the symphony. Did he mean it? Did this insanely powerful man mean it?

I'm loving you.

She took his hands, held them to her breasts and dared him with her eyes. "Two handfuls, Wyatt."

The laughter rumbling from deep within his chest pierced all the hard walls she'd erected around her heart. That unadulterated laugh was so rare, and because of her, for her, and only her. She ground into him, taking over the rhythm, beating him at his own game. Before she knew it, their joining had her mindless, breathless, and unable to move. His hands dropped to her hips and steadied her trembling pace. Between the two of them, they hit every spot, every nerve and every inch of her soul. When she felt that telltale knot of sensation, tightening inside her again, her muscles clamped down hard. Feeling invincible like a goddess, she lifted her soggy hair from her neck and arched. She tipped her face to the rain and let go, shattering apart while he held on, two hands like he promised.

While she went limp, sated and satisfied, he rolled them again so she was on the bottom. He drove into her hard, increasing intensity until he tensed with need, slammed himself to the hilt and cursed his release, muttering in her ear.

He languidly kissed around her neck and continued to mutter curses, as if his release had taken him by surprise, as if he was angry it was over. She laughed at his fierceness. "If I had known sex would always be like this with you, *koteczek,* I might have given you a different nickname. Perhaps little savage is more appropriate. What do you think, *dzikusku?*"

"What does it mean?" he mumbled. "*Koteczek,* I mean."

"Kitten."

His laughter roared so loud it shook the tower.

THEY SPENT the better part of the next hour indecently fooling around on the top of the water tank. Eventually the rain eased, and the wind picked up and even the heat of their love making wasn't enough to keep them warm. Their clothes were drenched, but they somehow managed to put them back on. It made Misha laugh. They'd really lost track of time. But what made Misha the happiest, was the permanent smile plastered on Wyatt's handsome face.

That smile was still there as they walked back to the studio, his arm slung casually over her shoulder, heedless of their soaked attire. Wyatt even stopped to point out a group of sparrows hopping around a puddle, taking a bath.

It neared lunch time when they approached the door to her studio, and she was surprised to see a group of people milling about. Misha recognized some faces, and it hit her—she'd forgotten about a scheduled class. She was twenty minutes late.

"Oh my God," she exclaimed. "I'm so sorry guys."

Her clients turned to her, grinning in various states as they noticed her disheveled appearance, and who she was with. She'd made it well known that she wasn't a walking hand in hand kind of gal, and some of her older clients had always teased her about finding someone to settle down with.

Wyatt stood back and gave her the space she needed to make things right.

"How about," Misha said, "I give you all a free make-up session tomorrow? I'll make it twice as long and—"

"That won't be necessary," a deep voice spoke from behind the crowd. "I'll refund their fees for today and carry you through until the end of the week. Your studio will be closed for the duration."

What the hell?

No one told her to close. This studio was her life.

"I don't know who you think you are—oh. Hi."

A tall man with long auburn hair in a designer suit appeared. It was Parker, Wyatt's brother, and he didn't look pleased.

The last time Misha had seen him, he'd been partying it up with her and the rest of his family at his nightclub's opening night. That was about the time Dimitri had ordered her to work as an exotic dancer in return for her family's protection. Looking back at it now, Misha wouldn't be surprised to learn Dimitri orchestrated the attacks on her family, all so he could swoop in and appear the savior.

Parker today was a far cry from the man who let loose on the dance floor. That playboy was the same public version gossip rags talked about on the news networks and in the papers. Now knowing about their sins, this arrogant version was probably the first time she'd ever met the real Parker Lazarus. What was the bet he fought the sin of pride?

Wyatt came forward and the two men scowled at each other.

"We give you space only to find you've been whiling away your time doing God knows what." Parker looked down his nose at Misha. "Or should I say, *who* knows what. While I'm all for spreading your wings, it's not really the time nor the place for such deeds, is it brother?"

Wyatt clenched his jaw, fury flamed his eyes, and he pointed in Parker's face, ready to chew some words out. The two of them faced off—Wyatt's brutal wrath, to Parker's nonchalant power. Where Wyatt was tall, lean muscle, Parker's bulk was brute strength, but he carried it with the languid fluidity of a well-oiled machine. It wasn't only Misha who noticed the silent power struggle, but the rest of her yoga clients. Some of them nodded awkwardly at Misha and made a quick exit. To the rest, she sent a few placating words of peace and told them she would contact them during the week.

She would deal with Parker's assumptions he owned her studio once they were alone.

Turning back to the brothers, Misha expected an explosive show, and was preparing herself to have Wyatt's back. Maybe she could jump on Parker, somehow get her hands around the strong column of his neck. Before her plan of attack finished, before Wyatt uttered a word to Parker, he bit down and unclenched his fists at his side. He nodded, conceding. When he turned to Misha, there was an apology in his expression.

Parker adjusted his cufflinks and then waved to the awaiting black Maserati SUV, double parked on the street. "Your chariot awaits. Try not to drip all over the leather." Seeing Wyatt search for his motorbike, Parker added, "God knows why you swapped your old ride for that piece of junk, but Evan's taken it home."

As Misha followed Wyatt into the back of the vehicle, she couldn't help feeling that she was a school girl about to be reprimanded for kissing under the bleachers. She opened her mouth a few times to defend herself, but decided this naughty school girl thing could be interesting. There wasn't much she could do about her yoga classes right now. No use getting worked up over it. The positive in the negative? She glanced at her brooding man while he buckled her seatbelt for her.

"Are we in trouble?" she whispered as Parker got into the front driver seat. Wyatt shook his head, and she deflated. "Oh, well, in that case, will you promise to spank me later, anyway?"

She knew that, like Parker had said earlier, it wasn't the time nor the place for such frivolities, but a small part of her had to know how Wyatt would react. Any man she considered dating must be able to take all of her, including her facetious humor.

When he returned her words with a smolder—yep, definitely a

smolder—she grinned widely and cuddled into him, making sure to rub her soggy pants into the leather. The unmistakable shake of his silent laughter warmed her. If they were getting in trouble, the fun was well worth it.

twenty-seven

WYATT LAZARUS

WYATT FOLLOWED his sauntering brother through the dark basement hallway of Lazarus House. The way his arrogant brother had picked him up from Misha's studio didn't make things easy. Parker treated Wyatt like a recalcitrant teenager, not a full-grown adult capable of making his own decisions. Yet, somehow, Wyatt felt no anger toward him. Without Misha by his side, he knew the outcome would be very different.

No tears. No flying fists. *Let's see where this is going.*

Lazarus House was a multi-level building owned by Parker, reserved for their family living quarters, their public hospitality establishments, and their secret base of operations.

Misha followed a step behind, her tiny hand enveloped in his, blocking out all sense of wrath with her calming contact. After the mind-blowing morning they'd shared, trusting their innermost secrets to the other, their connection was stronger than ever. But now... as they emerged from the hollow tunnel and into the operations room filled with blinking computer screens, weapons tech, and tall glass cabinets displaying lethal battle uniforms, he wasn't so sure.

The unmistakable glint of alarm entered Misha's eyes, and she tugged on his hand to inspect the room. Not one of Wyatt's family was present which meant they probably waited upstairs. The only sound came from the dull drone of a police scanner in the corner next to Flint's workbench littered with broken pieces of machinery. The only movement came from the screens on the walls, flashing CCTV footage from around the city and local news networks. The center bench was reserved for planning battle strategy, but today, lay empty and clean. Wyatt let Misha draw him to the glass cabinets surrounding half the room. Each housed a hooded suit on a black mannequin. Seven mannequins. Seven suits.

New designs, he noted. Gone were the black rudimentary leathers. These suits were dark gray, made from something leather-like, and with contoured trimming that flowed with the shape of the body. At the belt, and no doubt on the back, was an emblem Wyatt guessed Parker created to signify their team—a circle with a seven in the middle. Wyatt inwardly groaned. A logo? What next, incorporate the group and list them on the stock exchange? Still, as he cast his eye over the suits, he couldn't help appreciate the expensive looking material. He had no doubt they'd be a dream to wear in the field.

A dream to wear in the field?

Had he already taken that step? Back in the team, just like that?

Parker put his hands in his pocket and stood behind Wyatt, a mountain of responsibility.

"You've been gone a while," his voice rumbled.

Too long.

"There have been some upgrades," Parker continued. "The material is made from a graphene spider-silk polymer blend. Flexible, thin, flame retardant and they absorb kinetic energy." He arched a brow at Wyatt. "Although I hear it would be wasted on you."

So word had traveled back about Wyatt's new invulnerability.

"Still," Parker added. He opened the cabinet and pointed down a line running inside the sleeve seam. "You might enjoy the new capabilities for base jumping. Lock your arms to your body, your legs together, then tell AIMI to activate the wingsuit. A membrane is released from the container in the seam, and you're good to go."

"AIMI is loaded into the suit?" he asked, awed. AIMI was the artificial intelligence computer Flint, Sloan and Parker jointly created. But the last Wyatt heard, she was only available in the old school ear comms.

Parker nodded. "Speaker and mic attached to the hood. Shielded computer chips and flexible circuit boards layered throughout. She monitors your vitals and sends real-time data back to Flint. Except Griffin. His suit's more mechanical, and his power can disrupt everyone if he's not careful, but we're working on it."

"Fuck."

Parker snorted.

Wyatt felt as though he'd missed too much. Half expecting Misha to freak about the glaring reality of Wyatt's dangerous second nature, he waited for her to make an excuse and leave. As it turned out, she sidled up to him with mischief in her eyes, and ran a hand seductively up his front to wrap around his nape.

She whispered in his ear, "Please tell me you get to take your suit home. You might need to rescue me in the bedroom."

A warmth spread through him. Trust his girl to turn everything into a positive.

Parker gaped at the smile on Wyatt's face and then lifted Wyatt's wrist to inspect his balanced Yin-Yang tattoo. He shook his head. "I had to see it to believe it." To Misha, he said, "Welcome to the family. Wyatt, spare clothes are on the table. Misha, Lilo has you sorted upstairs. Here's a robe for now."

"Oh, thank God for Lilo!" Misha gratefully accepted the robe from Parker before he left the room. Turning to Wyatt as she put it on, she pursed her lips. "What did he mean?"

"That we can finally get changed out of our wet clothes."

She slapped him on the chest. "You know what I'm talking about. Why does he think I'm part of the family? It's a little, I don't know, soon for that, right?"

He gathered Misha into his arms. "There's only one way this is going to end between us. Together."

A distance formed behind her eyes.

Obviously, she still needed convincing he wasn't going to leave her, despite the dangers of his job. She needed to believe that love was worth it all. And to do that, he had to be everything she'd never had in her life. A supportive influence, a lover who would never leave, and a loyal protector. He leaned down and kissed her gently, tasting her lips. It was only meant to be a sweet touch, but the instant her salty tongue pushed through to his, arousal speared through him and he deepened the kiss until she gasped for breath.

"You really need to quit doing that," Misha murmured into his mouth, clutching onto him.

"Doing what?"

"Kissing me to distract me."

Wyatt nibbled her jaw. Licked her perfect skin. Sucked her ear lobe. Couldn't help himself. She drove his instincts with her scent and her very proximity. There was nothing for him to feel in that moment, no wrath, nothing, but her consuming presence. His hands slid down to cup her ass. Her clothes were wet. Soaking. Abruptly, he broke the kiss. "You're right. I'm distracting you from changing into dry clothes."

Misha's eyes had glazed. "No, from the pressure of meeting your family."

His palm ran down his face. This was serious. For Christ's sake, he was on his way to reunite with his family. But she made him mindless.

Trying to keep his back to her, he stripped and quickly changed into the clean clothes that had been sitting on the workshop bench. A pair of sweat pants and a black T-shirt. They knew him so well. When the soft cotton slid over his skin, he registered how irritating the damp fabric of his jeans had become. He scrubbed his hand through his hair, took a deep breath and turned back to Misha.

She stood near the exit, hugging her robe, eyeing him appreciatively. "We'll be revisiting *that* later. But first, I'm starving and kinda cold."

Lips curving, he guided her toward the hallway, past the workout room, medical room, and then to the elevator at the end. When they got inside the car, he stood back while she inspected her appearance in the mirrored wall surrounding them.

She was in his house. His home. He couldn't wait to cook her a good meal. None of that homey shit, but a taste bud exploding gourmet meal. To show her everything he'd learned about being a five-star chef. People fucking went on a wait list to eat his food.

Her hands trembled as she tucked hair behind her ears.

He opened and closed his mouth multiple times before saying quietly, "I know this is a lot to take in."

After checking her teeth, she turned to him with a blank face.

"The inside look at our headquarters," he elaborated. "And staying here… but it's safest for you here. At least until we work out how to deal with Dimitri. We have a spare apartment, so you don't have to stay with me if you don't want. I mean, I'd like you to, but you don't have to."

A blush tinged her cheeks. "Thanks, Wyatt."

That wasn't a definitive answer, but he didn't push her. It might take her over the edge and the last thing he wanted to do was frighten her away.

He took her hand and drew her to his body. "Have dinner with me tonight."

"Like a date?"

"Yeah. I'll cook. We can watch a movie. You can call your family."

Finally, peace seemed to settled over her. "I'd like that."

A ping announced the elevator's arrival at the third level. Wyatt stepped out with Misha shortly behind. He took a deep breath of courage, took Misha's hand, and walked into the common apartment to explain to his family of deadly heroes why he hadn't contacted them in five months. He'd left a broken, betrayed man, and returned with his mate. But they'd continued to fight the Syndicate without him, continued to do the right thing while he'd run from it. He owed them.

They followed the noise of chattering from the foyer into the large open space living room where the family sat around an enormous gray sectional sofa. The big television screen they faced displayed the local news station on mute. Further into the apartment was a billiards table, and a shared kitchen they used when entertaining in the common apartment. He remembered many nights when all seven of them, plus Flint and Mary had gathered to share a good meal and shoot the shit.

A quick count of heads showed Tony and Grace as absent.

Behind the couch, at a small round table, Griffin sat with their parents Flint and Mary. Sloan hunkered down on the couch, half underneath a blanket, plugged into a handheld device, glowing cat-ear headphones, and playing a game. Evan sprawled next to her, one eye on her progress, the other vaguely interested in the conversation Parker was having with Liza and Lilo next to him.

Upon their arrival, all noise vacated the room. Everyone stared at

Wyatt and Misha. A few gazes darted to their joined hands and then a chorus of smiles flowed around the room. Flint and Mary stood stoically at the back. Griffin came around to give Wyatt a handshake and clap on the arm. Lilo jumped up and raced to her friend for a hug, despite Misha's wet clothes. They spoke too fast to ascertain, more at home with each other than Wyatt felt in that room.

"I knew it." Evan stood up, fist pumping the air. "You tried to deny it, but I knew it." Then he turned to Liza. "Pay up, sis."

Smug little bastard.

The tall brunette rolled her eyes and fished into her pockets, pulled out a fifty and slammed it into Evan's waiting palm. His cocky elation wasn't shared with their sister. "I'm not betting against you again. You cheat," she simpered.

"Don't hate me because I'm smarter than you." Upon seeing Wyatt's glaring attention, Evan elaborated. "She bet that you'd hold out for longer, but she doesn't understand what it feels like to find your mate. There is no resisting."

Misha tensed beside Lilo, both had fallen silent.

"Whatever, Sparky." Liza turned to Misha. "Nice to meet you again. Tony will be sad he missed you."

"Nice to see you all again." Misha stepped closer to Lilo.

"Oh, you poor thing. You look drenched," Lilo said. "Come on, I'll take you up to our apartment. You can have a hot shower while I find you something to eat and wear. Obviously I know why you've been ignoring me now, but we can talk about that in a minute. Oh, how silly of me." Lilo turned to everyone in the room. "You all remember Misha from the opening night of Hell, right? Do I need to do introductions?"

"No, that's not necessary. I think she's met everyone." Parker came over to stand next to them. "I'll have some food sent up for lunch. We might be here a while."

"Great." Lilo stole Misha away, and a jolt of panic went through Wyatt.

Their idyllic morning was officially over. He intercepted them just before they entered the elevator. He wanted to tell them to go up to his apartment, because that's where she belonged, but he reined in his urge.

"Don't be long," he whispered to Misha.

Seeing the alarm in his eyes, she gave him a quick kiss on the cheek. "You'll be fine. Don't overthink it."

He watched the doors close, wondering how the hell he matched with such an easy going woman, and how the hell he seemed to like it.

Wyatt went back to his family.

Mary immediately left her husband's side to round the big couch. As she passed Sloan, she slapped her on the head, dislodging her headphones and mumbling for her to get off the game.

Grimacing, Sloan rubbed her dark shock of messy hair. It was long, split-ended and possibly matted. Her disheveled hair wasn't the only worrying sign. The weight she'd stacked on when Wyatt had last seen her was now gone, but not in a good way. Knowing her sin was sloth, she most likely had lost the will to keep herself fit, fed and washed. She slowly wasted away. Her trickster attitude was nowhere in sight.

Feeling his eyes on her, Sloan looked up and scowled. "What? You're the only one allowed to have a mental breakdown?"

Wyatt's jaw dropped, but he failed to speak.

Sloan slid belligerent eyes toward Parker. "Can I go now?"

"What do you think?" he shot back.

Liza had returned to her phone, swiping and making sexual cooing sounds. When Wyatt turned to Griffin for answers, he replied awkwardly, "Tinder."

Right. His two sisters were falling under their sins hard, and his absent brother... "Tony?" he rasped.

Shocked eyes snapped Wyatt's way.

"Yes, I can talk," he said, cleared his throat, then met eyes with Evan. "Thanks to Grace's handiwork and our biology. Remind me to thank her later. And you, Evan. I owe you an apology."

Evan's cheeks pinked, and he nodded curtly. "Grace'll be back tonight. Tony's on set. Filming for some new movie he started. Haven't seen him around much since Hell opened."

Mary pushed through the large men crowding around Wyatt. Flint wasn't far behind. The two of them had aged. He was used to them being so energetic and youthful. The last he'd tried, Mary could still master him during a sparring session. But the past few months had been hard on them. Sara had blown a hole in their family dynamic, and their children were flirting dangerously with their sins. The Syndicate was knocking at the door, threatening to make Mary's foreseen diabolical future a reality.

New worry lines were etched around both sets of eyes. Flint had more gray at his temples, and Mary's slick dark braid had lines of silver streaking through it.

"*Mijo*." Mary cupped Wyatt's face, her brown eyes turning liquid. The woman knew how to kill him a hundred ways, but the tears of gratitude glistening in her eyes hit him the hardest. "I'm so happy you're home."

Wyatt drew her small but strong, muscular frame into his body and hugged her tightly. The only mother he'd ever known, she'd been the first to understand the self-destruction and devastation in their futures. Her clairvoyant powers had pointed her in their direction as children and rescued them from the lab and the Hildegard Sisterhood —another faction of fanatics who wanted to use them. It was Mary and Flint who took it upon themselves to give the Lazarus children a semi-normal childhood and then taught them to be warriors for good. Never forced to do anything they didn't want to—except of course the seven years of combat training—after that, it was up to them who decided to team up and fight crime. Mary and Flint supported them when they fought, they supported them when they all took a few years off after Sara's first death. And they supported him now. Without the unconditional love from Mary and Flint, Wyatt might have lost faith completely after Sara. Seeing the two of them now, with love for each other still in their eyes, it gave him hope.

Mary pulled away, and then surprisingly, Flint drew Wyatt in for a hug, clapping him on the back proudly. "Good to have you back, son."

twenty-eight
WYATT LAZARUS

"RIGHT," Parker said loudly. "Let's get to work. We need to inform Wyatt about what's been happening, and he needs to explain what the fuck is going on with this Bratva mess." He frowned at Wyatt. "Do we need to be worried?"

"He's in league with the Syndicate," Wyatt rasped, then cleared his throat when his words caught. "The silver-haired woman was there. They tried to get a sample of my blood, but—" Wyatt strode over to where Liza sat and pulled her pistol from her holster.

Being a Cardinal City detective, she carried one on her most of the time.

Wyatt pressed the pistol into his palm and fired. He bit his tongue at the excruciating pain, and for a moment, when he tasted blood in his mouth, he worried that his invincibility had worn off. But when he pulled the gun away and opened his fist, a squashed bullet fell out. He shook his hand out. Fuck that hurt.

He licked the inside of his teeth, tasting blood. Must only be his outer skin that was invulnerable.

Evan whistled in awe, and a few collective "Oohs" went around the room, but Liza put her phone down and scowled at Wyatt. "You discharged a government-issued weapon, you dick. Now I'll have paperwork."

"Get some more rounds from downstairs," Griffin said, ever the pragmatic one. "No one will know."

"That's not the point," Liza grumbled.

She was acting off today, or maybe it was more noticeable now that he wasn't in a perpetually foul mood. As a matter of fact, any of the seven who weren't matched with a mate were snarky. What a difference some time with Misha had made, even more evident now with distance from his past self.

"So," Evan said. "She didn't get a drop of your blood."

Wyatt shook his head.

"Well, she'll be back for more," Parker said. "This Falcon woman doesn't seem the type to give up."

A ping sounded at the elevator. Suzi from Heaven's kitchen came in with a bag of takeout. She'd been Wyatt's sous chef, and a talented one at that. He was surprised to see Parker had given her access to their private rooms. Must trust her.

The robust woman had blond pixie hair and blotchy rosy cheeks from the heat of the kitchen. As she approached, Wyatt noted she wore the uniform of the head chef—his old position.

Upon seeing Wyatt, she froze. "Chef."

He made a pointed look at her uniform. The old Wyatt would have made some passive aggressive statement, but he honestly didn't care that she'd taken his job. It wasn't for him anymore. He loved cooking, but he didn't want to work in a big kitchen. He didn't know what he wanted to do with himself. Getting back into his battle gear would be a good start. He had a lot to make up for. All those bodies he'd wasted during his tour across the country with Betty... it did no good except incite more violence in the bars he'd left. Perhaps now, he could approach his sin with a calm head. He could do some good.

"Suzi," he said. "Uniform looks good on you."

Her cheeks brightened. "Well, I had a good teacher."

He folded his arms and snorted. "I was an ass, but I'm glad you think so."

She handed him the bag and gave Parker a short salute, then left. Once they were sure she'd safely gone, they continued their conversation.

"How did Falcon know about your DNA unlocking so soon after the fact?" Liza asked. "I mean, the Syndicate only want our blood *after* we've met our mate. With Evan, Sara discovered his blood had changed purely by accident. With Griffin, he had a public display of power, but with you, Wyatt, did that happen? How did they get wind of your situation?"

Wyatt cast his mind back over the past few weeks to determine whether anyone other than Misha had witnessed his transformation, and then it came to him. "The fire. I walked out of a burning building unharmed. It wasn't exactly a secret. I think Dimitri was already working for the Syndicate, so he probably passed the information on."

"They're everywhere." Liza threw her hands up in defeat. "It's like they have someone who knows us as well as they do. They know our habits, they know our places of work, they probably know what we eat and who we fuck."

"No need to get crude, Liza." Parker arched an eyebrow. "But I get what you're saying. It might even be possible that they know about the importance of the mates. They know too much about us, and we're still yet to learn about them."

But maybe, Wyatt did know something about them.

"Falcon looked familiar," he said cautiously.

"I'm assuming you mean beyond the interactions we've had with her over the past few months." Griffin nudged Sloan aside to make room for himself on the couch.

Wyatt turned to Parker, the only other one old enough to remember. "Does she look familiar to you?"

Parker's brow puckered as he inspected the food bag. "No."

"What if you imagine her with dark hair, instead of silver-white."

"I don't pay that much attention to other people," he replied.

Wyatt walked over to the window, pulled aside the curtain and peered down the three levels to the center city park. "Maybe it's nothing."

Mary came to stand near him. "It's not nothing. Tell us what you're thinking."

"She reminded me of Despair."

Mary gasped, as did the other members of the family.

"Come to think of it," Parker said, eyes narrowing. "She does look familiar. Is this possible, Mary... Flint? Could she have survived the fire that killed our biological mother?"

"It's possible." Flint came forward to stand next to his wife and rub her shoulder. "You can all heal extraordinarily well. We've seen them make clones that grow in tanks. There was a friend of mine who worked at the lab—Barry—he was almost as big of a genius as your mother. He grew limbs from cells in a tank. Anything is possible."

"No. It's not. It can't be Despair," Mary said firmly. "I would have seen her in my visions."

"They know how to circumvent your visions, Mary," Parker said. "Not to mention, your visions are drying up. Evan only dreams about whatever is on his mind the most, so it's definitely possible you've all missed the connection. But me—" He sat up straighter. "There's no way I'd have missed it. Despair is dead."

"That's your pride talking, Parker." Griffin narrowed his eyes. "You're not all seeing."

The tension thickened. Wyatt could feel the hostility on his skin, and for once, it hadn't come from him.

"We need to get Falcon," Wyatt said. "Whether or not she's our sister, she holds the answer to everything. She will be the key to stopping the Syndicate, once and for all."

"I agree," Evan said.

"Me too." Liza helped herself to a bread roll from the food bag.

"And how do you propose we do that?" Parker asked, although it seemed like he already knew the answer but was holding back.

"Since we know nothing about them, except she's working with the Bratva, we set a trap." Wyatt also took a roll from the bag, and turned it over in his hands, thinking. The trap had to be good. Unpredictable. "We neutralize Dimitri's threat to Misha's family, and then we take Falcon. Maybe Dimitri can be the trap."

"Except we know the Syndicate are smart," Liza added. "If we go in guns blazing, they'll be prepared. If we go in quietly, they'll see us coming. They know what we all look like."

"Liza is right," Griffin added. "The Syndicate were the ones who paid Lilo's father to gather photographic evidence of our true identities. We intercepted those pictures, but who's saying there weren't more? It's obvious they know who we are."

Liza continued. "The Syndicate has the numbers, they have Faithful coming out of their asses. Even if we do manage to stop this Dimitri dude, Falcon will get away."

"So what do we do?" Wyatt asked.

This was the point Parker decided to share his plan. The fact he saved it until they'd all made suggestions, reeked of hubris. "We go in disguise. Tony is perfect for this. He has makeup artists on speed dial, he knows how to act… it's a strip club. It's like this mission was made with his name on it."

Griffin wasn't so sure. "Still, there's only so much intel he can gather as a patron."

"I need to go back."

Wyatt spun around at the sound of Misha's voice, his heart tripping. "No. Absolutely not."

Misha had returned with Lilo and both stood by the exit. "Think about it, Wyatt. Dimitri has an unhealthy obsession with me. It goes beyond the fact we used to go to school together. I used to think his warped attention was because I was nice to him back then, but now I'm not so sure. He needs me for something. I don't know what, but he does. We can use that."

"That's exactly why we can't use you. We don't know what's going on in his mind."

Misha wasn't swayed. "I can claim that you kidnapped me against my will, that you're even scarier than he is, and that I need protection from you. It will appeal to his ego, you know it will."

"That man doesn't have an ego. He's pure psychopath." Wyatt folded his arms.

"I've been inside his office many times. I know where he keeps his ledger book. If I can get some solid evidence of his criminal activities, you can put him away for good, right?" Misha said to Liza, already discounting Wyatt's opinion, and that grated at his nerves.

Liza frowned in return. "Stealing his ledger won't be enough. We need to catch him in the act, we need supporting evidence, or we need a confession."

"There is a girl who went missing," Misha added. "I'm sure he got rid of her after a private party went wrong. If she is dead and we can tie her death to Dimitri…"

"That could work," Liza said, tapping her chin. "A homicide connection would also involve me professionally, all above board."

"No," Wyatt tried again. "I'm not accepting this."

"Good," Misha said as if Wyatt hadn't spoken. As if he had no voice again. "Me groveling at Dimitri's feet will make him feel as though he's won. It will take him by surprise. As long as I'm out here, on the run and evading him, he'll be paranoid that his people think he's weak. He burned down our restaurant to prove a point to his followers. When I went back after that, he was grateful I kept my head down and went back to work, just like he'd publicly ordered. I know how to placate him. I know how his mind works. Not only can I get some evidence of his crimes, but I can get close and get information about this woman you want. I've seen her there many times."

Wyatt couldn't believe Misha was saying this. Dimitri burned down her place to prove a point, and that was only because of an unpaid debt. This time, personal humiliation was involved. "And what happens if Dimitri decides to punish you on the spot—to eliminate you this time?"

"He won't do that. He likes to have power over me. And if it comes to that, Tony will be in the club, right? He'll be my backup."

"You're a civilian, Misha. You're not prepared for this kind of subterfuge." Wyatt stepped toward his mate.

"You have no idea what I'm prepared for. You hardly know me."

Her words were an arrow to his heart. The two of them glared at each other.

Seeking to keep the peace, Parker gestured at Sloan. "Sloan, you can take Misha's place. Get a job at the club."

Sloan didn't respond. In fact, she'd failed to utter a single word the entire time Wyatt had been there.

"Are you kidding me?" Liza said. "Have you seen Sloan in a bikini lately? Then again, maybe if you say she's working for V-bucks, she might get off her ass."

Sloan poked her tongue out at Liza.

"Aw, come on, Sloanie. That's gotta get you laughing." Liza stretched out her foot to nudge Sloan across the couch. But Sloan just ignored her, as if she didn't have the energy.

Lilo piped up. "I'll do it. I know how to defend myself. I know how to gather intel."

"No, Lilo." Misha gave her friend a soft smile. "This isn't your fight."

Lilo folded her arms and cocked her hip. "Oh, so it's okay for you to put yourself in danger, but not me? I want your family protected as much as you. They're my family too."

A low growl rumbled from Griffin's throat as he crossed the room to be with his mate. "No. Definitely not. You're not going in."

"Don't you start." Lilo glared at him. "You know once I set my mind to something, there's no stopping me."

Griffin shook his head. "Your face is on the video news networks now. You're too recognizable."

"So is Tony!"

"He can act."

Uneasiness rolled in Wyatt's gut. He didn't want to come between Griffin and his mate. "What about you, Liza? You worked in vice. You had girls in the trade as informants. Can't you get one of them to go in for you?"

"Don't look at me. I've been working homicide for years now. And I have a job. I can't just disappear to chase down some old contacts. Although, playing stripper does sound like fun." She shot a worried glance toward Lilo, and then Misha. "And I would prefer not to rely on Lilo. No offense, Lilo."

"None taken."

"No. Too risky. The Syndicate knows what we all look like," Evan added.

"Well, if Tony can go undercover, so can I," Liza simpered.

"Tony's an actor. You can't act for shit," he shot back.

"She doesn't need to act. She just needs to dance," Misha said. "Can you dance? Shake your ass, you know, that sort of thing."

"Babe, when men see me naked, they fall to their knees and weep. When they see me naked dancing… let's just say we'd better have the paramedics on standby. Give me a wig, some clever makeup, and I'm there."

It was Griffin who pointed out the obvious fact they'd all missed. "The lust in that club will make you physically sick."

"Come on, it's not that bad," Liza drawled. "I'll be fine."

"Don't be angry at me, Wyatt," Misha said. "I think it could work. I can handle it."

"No." Wyatt couldn't accept it. She was right. He hardly knew her, and he could lose Misha before he'd had a chance to keep her. But with the look of defiance and stubbornness in her eyes, he knew if he didn't agree to this, he'd lose her anyway.

Shit.

And that's when the knowledge settled on him.

He didn't trust her. Not yet.

Wyatt turned on his heels and stormed out of the room.

twenty-nine

MISHA MINSKI

AFTER SEEING WYATT STORM OUT, Misha turned to his family, pleading. "You know me going back is a good idea. I know that club like the back of my hand. I know Dimitri's every mood, where he keeps his ledger book, and... I can't explain it. I just know I can handle him. I'll be safe."

She hated the feeling of guilt churning in her gut. She had to do something to help.

Parker rubbed the bridge between his eyes. "You probably can, but we won't go in blind. Sloan, hack the club's CCTV. Deep dive into Dimitri's financial records. Let's put him under the microscope. There has to be a reason he's working with the Syndicate. Maybe we can find a trail that will lead us right to them."

Sloan whined, but one cutting glance from her intimidating eldest brother, and she shut up. She pulled out a laptop from between couch cushions and opened it. "On it."

"Evan, Griff, I want you shadowing Dimitri's men and the Faithful at the club. See if you can find another base of operations.

One thing we learned from Sara's time as a member of the Faithful was that they hole up somewhere to plan. She had a nest, remember?"

"That's right," Evan said. "She took me to her dingy room where she kept notes and surveillance gear. She was a cloned replicate, though. I destroyed them. Would all Faithful act the same as the clones? Some of them are just normal people working for the Syndicate."

"That's what we assume. But we could be wrong. We won't know unless we follow them. At the very least, one of them might lead us back to the Syndicate's base of operations. We know they're working out of the city somewhere."

Griffin nodded grimly. "They've got serums and other biological weapons in production. We saw what a couple of injections did to Lilo's ex, Doppenger. It gave him super strength, speed and even the ability to sense sin."

"We need to get on this right away." Mary stepped forward. "I'll get Tony in for a debrief."

"Lilo," Parker continued. "We appreciate your offer to join Misha, but we're going to need you on standby to feed anything we find to the networks."

"I thought we were doing this the right way," Liza added. "What do you need the networks for?"

"Sometimes the right way doesn't work. If that happens, I want every newspaper or station in the country publishing the Bratva's dirty laundry. Your department is full of dirty cops, Liza. We can't be sure their crimes will go unpunished if Dimitri is captured through the proper channels."

"That's why I'm going in with Misha," she replied. "I'll make sure he receives justice."

"It might not be enough. Between us, we've got some of the smartest minds and strongest warriors in the world. I'm done being one step behind the Syndicate." Parker turned to Misha. "For now, you sit tight. I'm not going to be responsible for Wyatt losing his mate. If we do this, we do this right."

Once he was finished barking orders, he picked up a bite to eat and casually nibbled. "Oh, and before I forget, I've hired a security firm to protect our public establishments. They'll be setting up shop across the street. We'll be meeting them in a few weeks. Lilo's kidnapping on the opening night of Hell made it glaringly clear we can't be two people at once. We can't be the Deadly Seven and our public identities at the same time, so for all the times we need to maintain our cover, we'll use the firm as protection."

He took another nibble of his food, effectively dismissing them all.

Lilo took Misha by the hand. "Come on, I'll show you where you can stay." She paused. "Do you want me to take you to Wyatt's apartment, or the guest rooms?"

Part of Misha wanted to go to Wyatt. She completely understood where he was coming from, but at the same time, she'd been right. He didn't know her, and Misha would do anything to protect her family. If he couldn't understand that, then their relationship was doomed before it began.

"The guest rooms," she said. "I think I need to give Wyatt some space."

thirty

WYATT LAZARUS

PUTTING Misha back in the line of danger wasn't sitting well. To cool down, Wyatt had retreated to the basement operations room. But after staring at the mannequin that held his Deadly Seven combat suit, a plan began to take shape in his mind. If he could work out the mechanics of the suit, then perhaps he wouldn't need Misha's help with Dimitri. Perhaps he could do it on his own.

Unease squirmed in his gut, along with a grimy sense of wrath he felt above the basement HQ, perhaps in the restaurant. Someone was angry. Another wrath signature blinked into existence behind him. He turned toward the elevator entrance as it approached. When it crested the room, Wyatt jolted, surprised to see Sloan shuffling in, a blanket wrapped around her shoulders.

Not who he expected, but still… she could give him a rundown of how to use the suit. "Good. You're here. I need your help, Sloanie."

She paused. Blinked. For a moment, he thought perhaps her slothful sin had petrified her, but then her wrath flared so sharply that his eyes watered. His little sister's eyes shifted from glazed vacancy to bright and vehement.

"I need your help, Sloanie?" She repeated in a mocking tone laced with bitterness. Her blanket fell to the ground revealing the devastatingly slim body wasting away. Her sweats hung from her hips. Her camisole sagged over her shoulders. There was no meat left on her. No muscle. *"I need your help?* Where were you, Wyatt, when we all needed *your* help? Where were you when I needed your help!"

Stunned into silence, Wyatt's mind scrambled with the realization, all that wrath was because of him. "Sloan?"

He stepped forward, and she backed off. "Don't."

"But..."

"Screw you, Wyatt. You know, maybe Sara was right. Maybe you really are a dumbass."

He narrowed his eyes. Really? But then her bravado collapsed. Tears overflowed from her eyes. "You used to cook for me. I confided in you. You were the only one who knew what I was really going through, and you just left! You left!"

Wyatt winced. While he'd been running around the country, stewing in his own anger and hatred, his sister was slowly fading away. Fuck, he'd been selfish. He'd been so caught up with his own miserable life that he'd never stopped to consider he should have been helping his family too.

She sat down on a stool next to the operations table and looked at her feet. For fuck's sake she wasn't even wearing shoes. He couldn't make up for his dumbassery, but he could comfort her and make amends. He went to her and enveloped her skinny frame, hugging tight. She didn't try to resist, just sat there, bone weary.

"I'm sorry," he said into her hair. "I thought you were dating someone. I assumed it was all fine."

"Never assume, bras."

"I know. It makes an ass out of—"

"—You and me."

They laughed half-heartedly. It was a Flintism. Something he used to say to them when they were younger. Apparently, he'd made an assumption growing up, and it cost people lives.

"It wasn't fine," Sloan sobbed, wiping her eyes. "And I only dated that loser because I couldn't be bothered saying no."

"You're right. You needed me, and I wasn't there."

"It's nothing."

"It's not nothing," Wyatt replied. "I was too bullheaded to admit it then, but heartache is heartache. It hurts everyone. I'm sorry he stood you up, Sloan."

She leaned into Wyatt and sobbed, her arms finally moving around his body and clutching tight. He ran his hand down her head, muttering soft words to her. A few years ago, the same time Wyatt had been dealing with the betrayal of Sara, Sloan had suffered her own betrayal. A man she'd fallen in love with, her best friend she'd only known from a distance, had agreed to meet in real life. There was a time when all Sloan talked about was her Max. Someone as quirky, as vibrant, and as energetic as she once used to be. They'd spent hours playing online games together, hours chatting online, hours video calling… years falling in love.

At the time, Sloan and Wyatt were the only ones in the family in a relationship. They'd been happy. Wyatt had to give Sara that. For a little while, he'd been happy, and that happiness had bled through to his relationship with his youngest sister. The two of them had bonded, had each other's backs when the rest of the siblings expressed their skepticism for love.

And then Sara had died. The Deadly Seven were blamed for the explosion that killed others. Sloan's man never turned up to meet her, and she was convinced it was because he believed the news reports, that he'd discovered Sloan's true identity and decided she wasn't worth it—that she was evil. For two years, Sloan and Wyatt shared in each other's misery. When Wyatt left, he had no idea he'd been the one holding Sloan together.

"I'm sorry," he whispered. "If there's one thing I've learned from my mistakes, it's accepting help from the ones who love you. If I had done that in the first place, instead of leaving, we wouldn't be in this mess." His throat tightened when he thought of Evan's persistence about Sara's true nature, his unwavering faith in Wyatt, despite Wyatt treating him like trash. Fuck, he owed Evan a lot. "So, I'm giving you my help whether you want it or not."

Sloan pulled away from his embrace and looked up at him with suspicion. "You're not going to make me run laps around the block and record my times on a spreadsheet are you?"

"Let me guess, Griffin?" A smirk lifted his lips as she nodded. "No. But I am going to start cooking our weekly family dinners again."

"Really? You're going back to work at Heaven?"

"No. But I'm sure they'll let me borrow the kitchen for a bit, and if not, we can have dinner at one of our apartments. Hell, we've got a dozen kitchens I can use in this building."

She gave him a small smile, wiping her nose with her wrist. "I'd like that, bras."

"Can you show me these new suits?"

"Yeah, but you gotta try it on."

Each battle suit used to have a different colored trim in the leather piping, that's how they could tell each other apart. But now, each suit was the same dusty gray—the color of shadow.

"Yours is the one with the black *fukumen*," Sloan explained, pointing to the cabinet, revealing a black scarf around the mannequin's neck. She went to hers. "Mine is yellow."

Right. After he stripped to his boxers, he relieved the mannequin of his suit and put it on. It was too big.

Sloan, now also swimming in her suit, sighed. "I haven't been fitted for mine either."

Both of them looked ridiculous. The gray arms hung past their wrists. The fabric at the legs gathered around their ankles. Catching his reflection in a mirror behind the glass cabinets, Wyatt could see that, fitted right, the suit would look wicked with its Deadly Seven emblem on the breast pocket. He began to remove the surprisingly light-weight suit when a big, laborious sigh came from the direction of the workshop. Neither of them had noticed Flint arrive, but he'd been tinkering with a gadget. He unfolded himself from his bench and lumbered over. Humor bounced in his eyes as he looked down at them from over his worker's spectacles.

"Sloan," he said. "If you had been paying attention when Parker completed the demonstration last week, you would have known that the fit is self-adjusting. Here." He tapped the round logo emblem on Wyatt's chest. "AIMI, Flint here."

"*Good afternoon, Flint*," came AIMI's voice from somewhere in the hood around Wyatt's neck.

"Lift that over your head and you'll hear her better. There's an earpiece attachment," Flint said, and then addressed AIMI. "Adjust Wyatt's suit to fit."

"*Adjusting now.*"

Immediately, air blew out of Wyatt's arms and legs as the suit shrank around his limbs, stretching and contouring his frame like a second skin. When it was complete, he checked his reflection. *Amazing*.

"Now you know, Sloan," Flint said. "You can't complain about your suit not fitting anymore."

"Damn Parker," she muttered, adjusting her suit.

"Where do we put our weapons?" Wyatt asked.

Once again, Flint gave an amused look their way as he handed his screwdriver to Wyatt. "AIMI, Flint here again."

"*Hello again, Flint.*"

"Wyatt's holding a weapon he wants synced with the suit. Please instruct him on how to do this."

"*Wyatt, are you listening?*"

Wyatt's brows lifted. "Yes, AIMI."

"*Good. Hold the weapon to the suit for three-seconds.*"

"Anywhere?"

"*Yes.*"

Wyatt pressed the screwdriver to his sleeve.

"*Syncing now. Three, two, one. Your weapon is synced. You may let go.*"

He did, and the screwdriver stayed put. *You've got to be fucking kidding me.* "This is incredible. But do we have to sync every time we need it to stay?"

"No. Just once," AIMI replied. "Pull with a firm grip, and the suit suction will release. Hold it back there and it will stay."

Wyatt pulled the screwdriver, and it came off. He pressed it again, and it held. Wow. He turned to Sloan, and she smiled back.

"Who came up with this?"

"Actually," Flint said, retrieving his screwdriver and walking back to the bench. "The base code for that operation was Sloan's."

"It was?" She seemed as surprised as Wyatt. "I don't remember."

"That's because you didn't finish it."

"Oh."

"See?" Wyatt punched his sister lightly on the arm. "You've been doing better than you think."

A small smile tipped his way. "So… Misha, hey?"

He fiddled with his sleeve.

"Yeah, Misha."

"She's the one?"

He nodded. "I should probably go and find her."

"You should probably give her space, bras."

His gaze snapped up. "What?"

"Well, you were a bit of an alpha-hole before. Maybe let her chill with her girl for a bit."

"Maybe you're right." He nodded. He was still pissed about her volunteering to go back to The Kremlin. In his mind, there was no other solution, but to keep Misha locked up in this place, safe. And that wasn't right. "I think we need some space."

thirty-one

MISHA MINSKI

A WEEK LATER, Misha still lived in the guest apartment at Lazarus House. Parker had forbidden her to open yoga classes, and her family were still on an all-expense paid vacation to an unknown location. Wyatt had tried to soften the fact that she was in a virtual prison by delivering her a box of belongings he'd collected from her city apartment. She should be grateful for the help, but the overwhelming sense of helplessness grew inside her.

As instructed by Parker, she'd contacted Dimitri and explained her fake situation. Dimitri was suspicious, and at first had threatened her life, but she'd expected that. She also expected the second time she called and he threatened her, but the thing was, he kept taking her calls. After the third and fourth time, she finally got him to agree to a meeting at the club.

Now, it was the morning before the big meeting, and Misha had just showered and dressed. There was nothing else to do but wait and pore miserably over the items Wyatt had delivered days ago.

She sat at the table, staring at a photograph of her mother and father embracing. They were so happy together. She probably romanticized things, but she rarely remembered them arguing. A vague memory popped into her mind of bath time when Misha was young. Her mother was giving a speech about how, being a girl, she had to respect herself, and that no decent man should ask her to do things she wasn't comfortable with. Looking back, Misha had always assumed it was the obligatory stranger-danger speech, but now, she thought maybe her mother had been in a tough relationship before her father. She was too young to pick up all the signs, but she had picked up enough.

As far as Misha knew, her parents were the loves of each other's lives. After her mother died, her father had never re-married, or even dated. But for the years they had together, their love had burned like the sun, warming everyone in their orbit.

Her stomach clenched, reminding her she'd not eaten breakfast. God, she'd kill for a walk down to her favorite coffee shop. But today was the day. She had to stay out of sight. Her nerves were on edge and she was feeling sick in the stomach at the thought of seeing Dimitri again. She knew she'd convinced everyone that she had what it took to get back into his good books, but deep inside, doubt had set in. Dimitri was unpredictable. She used to think she knew his motive—that he wanted her in his control, but there was a very good chance Wyatt was right, and Dimitri would kill her on the spot.

Thinking of Wyatt caused another layer of apprehension to coat her insides. Wyatt had checked on her every morning at nine, and every morning he'd asked her not to do what she planned to do. When she'd held her ground, he'd left.

She should be okay with his avoidance of her, but after they'd made love in the rain, and he brought the heat of the sun, Misha had dropped her guard. She'd fallen for him. So hard. It had been good—maybe too good.

Misha put the picture frame down.

God. What issues must she have if her relationships lasted no longer than a day?

A lump formed in her throat for the millionth time that week. Misha pushed thoughts of Wyatt from her mind and set to work on the mystery location of her family. It was a fun puzzle she could focus on. Since her phone was still in her locker at the club, Wyatt had called them for her. They weren't allowed to disclose their location to anyone. Griffin had said it was safer that way, but their absence left a gaping hole in her life.

She should take solace in the fact her family sounded happy. Her grandparents were still playing their perpetual card game. Her father told her he'd been relaxing by a pool, enjoying the first vacation of his life, reading a book of all things. Roksana was reluctant at first—she'd missed a rehearsal but, apparently, being in day spa heaven with Ciocia sorted that out.

Alek was another case. He had texted Wyatt his frustration at not being allowed to help Misha out. As the kid grew up, he was taking on more of a protector role. His self-defense lessons had given him the spark. Part of Misha was relieved he was old enough and capable of taking on more responsibility, but another part was terrified. He was her baby brother. Mostly deaf, mute, and still at school. He already hero worshipped Wyatt. What would happen if he learned Wyatt's true identity? He'd want to join the team.

No way.

A sharp rap at the door had her jolting out of her seat. A glance at the clock in the kitchen told her it was that time again. Nine o'clock. Wyatt time. She took a deep breath, steeled herself and went to open the door. Sure enough, standing in the hallway, looking as devastatingly handsome as the first day she'd met him, was Wyatt. Ebony dark hair, cobalt eyes, tight gray T-shirt stretching over flexing muscles as he lifted two bags of groceries. Misha blinked, surprised.

This was the first morning he'd brought something other than his dark mood.

"Hi," she said.

"Hi." Weirdly, he closed his eyes and inhaled. On the exhale, his shoulders relaxed, and he opened his eyes. Lifting the bags, he said, "Peace offering."

The groceries? She eyed them suspiciously. Really? "So... you're giving up on your crusade to stop me from returning to the club?"

He gave a curt nod, but from the set of his jaw, he still wasn't happy about it.

"What changed your mind?"

"Can I come in?"

"Oh, yeah. Sorry." She stepped aside. "Of course."

He moved through the living area and into the modern stainless steel kitchen where he unloaded his heavy bags onto the granite bench.

Unable to help herself, Misha went to the table and picked up the picture of her parents. She held it like a security blanket. "Why are you here, Wyatt?"

He began unpacking the bags, ignoring her, so she stalked up to him. "What changed your mind?"

Some apples rolled from the bag. His hand expertly shot out to catch them. Once he put them back in place, he braced himself on the bench, head dipped, almost defeated.

"I got back to my apartment," he said, voice low and rough, "for the first time in almost half a year last week. Do you know what I found?"

"A lot of dust?"

He smirked, but his eyes turned soulful. "Evidence of Sara everywhere. Pictures of her were still on my fridge. Her clothes in the laundry basket. Nothing had changed."

Misha tightened her hold on the picture.

Wyatt noticed. "It took me this past week of erasing her from my life to realize that you were right."

"I was?" Misha took an involuntary step back.

"I didn't know her, and I don't know you."

"Okay." Another step. "Can't say I'm a fan of you drawing similarities between me and the woman who tried to kill you."

Eyes flashed in alarm. "No, that's not what I meant. Please stop walking away. I… I want to get to know you. Um. That's what I want."

"Okay. I'm listening."

"Do you know the second I get within a few feet of you, I feel calmer? It's a physical reaction in my body. And when we touch, I can't sense that ugly sin at all. It's like your aura is a balm over my senses—like someone injects valium into my veins. My reaction is that visceral, that real." He took a deep breath. "I'm not telling you this to pressure you, I'm telling you so that you know where I'm coming from, what I'm struggling with, and that I get it—you don't have this instinct pushing you into my arms. I get it now. It took me a week of looking back at my past with the wrong woman, but I get it."

"Do you know that's the most I've heard you speak since I met you?"

A shy meeting of the eyes, and he blushed. "I don't want to pressure you. And I don't want you to pay any attention to this welcome-to-the-family-shit. I just want to cook you breakfast. And talk. Simple. Easy."

The picture frame cut into her fingers. When she looked down, she was reminded of her behavior with her family over the past few years, and the knowledge that she had massive commitment issues, but that didn't mean she wanted to be alone for the rest of her life.

She wanted that all-consuming love, no matter the risk. And—she looked back at Wyatt—she wanted it with him.

She put the picture down. He took the first step. She could take the next.

"I'm a vegetarian."

He grew even more alarmed. "Are you joking?"

Laughter burst from her so hard she had to hold her belly. He must have thought she was joking, because he began to laugh too, shaking his head incredulously as he unpacked the pounds of sausage, bacon and some other nameless meat.

"I'm not." Her laughter died. "I'm not joking. I really am a vegetarian."

All humor dropped from his face until he deadpanned. When it was clear she wasn't kidding, he exhaled in a huff and blew out through his teeth. "Fuck."

"Is that a deal breaker?"

"No. No. It's just that…" He stared at the groceries with devastation. "We really are opposites. What am I going to do with all this sausage?"

"Eat it."

"You don't mind?"

"Why would I mind?"

He shrugged. "Some people mind."

"Well, in case you haven't noticed. I'm not like most people." She sidled up to him and tipped up on her toes to whisper in his ear. "But just so we're clear, the only sausage I want in my mouth is yours."

He snorted, but his eyes turned dark and darted down to her lips before lifting again. The message was unmistakable: *I want you.*

She traced her fingers gently down his back, around his waistband to the front, and tugged until their bodies were flush.

When his words came out, they were deep and rough. "So… omelet?"

Misha released him and then hopped up onto the granite bench and smiled. She picked out an apple and bit into it. Juicy goodness exploded in her mouth. "Nah. Eggs are like baby meat."

"Heaven help me now." He prayed to the ceiling, and she laughed. Teasing him was so much fun. "Pancakes?" he offered.

A moan caught in her throat, almost making her choke on the apple. "Yes, please."

For the next few minutes, she watched him move about the kitchen while she nibbled on her apple. He was incredible. Confident. Talented. Goddamned sexy. Even the way he casually tossed the towel over his shoulder while he flipped the pancakes in the pan had her heart hammering. Little beads of sweat dotted his top lip, and he had a look about him that was both passionate and focused. Seeing him all eager to cook and feed her was the most arousing thing she'd faced in years. She wanted to stop him, tear his clothes off and have her way with him right there on the kitchen floor.

"Um, Wyatt?" she asked quietly.

Enthralled with his cooking, he grunted, stirred something in a pot, and then enthusiastically lifted the spoon to her lips, expectantly watching her reaction.

She tentatively touched her tongue to the spoon and the berry flavor exploded in her mouth. She snatched the spoon and licked the lot, moaning. "Oh my God that's amazing. Where did you learn to cook?"

Wyatt's sultry gaze locked with hers before he collected the spoon and wrenched it back to the pot. "France."

"Right. Well. You're gifted."

"I know."

Her lips curved, and she became entranced by the way his defined forearms flexed as he whisked.

He shot her a sideways glance. "What were you going to say?"

"I… um." She went all shy. "I was going to say that you were right, too."

"I was?"

"Yes. About me going tonight."

He stiffened, but kept his eyes on the stove, stirring his coulis.

"I may have been a little rash in my decision to go back. I should have discussed it with you first. I heard what you said about your situation, and… I get it too. It's hard for you. I don't want to start a relationship built on distrust."

thirty-two

WYATT LAZARUS

WYATT TOOK his pot from the heat and focused on Misha. Sitting on the bench, with her legs dangling, she looked picture perfect. Blond ringlets bounced playfully, thick lashes surrounded her blue eyes, and pink pouty lips sucked a round apple. The same lips he'd been dreaming about every night for the past week. He'd tried to stay away from her—but it was useless. His attraction hadn't dimmed since the first moment they'd met. If anything, it was stronger.

Every night, he'd gone to sleep without her by his side, and the temptation of his sin had seeped in until it stewed his insides. It built in his blood, making him toss and turn, until by nine the next morning, he'd been craving her fun, light-hearted attitude and calming aura. But every time her presence washed over him, dampening the sensation of wrath, every other sense in his body was free to feel more. So when she said no—that she still intended to go back to the club—he knew that losing her would be the hardest thing he'd ever face.

When he had awoken this morning, he'd realized he was already losing her, and it was his fault.

"So… what made you change your mind?" he asked, echoing her earlier question to him. His outwardly steady voice belied the inside voice, screaming *thank fuck for that.*

She shrugged. "I realized that maybe I was a little freaked out by us. I have some pretty intense feelings for you, Wyatt. Feelings I've never had about anyone else, and it scares me."

"Why does it scare you?" he asked gruffly and then pulled out two plates, trying not to let it show how much he enjoyed hearing about her intense feelings for him. If he acted casual, carried on with a menial task, maybe she would continue.

When she spoke, her voice held a note of strain. "When Mama died, it was hard. I was pretty young at the time, and I still remember sitting at the hospital with Ciocia and little Roksana, waiting to meet our new baby brother. Even Babcia and Dziadzio were there."

While she spoke, he dished up a stack of pancakes onto each plate, then drizzled the coulis.

"When Tata came out holding Alek in his arms, he had this look on his face. It was pure devastation. His eyes were puffy. There were tear tracks down his cheeks. He could barely hold on to the baby with his trembling arms, and then he just handed the little bundle to me. He told me mama went to heaven and then walked out."

"I'm sorry." Wyatt handed Misha some strawberries to hull. When their gazes collided, sorrow was all he could see.

"He didn't hand Alek to Ciocia. He handed him to me, a child." She glanced down at her strawberry, turning it over in her fingers. "He was such a quiet baby. So peaceful. It took us months to learn he couldn't speak or hear. Tata was never the same after Mama's passing, and I wanted to make sure Alek never felt that lack of love. After that, I spent my time trying to fill my mother's shoes. I didn't go to my prom. I never went on dates. I worked in the restaurant and took Alek to his doctor appointments, and Roksana to ballet lessons. I helped them with homework. I was their mother." She sighed and took a bite of the strawberry she was supposed to hull, chewed it over for a bit. "When Roksana finished high school and went to college, I realized I'd spent my entire life looking after them. There she was, getting a college education, and I had nothing. I was resentful. I moved out, started my own business, focused on my happiness and didn't look back. Well, I didn't until the attacks on the restaurant started, and since then, it's been an avalanche of bad karma. I feel like it's all because I left. All because, instead of sticking it out with my family, I was selfish."

Wyatt's heart ached for her, and he couldn't resist lifting his hand to cup her face, thumb brushing across her cheek.

She leaned into his touch, brows puckering. "I don't want your pity, Wyatt. Like you did earlier, I'm saying this so you know where I'm coming from. Losing someone you love doesn't just affect the partner, but the children, parents, aunts, uncles. It has a knock-on effect. So, this"—she waved between them, and pulled away from his touch—"whatever it is, is a big risk. Not only am I afraid of losing you, but... I'm afraid of making it work."

"Of making it work?"

"Yeah, because it's hard. You give so much of yourself to another person—other people if there's a family, like in my experience. It's harder than anything I've ever done before and if I fail at it with you... what will be left of me?"

They were silent for a moment, but Wyatt couldn't help the question brimming on his tongue. "Do you? Want to make it work, I mean?"

In answer, she captured his mouth in a needy kiss that left him panting with ragged breaths. Every emotion she felt came through that kiss, and when they broke apart, the hunger in her eyes left him no doubt.

"I can't help myself when I'm around you, Wyatt," she murmured and tugged on his shirt. "I'm selfish. I want this all for myself. And I'm afraid what knock-on effect that will have. This past week away from you was a hell I never knew existed."

"I know. I hated it too."

She pulled his lips to hers, this time teasing him with little licks and nips that sent pleasure shooting straight down his spine. He hardened instantly. A sound caught between a growl and a moan came out of him, and she sighed in delight.

"Let's not separate again," she mumbled into his mouth.

"I agree. Move in with me. Now, don't freak out," he said with a hint of humor lacing his tone. "It's not like we're getting married."

She raised a cocky eyebrow. "I see what you're doing there. Using my own words against me."

He shrugged coyly.

"Okay." Her lopsided grin melted his heart. "I'll stay with you. If only for the gourmet breakfasts, you'll cook me."

"And lunch." He pecked her on the lips. "And dinner."

"Oh, now you're talking dirty."

Wyatt chuckled and then had to step away in case he forgot about the meal he'd cooked and take her straight to the bedroom. "Breakfast is getting cold. Come on."

He served their meal on the table beside the kitchen bench and then helped Misha down from her perch. Instead of walking, she clutched him like a baby koala.

She grinned playfully. "Take me for a ride."

"Oh, I'll take you for a ride, all right," he replied darkly, sensual visions already swimming through his mind.

Damn it.

Pancakes.

"Promise?" She winked up at him as he deposited her in her seat.

As they enjoyed their first official meal together, Wyatt couldn't help his thoughts wandering back to her confession. Raising Alek when she was still a child herself must have been tough.

After his family's extraction from the lab, he'd had an idyllic childhood with Mary and Flint. With their new identities keeping them safe, they worried about nothing except managing the internal sensations of their sin. They went to school. They dated. He never went to prom because of the years training in combat, but he went to culinary college afterward. It had been one of the things Mary and Flint had insisted on, that they had half a life of normalcy.

He'd had time to focus on himself. Misha had only just begun.

He could help with that. Get rid of Dimitri. Get her back to her yoga. Help with her family.

It felt good to have a purpose again.

"So," he said in between bites. "Alek has been texting me."

"Oh?"

"He hasn't mentioned it to you?"

"No. I've hardly said a word to him since they've been gone. Just that one phone call."

A tickle of unease washed over him. "I thought you were in contact."

"No." She pushed around her food with her fork. "My phone is still at the club. I thought you knew that."

Wyatt's fork clattered to the plate loudly, and for a few seconds, his heart stopped. "But he said he'd been texting you."

"What?"

"Shit." Wyatt pulled out his cell and dialed Alek's number. Alek couldn't speak to answer, but he might text back. He might hand the phone to Roksana.

"Wyatt?" Color rushed from Misha's cheeks. "What's going on?"

Abruptly, he began pacing as he listened to the dial tone ring. And ring. And ring.

"Wyatt?"

When their gazes clashed, he couldn't hide his concern, and they'd promised to be honest with each other. "Alek told me he'd been texting you. Your phone is at the club. He's not answering. It doesn't add up."

"But… but you said they're all safe. That my family is hidden where no one can find them."

A cold feeling washed over him. "He's not safe if he's been lured out of there."

"Oh my God." Misha's hand covered her mouth and her eyes watered. Then suddenly, she ran into the bathroom and closed the door.

"Misha?" He jogged after her and knocked on the door. "Don't worry. If he's missing, I'll find him." When she didn't answer, he began to worry. "Misha? Are you okay?"

"I'm fine," came her lackluster reply.

He stood before the door, finger tapping on his thigh, thinking back to the green look she'd had on her face. "Are you sick?"

Can't be my cooking.

A muffled sound and a toilet flushing. "I'm not sick."

He stood back and waited, but she didn't come out. More sounds in there—sounded like… vomiting. Why was she trying to hide it from him? He could help.

"I'm coming in."

"No!" she cried. Her voice was muffled. Tired.

"Are you sure?"

"Yes."

"Can I do anything to help?"

"Get Lilo."

Her harsh tone made him jerk back. It was an instant reaction he couldn't control. She still didn't feel safe with him. He turned the knob. "Lilo is at work," he started to say, but when the door slammed back in his face, he jumped back.

"I have my period," she shouted. "You can't come in. I need tampons. I need Lilo."

Oh. He froze. Tampons.

Um.

Okay.

"So. Um. Lilo?"

"Or… if she's working, get Grace. Actually, yes, Grace! Get Grace."

"I'll be back. And Misha—" he paused. "Don't worry. I'll find Alek."

A muffled response was all he heard, and then he left to find the doctor. The unease in his gut expanded. She had lied to him.

thirty-three

DIMITRI

WALKING along the corridor to his office, Dimitri glared at his previously injured hand—now gleaming with gold-plated armor and skeletal metal fingers. A week ago, Wyatt Lazarus had pulverized the bones, destroying his hand for good. All that had been left was a floppy skin covered mess they had to amputate to above the elbow. If it wasn't for the Syndicate and their special doctors, he'd still be healing. Humiliation had almost drowned him, but when they offered to supply him with the robotic prosthetic, he didn't ask what the price was; he asked them to plate it in gold. Show all those fuckers he wasn't to be underestimated, that if you beat him down, he came back more powerful, and more valuable.

His father once compared him to a little cockroach. Always there when he least expected it. Always taking a beating, always scurrying back. He didn't call Dimitri "little" when he was murdered. Dimitri could still see the look of surprise in his father's fading eyes as the knife stabbed into his gut.

He smiled wickedly.

He knew the arm would come with a price, but he was willing to pay it. As he got to his office door, Dimitri flexed his hand, still marveling at how his brain connected with the tech as though it was a real hand. He could feel the strength radiate to his shoulder, barely a twinge of pain left after the healing protein they'd injected him with. It was almost as though he had the power of the vigilantes... not almost, better. *The power.*

"Stare at yourself long enough and you'll turn into stone."

Dimitri whirled around, new fist flying toward his assailant. A small pale hand caught it mid-air. Dimitri's gaze traveled from the hand to the arm to the face.

"Apologies," he forced out and relaxed.

Falcon was dressed in her combat gear—white half-face bird mask, lips and nose exposed, white leather from neck to toe. Silver-white hair streamed around her shoulders. Blue eyes seemed violet in The Kremlin basement. Blood spattered under her chin, as if she'd come straight from another business meeting.

Other men would believe she left it there to instill fear, but he knew better. She just didn't care. She accused him of turning to stone, but she was already there.

She held onto his fist and his gaze, never wavering. The seconds ticked by, and yet she would not release. She held his new powerful and enhanced hand with nothing but her fist, as if to show him with one simple gesture where the real power lied. She didn't even break a sweat.

He tugged, testing.

She held strong, head cocking to the side, mimicking the bird of her infernal mask. Fucking ridiculous. Everyone who worked with the Syndicate knew her face, why bother hiding it? But he knew the truth. He could show her the full power of his fist, he could rip her in two.

Patience.

Soon, he would slice her smirking head from her shoulders. No. He would make her watch as he peeled open her chest and ribs. Give her real wings made of bone. Dimitri's ire sizzled and snarled inside, but he dared not show his true feelings. She was the one who'd given him his new arm, after all.

He hated her. *Filthy suka.* Always so calm, so smug. He was not a puppet. He was the master. But he owed her. For now.

Her lip twitched. Amusement lit her eyes, and then she let go and strode to his closed office door. "He is in here." A statement, not a question. Her palm rested on the surface of the door. "I can feel his sadness."

"Yes. He is in there."

"And what do you plan on doing with him?"

"That is none of your concern. I will fulfill my part of the bargain. The details will bore you."

Falcon turned to him, unnatural eyes settling on him once more. "You have failed us twice, Dimitri, and yet, we continue to gift you with our assistance."

Tension locked his shoulders. Fuck. She knew what he was capable of, that's why she gifted him with her fucking assistance. Fine. Biting down on his temper, Dimitri pushed open the office door and ushered her inside.

Tied to a chair facing his desk was Misha's brother. Bound, gagged, and furious. Everything about the kid made Dimitri sick to the stomach. Blond unkempt hair, slouch shorts, a shirt with holes in it. Why couldn't teenagers dress like they gave a damn?

Lazy, entitled piece of shit. Kid hadn't acknowledged him, hadn't paid him any respect. That's what was wrong with this new generation. No respect. Dimitri had respect beaten into him when he was young, maybe he should do the same. Teach the boy a thing or two, give him a family lesson.

A few text messages posing as Misha, and the boy had been eating out of Dimitri's hands. It was almost too easy.

Suspicion pricked the back of his neck, and he ripped the gag from the boy.

"Tell me, boy. Does Misha know you are here? Did you tell her?" Every muscle and electrode within Dimitri coiled tight, waiting to pounce. If she had gotten one whiff of Dimitri's plan...

The boy glared at him, but stupidly made no response.

Dimitri's fist slammed into his cheek, sending his head rocketing back. He and his chair landed on the floor.

"Answer me." Dimitri kicked him.

The kid coughed and choked, but still no response.

A mocking hiss came out of Falcon.

"What?"

She waved at the boy. "Notice anything?"

Dimitri's gaze snapped back to the kid, inspecting. Fucking looked like any other waste of space. "Just tell me what you're getting at."

"He has hearing aids in his ears, and you've dislodged them. He cannot hear you. Most likely cannot speak, and you have bound his hands, hence he cannot sign."

"Yeah, well, the little shit is feisty. He attacked my men when they collected him."

Falcon's steady gaze met Dimitri's wild eyes. Nostrils flaring was the only sign of her displeasure.

"I am ready for you to explain your plan, Dimitri."

"You'll get your chance for blood, and I'll get mine." Dimitri pointed at the squirming boy, still on his side on the floor. "He is bait. She will come, then she will be bait, and then he will come. *Vy khotite, chtoby ya zapisal eto?*"

"Writing it down is not necessary," she replied, and Dimitri flinched. He did not know she understood Russian. Didn't matter. He won't underestimate her next time.

"And when Wrath comes, the rest of them will, or did you not think that was relevant to tell me?"

Dimitri didn't give a flying fuck about the Deadly Seven. He wanted the city. He wanted it to choke. He wanted Misha to watch. Watch me lay waste. Watch my strength. He was just as good as she —better, even.

He snarled at Falcon. "You said you wanted the man. I'm delivering him. Debt paid. You didn't say I had to deliver him on a silver platter."

"Facing the Deadly Seven at once was not on my agenda."

"Relax," he crooned, eyes sliding to the large terrarium containing his snake. Its big length slowly coiled around a small animal, constricting with patience. "The second stage of our plan is currently being set in motion. The rest of the seven won't be an issue."

Her eyes narrowed. "Need I remind you I want most of them alive?"

Angry eyes snapped to her. "You give me this arm, you pay me money, you give me followers, all so you can get your hands on the blood of one man. I am not so stupid that I will kill these others. They will be occupied. Though why you don't just take them does not make sense."

"We don't pay you to make sense of our plans."

"*Da*," he replied. "You pay me to make mayhem."

He stalked to his desk and bent to inspect the CCTV monitors, effectively dismissing her. The club was about to open, and he needed it to look real.

Falcon moved to the exit, paused, and turned back to him. "We gave you power, Dimitri. We can take it away."

His top lip curled at her threat.

When she left, he went back to the tank and wrapped his mechanical hand around the snake's head and squeezed, watching curiously as the hunter became the prey. At the last moment, before he did lasting damage, he released and dropped the snake.

He'd like to see her try to take his new power away.

thirty-four

MISHA MINSKI

UNABLE TO LEAVE, Misha hid in the bathroom, puking up the lovely breakfast Wyatt had made her. Didn't feel so lovely the second time round. All the panicked thoughts whirring through her mind made her even more nauseous. Alek. Her sweet Alek. The kid didn't even know how to tie his own shoes until he was eleven, and he was afraid of the dark. When you couldn't hear, or speak, the darkness was a frightening place. If he'd been caught, if they'd put a blindfold on him...

She gagged into the toilet and a new wave of panic engulfed her. Why so sick suddenly? Her period was late because it always was, no need for her mind to go *there*. She had a contraceptive implant in her womb, and it had only just been put in a few months earlier. She didn't feel like she had a virus, so it had to be the pancakes, or the apple. Surely. There was no other reason for her unexplained sickness. None at all.

Then why did I call for Grace? Because whatever this was, she didn't have time for it. She had to find her brother. Wiping her mouth, she flushed the toilet and checked her appearance in the mirror. *Good God, girl, you look rough.* Eyes all watery. Pale as hell. And the queasiness did not go away.

A knock came at the door, and then Grace's sweet voice. "Misha? Are you okay?"

"Are you alone?" she asked.

Muffled voices talking—Wyatt was still there.

Oh, God. Burning behind her eyes had her squeezing them shut. This was all looking so bad, and she didn't have time for it. *Alek.* She took a deep breath, steeled herself and then plastered a smile on her face. She was fine. Nothing to worry about.

She opened the door. "Sorry, false alarm. No period. All good."

Wyatt, who had been walking away at that point, spun around with concern etched over his face.

Dressed in baggy sweats, Grace held her doctor kit in one hand and swept a stray dark hair from her ponytail with the other. It appeared as though she'd just gotten out of bed. Grace darted a glance between Wyatt, Misha and the bathroom, her shrewd eyes inspecting.

"I'm sorry we got you out of bed, Grace. I'm feeling much better now." Misha looked to Wyatt. "Did you find Alek?"

His expression shuttered. "He's at The Kremlin."

"You know so soon? Are you sure?"

"Sloan tracked his phone while I waited for Grace to get out of bed. It didn't take long."

"At The Kremlin. Why?" she asked, fear gripping her heart tight. "Why would he go there?"

"Most likely, Dimitri found your phone and lured him in, pretending to be you." His jaw hardened. "Obviously he wants reassurance that you'll turn up tonight. He'll get a nice surprise when we all come in your place."

"But what would he want with Alek?" What he always wanted. A display of power. Control. Pain. "Is Alek okay? Do we know if he's okay?"

"Not yet."

Another wave of nausea rolled over her and she slammed the heels of her palms into her eyes, holding until she heard Wyatt's calm voice. "Come on, we'll go down to the basement. The others are already down there running through a plan."

Wyatt walked ahead, but Grace stopped Misha with a hand to her shoulder. She leaned in to speak quietly. "I heard vomiting."

"It must have been breakfast. Nothing to worry about."

Her eyebrow arched. "Wyatt's cooking? Somehow I doubt that. Are you sure you're okay? He mentioned you needed tampons. I have some in my bag."

Misha checked Wyatt, and he moved to the exit to wait for them outside in the hall. When he was at a safe distance, she confessed: "No, I don't have my period."

A pause. "You're late?"

Dammit. "It's not what you think, I have the implant, plus, Wyatt mentioned he's not... um, you know."

Awkwardness flittered over Grace's face. "They're only sterile before they meet their mate. Apparently it's a security measure to stop them passing down unbalanced genes. Is your implant in utero? They've been known to fall out. Have you checked for the string?"

Her queasiness rolled, and every instinct in her body screamed that Grace was right. That the implant had somehow fallen out. Misha felt different. Her breasts were tender, her moods were weird, and Misha and Wyatt had never used protection. No. She was imagining things that weren't there. She was sick, that was all. She went to move, but Grace held firm.

"Grace." Misha's tone held a warning in it.

Grace let go. "I'm a doctor, Misha. Anything you tell me will be confidential."

Misha kept walking. She had other worries. Alek needed her. The last thing she needed to think about was having the same condition that killed her mother.

thirty-five

MISHA MINSKI

THE BASEMENT OPERATIONS room was crowded when Misha arrived with Wyatt. It still boggled her mind that they fit all this underneath two very popular cultural establishments in the city. Right above was the restaurant Heaven, and somewhere above and to the far right was the nightclub Hell. Misha had seen a weapons room, a workout room and a medical room as she passed from the elevator. There were more hidden places, but she'd not had the chance to inspect the place.

Following Wyatt, Misha stood near the entrance, hand on her quivering stomach and inhaled deeply to center herself. Activity in the room focused on a stranger standing near the glass cabinets containing suited mannequins. The tall stranger rotated as though he was on display. His bald head shined under the halogen lights, as did his long nose and pink tips of his big ears. His plaid brown suit came straight out of the seventies. The hastily tucked shirt barely containing a pudgy beer gut.

Most of the family were there. Evan and Griffin—both wearing their Deadly Seven combat gear—poked and prodded the stranger as though he were a museum artifact, or something under a microscope. To the back of the room, in the corner reserved for the workshop, Flint and Mary looked on with veiled amusement. With her arms folded, Liza watched the stranger from a safe distance.

Upon seeing their arrival, the balding man hooted at Wyatt. "Check me out, bro." And then his eyes slid to Misha, and he grinned, big ears shifting. "Misha, doll. Haven't seen you since Hell opened. Come here and give me some sugar."

Oh my God. It's Tony. The lady's man and current Hollywood heartthrob? She didn't recognize him with all that makeup on, but his buttery voice was unmistakable. And come to think of it, the shape of his square jaw, the little dimple in his chin… that cocky twinkle in his eyes. She tried to smile. She wanted to smile… but couldn't.

Wyatt stood in front of Misha.

Was he trying to protect her? "It's Tony. Don't you recognize him?"

Tony stood there with arms wide, waiting. "How good is my makeup artist, huh? I feel like I was born to play this role. Babe, I had no idea you worked as a stripper."

Wyatt's eyes narrowed, but he stepped aside.

"Exotic dancer," she corrected.

"Yeah. That. Serious, no wonder you pulled all the right moves on the dance floor." Tony made some gyrating dance moves as if to prove his point.

It all looked rather strange in his getup.

"This isn't a role in one of your movies, Tony." Wyatt scowled and stalked to where a uniformed Parker was at the strategy table, concentrating on something on a laptop computer screen. "It was serious reconnaissance, but things have changed. The recon mission is now an extraction."

"He's right," Parker confirmed, his voice a deep base. "You'll be needed in combat gear. There's likely to be conflict." He arched his brow at Wyatt. "Have you tried your new suit on?"

He gave a curt nod. "It's a bit of overkill for me, though. I probably don't need it."

"The suit isn't only for protection," Griffin explained. His dark gray outfit hugged his body like a second skin, giving Misha a good idea of his musculature underneath. Out of habit, his hand lifted to adjust his phantom glasses, then lowered, scowling when he must have remembered their absence. "You're part of the team, Wyatt. You're part of the family. The suit has comms links, AIMI's interaction, the vitals health monitoring, the—"

"Yeah. I get it. Sorry," Wyatt conceded. "I'll wear the suit."

Silence settled on the room and then Liza spoke up. "Did you just… apologize?"

"Fuck off." Wyatt's ears reddened. "We're getting sidetracked here. We've got details to hash out, and time is wasting."

"Wyatt's right." Parker ran his hand through his long auburn mane. He shifted the laptop he'd been eyeing out of the way and revealed some blue and white paperwork. "Tony, get out of that ridiculous disguise and get into your suit."

Tony groaned dramatically. "I dressed up for nothing?"

Misha bit her lip. "My little brother's in danger." *And it's my fault.*

"Way to be disrespectful, bro." The sarcasm dripped from Evan's tone as he clapped Tony on his shoulder. "The douche has her younger brother. We're assuming Alek is safe because Dimitri hasn't called with demands, but that might not be the case."

Please be safe, Alek.

Even through his makeup, Tony had the grace to look ashamed. "No one told me."

"You were too busy making us fawn over your disguise," Liza replied.

Tony approached Misha, and she couldn't help feeling awkward.

When they'd met on the dance-floor in Hell, he was up for anything. In fact... a bit too much. He had wanted to take things further with her, and to be honest—a one-night stand with a hunky movie star was right up her alley—but when she'd learned that his idea of partying included substances that weren't exactly legal, she'd declined. She was grateful for that missed ship now. It made her icky to think of Wyatt's brothers like that.

"Sorry, Meesh," Tony pouted as he tugged his big ears off. "My bad. We'll get your brother back, don't worry."

"Thanks, Tony," she mumbled. "I'm sorry you didn't get a chance to play."

But as soon as the words left her mouth, something clicked in her mind. Wyatt had said the recon mission was over, and that it was an extraction instead. Did that mean the original plan was being set aside for a new one, meaning she wouldn't be involved?

"I still have to go," she announced. Alek would need her there. She was his safety net, plus Dimitri was volatile. Who knew what he'd do if she didn't turn up as planned.

All eyes settled on her, and Wyatt's eyes blazed. "I thought we discussed this earlier."

"That was before I found out Dimitri took Alek to ensure my capitulation."

"The situation is worse, if anything. Even more reason for you to stay safe here."

Grace shot Misha a worried glance as she settled behind Evan at the strategy table. Misha knew exactly what she was thinking, but the truth was, Misha was wrong in her initial assessment. She could very well have caught a viral bug. Her vomiting could have been one of those hourly things. Sure, those were a thing. She was feeling much better. The fact she was late for her period could mean anything. The implant slowed all that down anyway.

"If I don't turn up, Dimitri will execute Alek," she stated. "I've told you how he is. The only reason he's keeping Alek alive is because he wants me there. He hasn't even announced it to us, has he? I mean, he hasn't contacted you to let you know Alek is there?"

Parker shook his head. "But that doesn't mean anything. Wyatt is right. Things have changed. You're a civilian, you should stay here where it's safe."

"Dimitri wants me to turn up for our planned meeting, and he wants to use Alek to get me to do something. Just like he always does. This sick game he has of using me as a puppet isn't working anymore, so he's gone to bigger lengths. You don't understand. He'll shoot my baby brother."

"We don't negotiate with insane people." Griffin folded his arms.

Panic welled inside Misha. This was all going wrong. She *knew* Dimitri. Understood how his brain worked. Once she arrived, she could distract Dimitri with whatever he wanted her to do, and then the others could swoop in and save Alek. Or better yet, she could convince him it was all unnecessary, and he was the man in charge as usual. God, she didn't care what outfit she had to wear, or what promises she needed to make, as long as her baby brother was safe.

"I can get the CCPD on it," Liza offered. "Call in SWAT. Do we have any proof that the kid is being held hostage?"

"Negative." Parker mulled over the table. "The family said he left on his own, and they haven't heard demands either."

"He's in there. I know it." Misha's eyes began to water.

Wyatt came to stand next to her and put an arm around her shoulder. "You don't need to convince us," he said.

"Where do you think Dimitri would be holding him?" Parker

pointed at the blueprints. "AIMI, pull up the heat map of The Kremlin on the surveillance screens."

A screen on the wall, previously showing a news network, changed to display a satellite image. It zoomed in, and little orange, red and yellow blobs milled about. Misha could only assume it was imagery of bodies moving about the club.

At that moment, Sloan shuffled in from the direction of the elevator. "Sorry I'm late. What did I miss?"

Parker checked the time on his watch. "Everything."

"Okay. I'll just go back to bed."

"No—" Parker grabbed her by the shoulder as she turned around. She jolted back into his hold. "You can man the comms. Flint is busy repairing the relay on the communications jammer you fucked up last week with the spilled soda."

"Can't AIMI handle the comms?"

AIMI? Misha mouthed to Wyatt.

"Artificial Intelligent Management Interface," he whispered to her.

"AIMI isn't infallible, Sloan. And, while we're at it, you should be out in the field, not mooching around operations. I think we've indulged your sin enough. In fact, when the new security team gets here, that's exactly what you'll be doing again."

Sloan whined dramatically and slouched over to where Mary and Flint worked. She picked up a headset and sat down near a laptop.

Wyatt ignored his siblings and turned to Misha. "We'll all be going into The Kremlin with bulletproof clothing. We'll storm the place, and before you know it—"

An alarm sounded and everyone in the room began talking at once until Parker shouted for quiet. His big voice boomed so loud that even the alarm turned off.

"AIMI?" Parker's face was staunch as he stared at the screen on the wall. "What triggered the alarm?"

A map of the city came up, stretching from the top to the tail of the city. A red dot flashed near the bottom of the map. *"There is a disturbance in the south-side of the city, here. It appears as though the South-Side Bank is under attack. Please hold. More incoming data. Triangulating the new location now."* She paused. *"Analyzing police scanners. Adjusting outcome. There. Another bomb has gone off in the Quadrant Center Park."* A red spot flashed when the woman spoke. *"That makes two disturbances."*

"Any footage?" Parker asked.

Screens flickered to CCTV footage of people in a park, running, screaming. Another screen showed gray dust blooming before a building, making it hard to see.

"Three disturbances."

"What the hell?" Tony muttered as he peeled his prosthetic nose from his face. More footage came to light. More attacks. One by one, on the screen with the map of the city, little red dots appeared at random intervals.

"AIMI, anyone reporting?"

A news network video feed replaced one of the CCTV footage screens. A female news anchor was speaking—not only reporting on the unexplained explosions, but on the white-robed fanatics creating mayhem in the streets, inciting looting, causing violence.

"Faithful." Tony spat the word out like a bad taste.

"Four disturbances."

"Holy shit," breathed Liza as she palmed the gun in her holster.

"It's like my building collapse, only on a bigger scale," Grace gasped.

Misha cast her mind back and remembered Lilo telling her that Grace lost her family in the Cardinal Bombing a few years ago. Many people died that day, all because—Misha turned to Wyatt as the memory of his confession slid home. His ex-fiancée set that bomb off and killed all those people in order to frame the Deadly Seven as the perpetrators. The city had turned on the disgraced heroes for years.

"This is different," Wyatt said. "We know the Syndicate is behind it now, and the Faithful are caught on camera. The city will know it's not us, either. They won't turn the blame on us."

"Bombs are going off everywhere!" Liza whipped her gaze to Parker. "I need to get out there. CCPD is short staffed today. I think it's better I go as a cop."

Parker nodded abruptly, and Liza disappeared down another corridor, presumably toward an exit. To Griffin and Evan, he spoke next. "You two are already geared up. Griff, you head here"—he pointed at a red angry spot on the south outskirts of the city—"where metal structures are in danger of collapsing. Use your power to keep those buildings up until survivors can get out. Take Tony. Stay in pairs. Evan, I want you here, near the Northside. I'll go with you."

"On it," Evan replied. He shot Wyatt an apologetic look and then gave Grace a quick kiss on the lips. "See you later, Doc."

"I'll come too." She collected her medical kit from where she'd left it by the door. "I'm not due at work until later tonight. They'll need a doctor down there."

"I'll meet you there." Parker waved them out.

The two of them were gone in an instant. Griffin and Tony stopped by the weapons room to load up before leaving at a run.

"What about Alek?" Wyatt said, jaw clenching. "You just going to leave him now?"

Misha was grateful for him, he'd said exactly what she'd been thinking.

"What do you want us to do, Wyatt?" Parker growled. "Just

ignore all these people? There are hundreds needing our help. We have priorities."

"Exactly. Family first, right?"

Mary and Sloan came over, and soon, all remaining Lazarus family members entered into an argument over who should go where. Wyatt hurled insults about Parker's pride and his drive to redeem the Deadly Seven's public name. Parker shouted back. Misha hated it. She never felt more out of place, and more useless.

And through it all, she stepped back, and back, and back until her rear hit the wall near the exit. This was her fault. If she'd just said no to Wyatt when he came for her at the club, Dimitri would never have been hurt, he'd never have lured Alek, and this incredible family of heroes wouldn't be arguing over her being a priority. Those victims of the video footage—blood, tears… pain.

Wyatt was invulnerable now, those people needed him. He could walk into a burning building and rescue victims. They needed him more than her.

Her worst fear had come true—she was a burden.

WYATT HELD PARKER by the scruff of his Deadly Seven combat outfit. Fuck him for saying Misha and Alek weren't a priority. "You need to get *your* priorities straight."

"What the hell is wrong with you?" Parker growled, his indignant eyebrow waiting for Wyatt to calm down.

He snarled through a clenched jaw and shoved Parker back. When they connected with the wall, screens wobbled and glitched. Wrath rose within Parker like a swelling tide, making Wyatt's stomach crawl.

"Put. Me. Down." Parker's teeth ground.

"Fuck you, Parker. You all say you wanted me back, but the first time I ask for actual help, and you desert me." They'd abandoned Wyatt. Fuck! A surge of fury flooded his bones. He wanted to rip Parker's head off. What was the point of it all if they ended up back where they started—a family broken apart.

"Wyatt," Mary's voice snapped harshly from somewhere beside him. "Check your wrath, *mijo*."

What?

He had trouble seeing straight through the cloud of anger.

But...

Why was he so angry?

He shoved off Parker and searched the room for Misha. Naturally, he craved her touch. Needed it. The wrath. It fed his rage. It was everywhere. He'd gone too far... and... "Where is she?"

"My guess?" Parker rubbed his throat. "She took one look at you losing your shit and got out of here."

She was gone. No wonder his fury had been so quick and violent to rise. *Fuck.* He scrubbed his face. Parker was right. She must have seen him, thought, what am I doing with this asshole, and left.

"No," Sloan muttered from her seat in the workshop, wrapping her blanket around her tighter. "She left a while ago."

Wyatt strode up to her. "What? Why didn't you say anything?"

Sloan shrugged.

Of course she wouldn't. Too fucking lazy to even lift her head.

"Fuck!" Wyatt shouted at the ceiling. He hated feeling like this.

"Settle down," Flint said. Always the cool one. Always so easy going. "You lot were going at it like a family of rabid dogs. It's a lot to take in. I'm sure Misha has just gone to get some space, and if she hasn't, she won't get far. We'll catch up."

"I'm leaving," Parker announced. "Who's on comms?"

"I'll do it," Flint offered.

Parker shot Sloan a withering stare. "Last time, Sloan. I mean it. Things are about to change around here."

"Yeah, yeah." She took the end of her pigtail and popped it into her mouth to suck.

Parker stepped toward Wyatt and straightened to his full towering height. "This isn't personal, Wyatt. When you get that, I expect an apology."

He lifted his purple battle scarf to cover his nose and mouth.

Golden eyes glared with the full focus of his proud center. Parker lifted his hood without breaking eye contact. "I'm traveling the city by roof. If this all blows over quickly, we'll redirect to provide assistance. I suggest you get into your suit in the meantime, Wyatt. You want assistance from the team, then act like you're one of us."

Wyatt bit off his snarky retort and stared back. It took all of his self-control to nod. Parker was right. Deep inside, Wyatt knew that.

"Good." The challenge faded from Parker's eyes, and then he strode out.

Mary let out a hiss of breath and pinched the bridge between her eyes. "I swear you lot will be the death of me, not some knife to the gut."

Flint snorted, pulled the spectacles down from his nose and refocused on the small black box he was pulling apart. "But we love them."

"Don't remind me." To Wyatt, her face hardened. "I'll come with you."

"What?" Flint's gaze lifted.

"There's still three of us here." Mary walked to one of the glass cabinets housing a battle suit. It was smaller than the others, black leather and weathered. "I haven't put this on for years, but it still fits."

Of course it did. She hadn't been officially working as an assassin for years, but that didn't mean she'd let go of her skills, or her physical fitness. She trained daily and put the seven through the wringer. She just didn't go out into the field.

"No," Wyatt said, and Flint agreed.

"You don't heal like the kids, Mary," Flint said. "You know this."

The look she sent her husband could have melted stone. "Forty years, Flint. Not one vital injury."

"Doesn't mean you can't get hurt," Wyatt added, his hand moving to his scar on instinct. "We regenerate. You don't."

Mary's eyes narrowed. "I've been doing this a lot longer than you. I can still kick your ass."

"Try it, and you'll break your foot." He was going for a laugh, trying to diffuse the situation, but Mary had none of it.

"I'm not having this conversation." She opened her cabinet and tugged her suit down from the mannequin. She began unbuttoning her jacket. "My son needs me, I'm going." Then she slid her don't-fuck-with-me eyes to Sloan. "You too, *mija*. Suit up."

Sloan's mouth gaped open and the soaked ponytail strand fell from of her mouth. "But…"

"No buts."

Sloan's desperate gaze whipped to Wyatt. "But, I'm a liability. My reaction time is down."

Wyatt forced his face to calm. Every second they argued, the more his panic rose. He had to go after Misha. Please let her be upstairs. "I'm not going to force you, and I'm not going to be offended if you decide not to go." He squeezed her shoulder. "But, I think you need to. Please."

"But I said—"

"I know what you said, and I don't believe it. Yes, you're out of shape, but the first step to fighting sloth is to get up and do something. So, you're coming with me to rescue Misha's brother. You're not a liability, Sloan. You're an asset, and I can't think of anyone else I want to have my back."

"Ugh."

He arched a cool eyebrow.

"Fine. I'm coming." She whined, but she did it with a smile on her face. "You're such a pain in the ass."

"Now let's load up and go and find Misha."

Hell, if she wasn't in her room. If she was out there…

Flint came to stand in front of the wall of screens. "AIMI, search for Misha Minksi in the building."

"Conducting a search now."

He dressed swiftly. It felt like old times. The routine of putting on their suits, loading up with weapons, launching into action. All three of them visited the weapon's room and synced various items to their suits—Mary went the old school route and strapped them to her fighting leathers.

"Misha Minksi is not in the building."

Wyatt's heart sank. Fuck. Why, Misha. Why be so rash?

Love made people do rash things. He knew that... or... a cold feeling flowed through him when a nasty thought came to him. Did she leave to help Alek, or was it all a ruse? Was Misha working with the Syndicate?

"AIMI," he asked. "Pull up CCTV footage of the front of the building. Scan for when Misha left."

Footage appeared on every screen, clearly showing Misha getting into a cab.

"Don't go there, bras," Sloan warned, watching over his shoulder. "She's not Sara."

She lied to you this morning in the bathroom. Sara lied all the time, and he never knew it. He thought—fuck, he didn't know what to think. He grabbed his hair and pulled, pacing, blowing air from his mouth. As the walls began to close in, and his breath thickened in his lungs, Mary slapped him on the cheek.

"What the fuck?"

"One, you don't curse at me. Two, Sloan is right. Misha isn't Sara. She's your mate. Have a little faith. Let's think about this clearly."

Screw Mary. You need to go. Go now. Find out for yourself.

YURI LET Misha into The Kremlin without a problem. The big Russian simply cast his cold eyes down her body and spoke into his comms by pressing the mic at his sleeve.

"She's here." Yuri neglected to look at her while he spoke—presumably to Dimitri. After shooting off "da" a few times, he lowered his gaze and nodded curtly. He didn't pat her down for weapons, didn't even say hi.

No *lapochka*. No sweetheart.

More bizarrely, he left his post at the door, closed it, and took her personally to Dimitri. When she walked through the dark maze of red hallways, already teeming with customers and staff, she barely received a glance of recognition from her fellow dancers. It made her feel as though her entire life at the club had been a lie. Sure, she only ever saw it as temporary until her debt was paid, but the acquaintances and, dare she say, friendships, she'd built were obviously just a means to an end. Did any of these people ever make lasting connections? The thought made her long for what she'd built with Wyatt.

With Lilo. With Grace. And what she was inevitably throwing away simply by being there.

As they passed through the main floor, she caught the eye of Joe as he packed away a fresh rack of cleaned glasses under the bar. Anastasia danced around a pole on the stage, fluttering her eyes closed, and hooking a leg on the pole to twirl away. On the adjacent pole, her sister Dominika danced with her back to Misha. Pity, regret, and resignation reflected back at Misha from all sides. In their eyes, it was clear Misha was already a ghost. The notion should make her afraid, but the reassuring weight of the gun tucked into her waistband, hiding under the bulk of her denim jacket, allowed her to relax. Whatever happened today, she would get Alek out of there. No matter what.

Down the dark stairs, through the cold corridor of blinking lights, watched by strange masked men, hiding in alcoves. They got to the end and Yuri knocked at the closed door of Dimitri's office.

"Da," he said from inside.

Yuri opened the door and exchanged a few Russian words with Dimitri, then stepped aside to let her in. She took a deep breath, hardened her resolve, and walked through, barely registering Yuri closing the door behind her until the soft click of the latch sounded as loud as a hammer.

Alek lay on his side on the floor, still strapped to a chair by the wrists. Bruising discolored his swollen lip and cheek. One black, puffy eye squinted shut, the other stared at the far wall. *Can't see me...* or... He didn't move. For a moment, her lungs burned from lack of oxygen. Then his chest lifted with breath, and she forced her lungs to work. *He's alive.*

Ignoring Dimitri at his desk, she went to her brother and placed a gentle hand on him. "Alek."

Immediately, an icy blue eye snapped to her with a vulnerable accusation that seemed to say, *"You shouldn't have come,"* the same time as, *"I'm so glad you're here."*

Before she could be stopped, Misha pulled at the rope tying Alek's hands to the arms of the chair. When they fell free, he rubbed his wrists gingerly. Misha helped him to a sitting position on the floor and then rounded on the man watching her with morbid fascination from beyond his big wooden desk.

"I knew you would come." His black soulless eyes locked onto her. "It is in our blood; this need to finish the game."

You're insane. And that was when she noticed his arm. The gleaming gold and metal piece of machinery was something out of a futuristic horror movie. It seemed so unreal that for a moment, she thought it was a costume, but then it moved. He could have hidden the arm, but he chose to expose it. He'd ripped the fabric from one suit arm, and the hideous monstrosity was for all to see.

Visible power. No one would dare say no to him again. But even as part of her mind jumped to conclusions about his motives, the other part was painfully chaotic, traveling back to his greeting words. Why her? Why this relentless sick game he played? It wasn't one she wanted to play.

Her shoulders slumped in defeat because it was true, in a way, she had come to finish his game.

"Yes, Dimitri. I came."

The snake moved behind him. It coiled around the tree branch, a slithering mass of muscle. All around the room, evidence of Dimitri's madness glared back at her. The obsession for gold. The blood stains left on the floor. The CCTV screens invading the privacy of his customers upstairs. Her hand began its slow path to the back of her waistband.

She'd always believed in karma, that if you lived a life full of anger, anger would come for you. With him, it had. The man had no love, no joy, no peace. That was his life by choice and, at the start, it was why she'd put up with his bullshit, because she always knew she'd already won. Toward the end, that willingness of hers to live and let live had only caused her pain and suffering. Now karma was coming for him, and it felt like the cold hard steel her fingers slowly closed around.

"Let my brother go." The words trembled from her lips, betraying her uncertainty. "And I'll do whatever you want."

Just a little more. Get a good grip around the trigger.

A sneer pinched his face. "Put your hand back where I can see it."

She paused and considered pulling the weapon to shoot him. Calculations zoomed through her mind, and it was that hesitation that cost her. Dimitri's jaw hardened, he moved. She gripped the gun, pulled it, swung it to—it was knocked from her hand. Shock petrified her body and made her a prisoner to her galloping heart. Adrenaline pumped and prickled her skin. *Get out, run,* her mind screamed, but she couldn't. She couldn't. Alek was still behind her. She couldn't leave. She couldn't even try.

He was there. In front of her. Menacing eyes and golden strength about to hurt, she flinched back, waiting for the inevitable blow, but the breath burst out of him and he took a step back. His eyes trailed to an outfit hanging from a hook on the wall. A French Maid's outfit. It had black cuff sleeves, a revealing neckline, a short black skirt with a white frilly petticoat with a tuxedo apron down the front. Obscene. "Put it on."

Tears stung her eyes at his request. Humiliation sank her heart.

Alek got to his feet behind her, and she knew the full shame of her actions would no longer be a secret from her family. But she'd done it for them and she would do it again. She had to get Alek out of there. Make him safe. Slowly, inch by inch, she stepped backward, shepherding Alek away from Dimitri and toward the door.

Dimitri's eyes flared with aggravation, and he stood. "You defy me still! I am the one making demands, Misha. Me. Not you."

"I'm sorry. I'll do anything you want. First, just let Alek go. Please. I'm begging. He's done nothing to you."

For some reason, that infuriated him more. "The entire Minksi family owes me."

One look at his mechanical arm clenching, preparing, and Dimitri's violent intent was clear. He wasn't going to let them go. A step forward. Veins bulged in his little head. Clenched teeth released his words. "I said, get dressed."

He shoved her sideways, back the way she'd come. She knocked against the wall and slid to the floor before she understood what happened. When her vision cleared, Dimitri advanced on her. The manic light in his eyes had gone beyond comprehension, and when his foot lashed out toward her abdomen, her first panicked thought had been the very thing she'd denied all week. "I'm pregnant!" she shouted, arms out to shield her.

The kick never came. She lowered her trembling hands. Dimitri's head cocked to the side, stunned. But beyond him, near the exit, Alek's eyes were the most surprised. He understood. He'd read her lips. A fierce, loyal expression crossed his face before he clamped down hard. For a moment, Misha didn't see her younger disabled brother. She saw a man, strong and determined.

The word *run* was on the tip of her tongue, but Alek wasn't watching. His attention speared Dimitri's way. The hatred and fury burning through his posture stole her breath away, and she knew her brother was about to do something stupid. For her.

Dimitri snarled at Misha, bringing her focus back to him. "You think after your mother abandoned me that I give a shit about what's inside you?"

Huh?

Thoughts scrambled in her mind as Misha tried to make sense of his words. The room spun around her. The floor tilted. Was he insane? Was she in some sort of movie, or a dream? How could her mother abandon him? While her eyes wildly darted about the room, they landed on hope. Her pistol was underneath the fallen chair, not even a yard away from her. Forcing herself to calm, she straightened her spine. Chin out, she caught her brother's eye. He noticed the gun, too. A plan formulated in her head. Distract Dimitri. Get the gun. Live.

"You're insane, Dimitri, and you're a liar."

Misha barely finished her words before Dimitri careened to the side. One second, he stood there, about to unleash fury, the next he was knocked to the side. Alek had launched himself at Dimitri's torso, tackling him. The two of them hit the desk. CCTV monitors scattered to the ground. Dimitri's metal fist hit Alek with a sickening sound, but Alek made no cry of pain. He couldn't. Launching across the old carpet, she retrieved the gun from under the fallen chair, but the tangle of limbs lashing at each other was too much. She couldn't see what happened, couldn't pick them apart. Only when that shining mechanical thing whirred through the air and landed on her brother's arm, did she get her chance. They both froze as Alek's mouth opened in a soundless scream of agony, and Dimitri pressed down harder.

She aimed. *Fired.*

Glass shattered as the terrarium exploded. *Missed.* She'd missed Dimitri, but it shocked his grip from her brother. Without missing a beat, she tugged Alek from the desk and shoved him at the door. She tried not to think of her brother's injured and bloody face. He would be fine. He was a survivor. She only took her eyes from Dimitri for a second, only enough to open the door and shove her brother out, but it was plenty of time for Dimitri to take hold of the gun, wrest if from her grip and crush.

"Go!" she shouted at Alek and pushed with all the might of the love bursting from her heart. "I'll hold him off. Get out, get—" She slammed the door shut and locked it. *Get Wyatt.*

If she escaped with her brother, Dimitri would chase them down before they got to the end of the corridor. The masked watchers would chase them down. Alek had a better chance of survival if she kept the boss busy, kept him from making that order to cut them down. Leaning against the wood, catching her breath, she turned and faced the spindly devil, panting and snorting with rage. Keep him busy. Yeah, right.

How? The crumbled remains of her gun had scattered across the floor. That arm of his had turned the metal into shavings, and Dimitri delighted in the fact it scared the living shit out of her. Before he moved to attack her, she pushed off the door and went to the outfit. Keep him busy. Give Alek enough time to get out of there before the alarm went off.

"Look," she said without turning. "I'm playing your game. I'm putting it on."

A snort of rage behind her made her think of a bull, and she tried to remain steady, knowing that any moment he could tear her head clear from her shoulders.

"Once I put it on, then what? What do you want from me?" She slipped the dress from the hanger. She shoved her pants down, ripped her top off, and slipped the skimpy dress over her head, all the while continuing to talk. "Why me, Dimitri? Why insist on putting me through this damn charade of yours?"

The heavy breathing seemed to subside.

Unable to zip herself up, the dress hung limply from her shoulders, like a rag doll. When she turned around, his eyes momentarily lost their fire, but then they hardened, once again turning to pure black hate.

"You still have no fucking clue," he said. "You're as dumb as your mother."

She gasped. Still, he brought up her mother? *Your mother abandoned me,* he'd said.

"She worked for us." Dimitri stalked toward her, his human hand jabbing in accusation toward her. "The *suka* worked for my father, cleaning our fucking toilets. He paid for her to come from Poland, and what did she do? She fucked him. Got pregnant. But do you think the whore wanted me? No. She got what she wanted—a life in this country. She stayed for two years, and then left me at my father's door, and abandoned me for her new family." His eyes narrowed in malice. "*You.*"

Nausea rolled in her stomach. The carpet rocked beneath her feet. "No. You're making this up."

"Nyet, Misha," he sneered. "I do not make it up. I lived with my asshole father for years telling me how unwanted I was. How a little cockroach like me wasn't wanted by his cockroach mother. And when I was old enough. I killed him. Stabbed him, then filled his puny mouth with cockroaches—made him choke on them. Then I tracked down this woman. To see if this was the *blyád'* he led me to believe. To make her see it was an honor to consider me her son. And when I find her dead, when I go to her funeral—" his dark eyes turned vacant. "I was…" He paused, stunned, eyes glazed as he relived the memory. "She had another family. One she wanted. A family who mourned her for being a *wonderful* woman." His face twisted and he spat on the floor. "I would have killed her if nature had not done it for me. Instead, I find you… a woman with the same face. Same hair. The one she had growing in her womb when she left me."

Denial pumped through her system, but she couldn't discount he might be telling the truth. Her parents hadn't met in Poland before coming to this country. They'd met here. Hannah Minksi had immigrated with another man, or there had been one waiting for her. She was a little rusty on the details, but it was entirely plausible. The instant her mind thought it, her heart threw up an argument. Her mother was too kind to be this heartless woman he accused her of being. She had always said their family was the best thing that ever happened to her, and Tata had said she was the best thing that happened to him. Family was important to her.

"No," she insisted again. "This is part of your sick game. We graduated school at the same time."

Dimitri laughed. "Look at me, *siostra*. I am puny. I could pass for a teenager, even now. You know it is true."

She shook her head. No.

"Yes," he said, delighting in her horror. "My father beat her as he did me, but instead of staying, instead of protecting me, she left me. And this is what you get now." He splayed his hands wide.

God. Misha squeezed her eyes shut, mind hurtling back to her childhood. All the times her mother admonished her for whining about her life, saying she didn't know how good she had it. It had all sounded like gratuitous parenting, but now, it held a note of truth.

A pounding at the door had both of them jolting to attention.

Damn it. Alek was probably still out there. He hadn't run. Misha's desperate eyes clashed with Dimitri's insane ones. There was no way he'd let her go. With a sinking feeling, her hand fluttered to cover her stomach. She should have trusted Wyatt.

thirty-eight
WYATT LAZARUS

SARA'S LAUGHTER haunted Wyatt's memories. *You're just a dumbass. It's why I picked you.*

Shutting her out, he raced down to the garage and climbed aboard Betty. Sloan and Mary rushed to keep up with him. Sloan with her iPad, chasing down the steps, shouting for him to plan his entry. Never go in blind. That was a rule drilled into them during training. Get eyes on the target. Know your enemy. A small part of him was proud of Sloan for her diligence, but he was already deep in a haze of uncontrollable emotion.

Everything Sloan said took him a step closer to the edge. There were too many voices in his head. He had to get out of there before he snapped. Wrath made his vision blur, just like it had that day he'd chased Evan and Sara down the freeway, running their car off the road and pulling Evan out to beat him.

Stop being so stupid, Wyatt, Sara had whispered into his ear, that night on the freeway. *Love can't conquer all.*

AS WYATT DROVE through the streets of Cardinal City, he stewed. The further he got from HQ, the more his dark thoughts tried to convince him that Misha had lied to him the entire time.

Never trust a woman.

Maybe the voice was right. Whether or not Misha was Syndicate, it was clear she'd been hiding something from him, acting cagey and distant all week. He wanted to be bitter about it, but as he raced toward The Kremlin, he only felt a hollow ache inside, an emptiness she used to occupy. It didn't sit right. It twisted his gut in a way he'd never felt before.

Regardless of Wyatt's feelings, Alek deserved his help. The kid didn't deserve to die by the hand of a psycho like Dimitri.

That's if Alek is really there.

Shut up! He hit his visor with a fist. *Get out of my head.*

Cutting through the night traffic, Wyatt whipped in front of cars, changing lanes without warning, burning rubber. His bike almost clipped another vehicle, and he wobbled as control wrenched from his grasp. The hit vehicle beeped angrily as he wrestled control back from Betty. Back tire spun. His boot slammed the ground for balance as the bike ran in circles. When he finally halted, his muscles locked up, aching from the intense strain.

Christ.

He'd come close to causing an accident. He would have survived, but the other car? Major damage. Shock snapped him out of his self-indulgence and he realized he was in the same headspace as last time. When Sara had set up Evan to make it look like the two of them were eloping. That had been a terrible lie.

Had he learned nothing? Still chasing his sin, still believing the worst.

If there was a tiny kernel of possibility that Misha had simply left to go to The Kremlin because she believed she had a better chance of rescuing Alek on her own, or that she didn't want to be a burden to his family, then her motivations were pure. She was just a girl looking out for her family, and in no way tied to the Syndicate. She was not Sara.

Sara was dead.

If there was a chance that Misha's life was in danger…

I want someone who can promise me they'll always be there. A better voice, Misha's voice, filled his mind. She'd said that before he'd made love to her, and he promised to hold on to her with two hands. He failed at his promise the moment they'd arrived back at his family home when he let her stay on her own in the guest apartment.

He shut his eyes and forced himself to calm, to breathe just like she'd taught him on top of that water tower. He conjured more of her words. More of her.

No, silly. We don't run from the rain. We make love in the rain.

And then…

If I let you in, koteczek, I'm not letting you go.

With each passing second, his heart rate slowed. The memory of her lilac and incense scent filled him with a longing. He wanted to be back on her family couch, to have her feet under his thighs for warmth.

He opened his eyes, thoughts clearing. This wasn't history repeating.

Two motorcycles pulled up beside him. The riders, clad in charcoal battle gear and black glossy helmets, idled next to him.

Sloan lifted her visor. "You dumbass."

Mary lifted her visor and said nothing. He experienced a rush of emotion at the motherly patience staring back at him. It was the same look she'd given him when he'd made his mistakes the first time. It said, *I love you.*

He sucked in a breath, lifted his visor. "You're right, we need a plan."

"I agree," Mary said. "We go in through the front and there could be innocent collateral."

"That's why I looked at this earlier." Sloan grinned and pulled a tab on her sleeve. A thin flexible screen rolled out from the hem of her inseam and she flicked it stiff. When Sloan tapped the screen, it lit up with computer data. "We tracked the cab Misha took to The Kremlin. She's definitely there."

Pain in his chest made it hard to breathe. Wyatt nodded. "She's gone to get Alek."

"Here." Sloan pointed to the digital blueprints of The Kremlin. "Roof entrance. There's a helipad up top. Doesn't look like it's used. We go in from there."

"All right." Wyatt snapped his visor closed. "Let's go."

CLIMBING the side of the building had been no problem with their grappling hooks and retractable rope. Getting through the roof emergency exit door had also been a breeze. It wasn't until all three of them hit the inside stairwell that Wyatt sensed sin coming from two people below. He recognized the sin-signatures of both Alek and Dimitri. The dual surge meant only one thing. The two were locked in battle.

"What is it?" Mary said, coming up next to him.

"I know where they are. Alek's in danger."

With steely determination set in their eyes, they masked their faces and lowered their hoods. Sloan released her bow from her holster and pulled an arrow from the quiver at her thigh. She nocked, pulled taut, held it ready and sighted. Mary withdrew her knives. Wyatt just went.

The flare of sin came from way down, and he had no time to waste.

Down the dark stairwell and into the thumping base, he dropped, two steps at a time. Saucy electro-jazz music pumped loudly through the club, giving them the cover of noise. Whatever happened tonight, there would be collateral damage, but as another burst of sin exploded from deep in the bowels of the basement, a surge of hopelessness flooded him. If he was too late… He pushed on, descending at an alarming speed. *Nearly at the next level. Almost there.*

If Misha was hurt, and Alek was… no. He could still sense Alek down there. His wrath simmered, providing Wyatt the beacon with which to find them. He hurtled from the stairwell onto the main club floor and stopped.

Despite their intel, despite the satellite heat map showing multiple bodies inside the club—it wasn't customers and dancers who greeted them. It was Falcon stepping casually his way, dressed head to toe in white, bird mask hiding her face, white bullwhip snapping at her side. Behind her, on the mirrored stage and from the curtained side walls, a white-robed army of Faithful stepped out of the shadows.

A trap.

His stomach dropped out. Misha's betrayal was clear as day. She'd led him here… to his death. His pulse pounded in his ears, roaring while his hot breath pushed at the cloth covering his mouth. Seconds ticked by and neither party moved while he came to terms with the situation.

If he truly believed his mate had betrayed him, then why did his heart still pull him toward the basement? Toward her. Misha was his *life*. He wouldn't survive without her.

Mary stepped around him and held her throwing knives ready. "We've got this, *mijo*."

"Go save the princess." Sloan took up a position behind Mary and aimed into the horde. The entrance to the basement was just to the right. He'd make it if they provided cover.

Wyatt hesitated. Neither woman had been in the field for months, and neither were bulletproof. *Family first,* had always been Mary's motto.

She must have seen the conflict in his eyes.

"Don't go soft on us now, Wrath." Mary's gaze hardened over her blood-red scarf. "We'll hold them off."

"I'll come back."

"We know." Sloan fired her arrow at Falcon and then all hell broke loose. But he didn't stick around to watch. He went down the steps to where he felt Alek's wrath pull at him, taking him toward the boy like a puppet string to the gut. Taking him to where he hoped Misha still remained unharmed.

When he came across one of Dimitri's men, he jabbed him in the throat, putting him down immediately.

He wasn't showy, like Tony. Wasn't flashy, like Evan. He was after the swiftest way to his woman and her brother. Anything in his path simply became an object to remove. Through the dark maze, he turned. He slammed heads. He poked eyes. He crushed kneecaps with a boot. He threw bodies over his shoulder. And when he got to the end of the tunnel—Wyatt pulled back at the last possible moment as a blur of wrath attacked him. He caught the fist before it struck his face and grinned with pride.

Alek, my boy.

The teenager was beaten, black-eyed and bruised, and he was alone in the edge of the hallway, standing before a closed door containing Dimitri's twisted wrath. Alone, beat, but insatiable. The kid had remembered his lessons, and when Wyatt had caught his fist, the boy adjusted his strike. *Turn the body, bend the knees, follow through, commit with the other hand—strike the open solar plexus.* Wyatt remembered vividly showing Alek what to do, and the boy did it without wavering.

Wyatt caught Alek's second fist.

A foot headed toward Wyatt's groin, and he was about to shout for Alek to stop, but couldn't. His mouth was covered. Alek couldn't read his lips, and with Wyatt's hands occupied, he couldn't sign. He released, shoved away and tugged his scarf down.

It's me, Wyatt signed and mouthed. *It's me.*

Alek flinched, and his bravado melted. His face crumpled, and he began to sign wildly, pointing at the solid door behind him.

Wyatt slid the fingers on his right gloved hand up the back of his left hand. *Slow down, kid. I'm not there yet with the sign language.*

Alek's bottom lip disappeared under his teeth as he forced himself to calm.

A cold realization settled on Wyatt. There was no way Misha worked with the Syndicate. Not with Alek so brutally beaten. She'd never stand for that.

"Misha's in there?" Wyatt asked quietly.

A nod, and then Alek's brows joined and lifted in the middle, clearly distraught.

"Is she…" he couldn't bring himself to finish the sentence, or to sign.

Alek shook his head and then signed, *She's alive.*

But that's where Wyatt's translation ended. He lost the rest. His skill wasn't enough, because the next actions made Wyatt think of a baby. The boy rocked his arms as though he held one, and then he pointed to the door.

"There's a baby in there?"

Alek shook his head and made a motion around his stomach, pointing desperately at the door. Misha was in there. Why would he make that motion toward the door unless—Wyatt's heart stopped beating. Misha's evasiveness and unexplained vomiting over the week became clear. She was pregnant, and she was in danger.

He froze. Rooted to the spot as the word bounced around in his head. Pregnant? His?

No time.

If Alek knew, he'd never leave her side willingly. "What are you doing out here?"

She locked me out. Blue eyes widened and Alek shook his head. *I'm looking for a weapon.*

"Kid, I am the weapon. Move."

thirty-nine

MISHA MINSKI

THE SICK MAN in front of Misha had been toying with her since high school because—if he was believed—he was her half-brother. Reconciling his view of their mother with her own version was not melding. She knew Hannah Minksi to be a kind and caring mother who would do anything for her children. It didn't make sense that she would give one up. Never. It didn't compute that she was this *whore* Dimitri made her out to be, even if she was beaten by her first husband.

Misha was in some kind of hell, a nightmare she couldn't wake from, but there she was, dressed in a cheap French Maid's outfit, with no weapon, and no protection from the madman with an impossible mechanical arm. As she stared at him, she couldn't help registering the real pain in his eyes.

"You're taking your anger out on the wrong person," she said, lifting her chin. "If what you said is true, I had nothing to do with my mother's decisions. I wasn't even born then."

"You had everything to do with it!" he shouted, face turning red with rage. "She wanted you, but did not want me."

"You want me to feel sorry for you?"

"No. I want you to pay for her sins." Dimitri drew his mechanical fist back, clenched his teeth and held it there, hovering—eyes so full of fury that Misha knew these next few minutes would be her last, and she didn't want to die, not anymore. She knew she'd already become a burden to Wyatt, and this child would make everything complicated, but damn her if she gave up now.

Dimitri released. Misha dodged and his metal fist embedded in the wall beside her head. Plaster crumbled. She tried to get out from underneath him but he grabbed her with his free hand and forced her in place while he yanked his enhanced hand free.

She had nothing. No weapons, but herself. She kicked and punched and scratched. The man was smaller than her, but strong, so strong. Hopelessly, every strike she made glanced off, and when her fist struck his metal arm, she cried out in agony. All she did was infuriate Dimitri further, and when he finally pulled his metal hand free from the wall, and drew it to strike, she shut her eyes and prayed.

This is it.

Had she lived life the way she wanted? Everything stilled and Misha's world slowed. Time stopped and all she could think was, I don't want to die. *I'm not ready.*

A loud bang exploded behind Dimitri and a shadow burst through the door, kicking it from its hinges. That's all she saw, the fast blur of a shadow, and then Dimitri cried out in pain, bowing his back as though he'd been hit there. Dimitri's face twisted, and he rounded on his attacker, mechanical fist flying.

Wyatt.

In his Deadly suit with the hood and mask down, his face was clear as day and… infuriated. His dark blue eyes were shrouded in animosity. He focused all that fury on the man who'd tried to kill her. Wyatt's hands moved in expert precision as he pummeled Dimitri, but when Dimitri's powerful arm collided with Wyatt—Misha's heart almost burst from her chest.

She thought he was bulletproof, but that right hook knocked the sense out of Wyatt—he shook his head, clearing the fog from the hit. A flash of red blood in his mouth revealed he wasn't infallible. Dimitri took advantage. He attacked Wyatt, over and over again, hitting her man with his unyielding metal fist. Wyatt blocked, two forearms and fists shielding his body and face.

Weapon. She needed a weapon. Her sight jumped all over the broken room, searching for something. Glass. The glass terrarium had broken. She ignored the tiny shards pricking her bare feet and ran to the desk, looking for a big shard she could wrap her jacket around and use to cut. But when she rounded the desk, she saw something even more frightening. The enormous snake slithered out of its container, somehow climbing over the fallen computer monitors, broken glass, and filling the entire floor space between the desk and the back wall. It was massive. Human killing size. She swallowed a lump in her throat, urgency speeding her pulse. There was no way she'd reach past that thing to find a shard of glass big enough to use as a weapon.

So what? What else?

Dimitri's damned golden gun.

Misha yanked open the drawer to his desk. Adrenaline surged when her eyes landed on the obscene glowing weapon winking in the artificial light. She picked it up and turned back to the grappling men. Wyatt had Dimitri in a headlock, and was trying to separate his arm from his body with his feet, but the mechanical arm was too strong and slippery to gain purchase. The two men rolled, grunting. There was no clear shot. They were so intertwined... but... Wyatt was bulletproof. Maybe not mechanical arm proof, but she could shoot, she could—

No time. With an infernal roar, Wyatt tore Dimitri's gold arm off.

"*No!*" Dimitri wrenched himself from Wyatt and stood cradling his shoulder. Wires dangled from the cyborg prosthetic, sparks ignited. Dimitri tried to irrationally hold the wiring together, but only succeeded in giving himself small electric shocks. "Give it back!"

Wyatt held Dimitri's broken metal arm. He flipped it to adjust his grip, holding it by the wrist, and then his hard eyes met Misha's. He swung the metal arm, baseball style at Dimitri's head, knocking the man out cold. Dimitri's body landed near the desk with a thud.

Panting, Wyatt dropped the dead arm, kneeled down beside Dimitri and raised his fist, aiming for his face.

"No!" Misha shouted.

Wyatt stopped, drawing back confused.

"Don't kill him."

"Why? After all he's done."

"I—I think he's my half-brother. I know he's insane. I know he's been ruining my life for years, but... I can't. I just can't bring myself to be the one responsible for his death."

"Fine." Wyatt stood up. "But I'm not leaving him like this. He has to pay for his crimes. He's—" Wyatt suddenly clammed up. His eyes dropped to her outfit, lowered to her stomach, and then lifted to meet her gaze. He stilled.

Everything stilled.

In that moment, Misha knew why. Alek must have said something about her earlier confession. She held her breath. This was it. The truth would come out.

"Is it true?" he croaked.

"I think so. I don't know. Maybe."

"Why did you leave?"

"Because I don't want to be a burden. My problems shouldn't be your problems."

"You're calling this child a problem?" The whites of Wyatt's eyes showed as he gestured toward her stomach.

"No. That's not what I'm saying. I'm not even sure if I am, but—" She sighed deeply. "It was wrong of me to leave like that. I'm sorry. I just heard you fighting with your family. You're needed by the people of this city. Parker was right. There are priorities, and you'd only just reconciled with your family. I didn't want to be—"

Wyatt was upon her in an instant, bright blue eyes imploring. "You are not a burden."

She tried to talk, but nothing came out.

He shook her gently. "Christ. Don't make me say it again."

But she couldn't face him.

"Misha Minksi, you're not a burden. You're a joy. Before I met you I was in a dark place. A broken man. I never thought I would be able to trust another person again, let alone a woman. But there you were, crashing into my bed." A small smile danced on his lips. "You challenge me, and you lift me up. You gave me a voice... got me to control my anger. I can't live without you, baby or not."

"Wyatt... I..."

"No. I mean it. And helping you and your family is an honor. I will guard them with my life. My family might have other priorities, but I don't. You're it for me, and believe me, Evan and Griffin would do the same for their mates, so... you come first."

She choked on a sob.

"You don't have to say anything. I'm not expecting you to feel the same way. I know I'm different, and to expect you to love me back right now is impossible. It's all kinds of fucked up. One of the things I like about you, Misha, is that you turn any dark situation into a positive." He grinned. "And you don't give a flying fuck what anyone else thinks of you." He took a breath, lashes lowering to her stomach once more. When he lifted his yearning gaze, Misha's heart squeezed.

"I know I'm this cursing, short-fused idiot with no job and nothing else to offer the world but his fists—"

"Shut up."

Startled, his jaw clicked closed.

Tears fell from her eyes now, but it all came through a smile. "You *are* an idiot."

"I am?"

"Yes, because I do love you." She cupped his stubbly jaw and lifted her lips to his, kissing him gently. Her fingers trailed his scratchy jaw, thick with uncut stubble. It made him so darkly attractive that she was already forgetting the words that had come to her mind. "You are so much more than your sin. You're loyal, strong, sexy, and when you fall, you go all in. I love that about you."

He buried his face into her neck and held her so tight she thought she might explode.

A clapping sound came from the door, and they broke apart.

Alek poked his frightened face in. He clapped again and pointed at their feet the same time something rubbed up against Misha's bare skin. When she glanced down, terror gripped her tight.

"S-s-s-snake."

"Jesus!" Wyatt pulled her back, out of the way of the fifteen foot anaconda slowly wrapping its way around Dimitri's body, crushing him in its massive girth. They could hear bones and metal crunch.

Wyatt scooped up her fallen clothing. "Come on. We have to go."

Misha took one last look at Dimitri and then averted her eyes. She should feel bad, but in the end, he got what was coming to him. There was no way of saving him now.

forty

WYATT LAZARUS

GODDAMN THAT SNAKE, was all Wyatt could think as he barricaded Dimitri's office door closed while Misha dressed back into her normal clothes in the hallway. When he was done, he told her and Alek to stay put until he returned. He'd had no response from Mary and Sloan, despite repeated attempts at contact on his comms. It wasn't right. Tugging his mask up to conceal his identity, he made sure Misha had the golden gun, and then gave Alek one of his daggers before continuing through the hallway. Midway up the basement steps, he had to step over bodies—fallen men and white-robed lumps covered in blood and gore. They'd been thrown down the stairwell from the main level. The smell was sticky, and the air was thick. He hadn't seen such a massacre in years. Stone cold unease unfurled in his gut as he stepped over more unmoving bodies—it was quiet. Too quiet.

He tried the comms again. "Sloth," he hissed. "What's your status?"

Nothing.

"Mary."

Silence.

Shit.

Picking up the pace, he stopped only to check the pulse on a few bodies. All dead. He recognized evidence of Mary's trademark puncture wounds in vital pressure points. Bled out from their femoral or carotid arteries from one simple stab. She must have been a tornado of destruction. He cautiously continued up the stairwell, and when he crested the top to land on the ground level, more silence greeted him. The music was off. The only light came from the green emergency exit signs lighting the path out. Deep into the club where the stage and catwalk was, it was a shadowed mess. He couldn't see jack. But if he concentrated hard, he could feel something.

Wrath...

The sin wriggled in his gut and picked at the edges. Just like always, the string pulled its puppet, commanding his attention. *That way. End the sin. Kill it now.* Too many sources. One, two... he counted silently. At least five more people he could tell were hiding in the shadows beyond. But who?

Preferring the safety of distance, Wyatt disconnected the throwing knives attached to his thighs. He palmed the hilts as he crept closer, keeping his movements stealthy and light. Toe first, heel second. Softly, softly, until the sounds of groaning and dying men wafted into earshot. The smell of blood filtered through his mask. If Mary and Sloan were dead, they went down fighting. His throat tightened. *Keep going.*

Don't jump to conclusions. Seek them out.

Both Mary and Sloan had a unique sin signature. He'd spent his entire life learning how their anger felt, and if he concentrated, he could work out whether the signatures he sensed belonged to them, or the enemy. He tracked around the room—focusing on where he'd felt them before.

Movement in his periphery.

He rapid-fire released his daggers, satisfied when they ended with a thud and gurgle of astonishment. *Got 'em.* Two wrath signatures winked out, and then... Sloan.

He felt her. Alive and simmering in anger—probably injured, but alive—thank Christ. But where was Mary? She was usually the most fearful in battle. An assassin that assassins feared. Even as human as she was, she was a force to be reckoned with. The dead bodies attested to that. Uncertainty spread within him. Why couldn't he sense his mother?

She was either controlling her rage, or...

A loud clang, and then light flooded the room revealing piles of dead bodies fallen in disregard over fallen furniture and broken glass. A gasp behind him sent shock-waves rushing through his system. He spun around—

"What are you doing here?" he growled through his teeth.

Misha stood arm in arm with Alek by a fuse box on the wall. She'd turned on the lights.

"I'm sorry!" she gasped, white faced as her gaze traveled over the carnage. "It was so quiet. I thought it was safe."

He bit down. "Get back until I say it's safe."

He waved them away and signed the same thing. It was Alek who tugged the stupefied Misha into the safe cover of the hallway. Good boy. He'd make a good soldier if they could work around the hearing and sound disability. When Wyatt turned back, his gaze traveled over the many bodies—some with arrows sticking out of them—to the main stage where two stood still, waiting.

His heart dropped into his stomach. Falcon had her bullwhip wrapped around Mary's neck, and the rest of it was looped around the rafters before landing back in her hand. She tightened her hold and stared down at Wyatt from an unmasked face. It must have fallen in battle. Mary was also without her mask, jaw set with determination, eyes hard but thinking. The cord around Mary's neck reminded Wyatt of the snake consuming Dimitri. Relentless, determined, and unyielding.

Why wasn't Mary fighting back?

The suspicion shouted at him. It was wrong. This scene was wrong. Mary's hard expression was almost impassive. Apart from her thumbs beneath the cord at her neck, she seemed not to notice, nor care about the stool holding her feet up, or the whip connected to her neck and the ceiling, preparing her for death.

A groan came from Wyatt's right, and he caught movement under a fallen table. Deep beneath a pile of red splattered bodies, a hand burst out, followed by Sloan's sleeve, then her shoulder and head as she pushed the dead weight from herself. Blood streaked down her face like macabre war paint. She groaned loudly.

With one cautious eye on the stage, Wyatt offered Sloan his hand, and he pulled her to her feet.

He tugged his mask down. "You good?"

She nodded curtly. "I'll heal."

"Arrows?"

"Gone."

Shit.

"Guns?"

"Nada. And before you ask, it's all gone. I'm out. You took your sweet-ass time."

"Sorry."

Her grim face hardened, and she nodded in the direction of the stage. "Do you think she realizes that won't work on Mary?"

Hanging Mary, probably not. All of them had spent time training their iron necks with the Shaolin Monks. It was well known in martial arts that to control your opponent was to control their head—whether that be mental or physical. So they spent hours, days, sometimes over weeks hanging from a tree by their necks. And then hours and days slamming iron plates against their foreheads, or to carry loads on their heads to strengthen muscles, turning their most vulnerable body part into an unexpected weapon.

But had Mary kept up her strength training?

From the look of calm on her face, he guessed yes, but he couldn't risk it. A fifty-something-year old woman's neck wasn't the same as it was in her youth—strength training or not. He had no idea what was rushing through Mary's mind—she felt no wrath in that moment. The turmoil of emotion bubbling in her eyes was not connected to anger.

But it was connected to sloth because Sloan flinched and whispered to Wyatt, "Mary's guilty about neglecting something."

Their stony gazes met and then Sloan gave Falcon a pointed look.

He exhaled in a rush. It could only mean one thing. When his eyes landed back on Falcon, he stepped closer and asked, "What do you want?"

The white-haired woman coiled the end of her whip around her fist, tested the torque on the hangman's noose. As the whip lifted, so did Mary's neck until she stood on tiptoes, hands straining at the cord for support. Her feet scuffled on the stool, precariously rocking with her slipping foothold.

Wyatt snarled and lurched forward, but Mary shot him a halting look. "Don't," she rasped.

He stopped, four feet from the stage, shocked. "Why?"

"Despair," was all Mary managed to hiss out.

Sloan hissed in shock, but Wyatt wasn't surprised. He'd suspected it before. *Despair.* The forgotten sin... back from the dead. If she—Despair, Falcon, or whatever they should call her now—gave any indication that she heard Mary, or cared, it was lost. The woman just stared down at Wyatt with cold eyes.

"Give me your blood, and I'll let her go."

"Despair?" Sloan asked. "As in… the sister we thought was dead?"

Wyatt took another step closer and narrowed his focus on the woman. She certainly looked related with her wide lips and delicate facial structure. Put her next to Sloan, and she'd be the light version next to Sloan's dark. Tall, like all of them. Strong. Another step closer and he noticed the burn marks down the side of her face, so pale and silvery in the light that he almost didn't register. They believed Despair died in a fire, and he knew as well as anyone, that although the Lazarus children could heal and regenerate, the scars remained.

"We thought you were dead," Wyatt announced gruffly, and then took a step. "We had a funeral for you. We gave you a name."

Almost there. The stage was within reaching distance.

"Stop." She wrenched on her whip, lifting Mary higher. "Last warning."

"Okay, okay!" He held out his palms, crouching as though testing a tiger. "I'm stopping. What do you need my blood for? You already have Griffin's and Evan's."

"You mean Greed and Envy."

"No. That's the names they gave us, but we chose our own names. I'm Wyatt." He touched his chest with his palm. "We named you Daisy, because you loved flowers."

"My name is Despair."

He narrowed his eyes. Interesting. Not Falcon, but Despair. She wasn't trying to hide it. Good. He was getting in her head. Keep going.

"He can't give you what you want," Sloan added. "He can't bleed. But I can give you my blood."

"You lie. He's bleeding in the mouth."

Christ the woman had sharp eyes to see inside his red mouth.

"Daisy," he said. "Let's talk about this."

The second her name came out of his mouth, it felt right. Daisy. Not Despair. But she had other thoughts.

Her face twisted with the most emotion he'd ever seen out of her and a desperation flickered over her features. "Despair. My name is Despair, and we don't want anyone else's blood but yours."

"Why?"

"I don't have time for explanations. Give me your blood, bite your tongue if you need to. Do it, or she dies. *Five—*"

"That's Mary, don't you remember her?" Wyatt said. "She cared for you in that lab."

"*Four—*" Despair's haunted eyes landed on Mary. "*Three.*"

"Don't," Wyatt shouted. "I'll give it to you." Tugging his gloves off, he bit his tongue. He clenched through the eye-watering pain and let the metallic taste of his blood flow enough so he could spit into his palm. Holding his red hand out, he stepped up to the stage. "Your turn. Spit and shake. I want your word you'll let her go."

She looked down at him. Not even a flicker of emotion remained behind her eyes when she said, "I'm not spitting. I need an unconta-minated sample."

"It's the only way you get what you want. Deal or no deal."

Wyatt thought she wouldn't go for it, but she caved. She secured her end of the bullwhip to a stripper pole. Confident her noose would hold, she spat onto her palm, stretched toward him and shook his hand. While they were still locked, she kicked out, pushed Mary off the stool and into the air, legs flailing and kicking. Mary choked and gasped, long black braid swinging behind her. Wyatt launched forward, vaulted the stage and lifted Mary by the hips, growing the slack on the noose.

"I got you," he said to Mary, then bellowed: "Knife!"

"Where?" Sloan frantically searched the fallen Faithful and mobsters. "I don't see one."

"There—" Wyatt pointed to where he'd felled one of them near a leather couch full of holes. "In his back."

Mary's jaw set in determination, and her face reddened with strain as she tried to say something, but while her lips moved, nothing came out.

Sloan rushed to retrieve the knife, tugged it from a man's back, twisted, aimed, and fired at the leather whip holding Mary. With precision accuracy, it sliced through the cord, snapping the tension. Mary dropped into Wyatt's arms. Frantically, he worked to release the whip around her neck. Her lips moved, but still no sound came out.

"Stop trying to speak," Wyatt said. "You'll hurt yourself."

Defiantly, Mary wouldn't listen, so Wyatt looked for Misha and called. With her brother by her side, they rushed over.

"What's she saying?" Wyatt asked, then said softly to Mary. "She can read lips. Don't speak, just mouth the words."

Misha watched, then said, "Find Daisy. Family first."

Fuck.

Wyatt snapped to attention and signaled for Sloan to take one direction while he searched the other. They went through the destroyed club, into the dressing rooms, around the bars, the store-rooms, and down the stairwells, but Despair was long gone. All that was left of her was the saliva drying on his palm.

forty-one

MISHA MINSKI

EXHAUSTION BATTERED Misha as she said goodnight to her younger brother and settled him into the spare room in Wyatt's apartment. Wyatt had insisted both of them stay there while he sorted out affairs with his family, and she was glad for it. Being away from him was not something she looked forward to, especially after the night they'd had.

The sight of the snake crushing Dimitri's body had burned into her memory. Every time she closed her eyes, it was all she could see. Green monstrous muscle, slithering and choking.

When they'd arrived earlier, she'd washed and changed into fresh clothes, and Alek had done the same. Wyatt had been gone for hours in the basement, seeing to his mother's injuries and conferring with the rest of the Deadly Seven, who had returned in dribs and drabs from their rescue missions. Grace had stopped in for a few minutes to check on Alek's wounds before she had to leave to work at the hospital. She had told Misha there were many fatalities that night. Many people had died, but many were saved.

After Grace left, Misha wanted to spend time getting Alek used to the unfamiliar surroundings, but as it turned out, Alek didn't need her much at all. He helped himself to food in the fridge and made Misha a hot chocolate before heading off to bed. He hadn't mentioned Dimitri and his revelation about being their long-lost half-brother, which meant—hopefully—that he hadn't heard or seen an iota of that confession.

It didn't matter now if what Dimitri said was true. He was dead. It would only hurt and confuse her family's opinion of their mother. Misha could only comment on what kind of person Hannah Minksi was to her, and that woman, the one who shelled beans with them in the backyard, the one who stayed up for hours sewing Roksana's ballerina costumes, that was the only woman she needed to know about.

After Misha finished her hot chocolate, and while she could still keep her eyes open, she went to check on her brother, her maternal instinct needing to see him safe and in bed. When she cracked the door to his room, she found his long lanky frame sprawled on his back under the covers of the double bed. God, he wasn't a kid anymore.

Emotion circled her heart and squeezed, spreading warmth throughout her body. She couldn't help but perch at the end of the bed to place her palm on Alek's chest. Feeling his breath was the most incredible thing. She remembered him as a child and having to communicate by touch to educate him.

Alek's eyes blinked open, saw it was her, gave her hand a half-hearted pat of solidarity, and then drifted back to sleep. He was so brave. She'd spent too much time thinking bitterly about parenting, instead of focusing on the amazing humans her siblings had become. She'd never stopped to think that regardless of her regret toward the loss of her prime partying days, she'd helped Alek grow into a strong, capable man, despite his disability. She'd also helped Roksana become one of the best ballerinas in the Tri-state area. Misha had done good. Her mother would be proud.

Misha covered Alek with the comforter and returned to the living area. She gathered a throw blanket and waited on the pillowy brocade sofa. Her eyes had only been closed a minute when she felt herself being carried in strong arms. Rousing from the haze of sleep, she found Wyatt placing her on his enormous bed.

"You're back," she murmured into the dark.

He shushed her and told her to go back to sleep, but suddenly, she wasn't tired. The smell of him lingered, and she became acutely aware of freshly showered man. Sitting up, she blinked at his silhouette, trying to let her eyes adjust, and when they had—her savage *koteczek* wore only a pair of low slung sweats, naked torso right there for her to see. The sight made every feminine muscle inside her clench in delight.

The two of them locked eyes for an eternity.

Desire thrummed in her veins as she soaked him up. Still hot, she thought. And she was still filled with want for the heroic man. Not bored after one night. Not at all. Everything about him screamed masculinity, from the dark fuzz trailing from his abdomen to the waistband of his sweatpants, to the bulge in his pants growing under the loving weight of her intense gaze. Every muscle in his carved body turned to stone.

"Come here," she breathed, but he wouldn't budge.

She needed to feel his strength around her body, to be caged in his arms. She reached out, and it was that silent gesture, not words, that had him coming to her side. The mattress dipped as he lowered. Curling a knee as he sat, he left the other dangling over the edge. Still not fully committing, he held back. He sat there and toyed with her hair. So serious and stern, as if he didn't want to break her... or scare her away.

The revelation zipped through her. This was her fault. She shouldn't have left him. Trust was a two-way street, and she had to work out any problems with him together. She owed him that respect. As his warm touch feathered behind her earlobes, she melted and leaned into him.

"Is Mary okay?" she whispered to fill the silence.

He nodded.

"Are you okay?"

He exhaled in a long slow burst and then adjusted her hair on the other side. Unable to stop, he trailed his touch everywhere. With his two big hands heating her blood, she felt completely at home. He once said that her touch was like a balm to him, like someone injecting valium into his veins, and from the way he visibly relaxed, she believed him. It was such a strong, visceral reaction that it was hard not to see she was made for him. One in millions. It made her feel empowered. Bold. Her internal sensations would never be the same as his, not a lab-created biological response, but she still felt it— the connection that drilled into her soul and basked in the heat of his sun.

Her hands slid up his chest and traced every feverish dip and valley of his satiny skin. Along his collarbone, up the thick column of his neck, around his earlobes, over his stubbly jaw, into his thick hair still damp from the shower. He'd saved her life today. He'd saved her brother. He would keep saving people because that was the kind of man he was, even if he hated himself sometimes.

Maybe she could love him enough for two people. Or three.

She continued to rub and massage, easing his anxiety, but he still held a note of restraint. He wanted to talk about the possible pregnancy, but she couldn't do it. It reminded her too much of her mother dying. She'd had enough adulting for one night. *Tomorrow.*

With a pained look, he opened his mouth to speak, but she shook her head, silencing him. She just needed to be close to him. To find that joy he spoke of and remind herself it would be okay.

To banish the nightmarish snake scenes still flashing behind her eyes, she kissed the corner of his mouth. He stiffened. She kissed again. His lashes lowered and he shuddered. She kissed again, closer to the center of his bottom lip. Her tongue darted out and tasted salty skin, licking and laving until he opened his mouth and she bit down on the plump flesh.

A hitch of breath and his restraint burst. He kissed back, tongue meeting hers in a demanding dance that made her mind spin. He cupped her head and held them locked together, unyielding in his ardor, until they dropped to the bed, breathless. Lying next to each other, feeling hot breaths between them, he rolled her so her back was flush against the front of his body. Deftly, he adjusted the comforter and sheets so they were both cocooned beneath. With a sigh, he rested his head on the pillow behind her and tugged her close as if he thought she'd slip away.

Staring into the dark, Misha closed her eyes.

Wyatt was the best blanket she could wish for, but it wasn't enough. Every cell in her body buzzed with him behind her. Hot, firm, smooth, rough. She traced her fingers up and down his forearm resting between her breasts, hugging her to him. In response, he kissed quickly and modestly behind her ear. All that did was ratchet her desire until all she could think of was his unyielding body against her soft rear end—that hard length digging between the two halves of her bottom.

Heat pooled heavily between her legs, her sensitized nipples grazed against her pajama top, making everything worse. She was going to die if he didn't touch her soon, and when he didn't, when he infuriatingly laid still, she wiggled and pushed back into him, demanding with her body. The expletive he shot out made her smile, so she took his palm and slipped it under her top to her bare breast, molding his fingers over her flesh, until he couldn't help himself but knead and plump and roll her puckered bud with his fingers.

A deep, sexual groan came from his mouth in a way that rumbled her entire being.

She urged him to keep going, but he hesitated. Getting desperate, she needed him, wanted to feel him inside her, wanted that connection to drive deep. She urged his touch from her breast down her flat stomach and below. They slipped together beneath her waistband until he hit her aching core. She wore no panties, and he approved with a grunt into her hair. When he took over driving the touch, she almost wept with relief. *Thank Christ.*

Yes. *Yes.* She lifted to his touch, and he pushed a finger inside. Little pleading sounds burst from her mouth as he pumped slowly, and toyed with her, spreading her wetness around.

"Oh, God, yes, *koteczek*. Play with me," she moaned, breathing heavily into the dark.

A rough, ragged breath into her ear told her he loved it, and that he was falling as hard as she. With each stroke and flick of his fingers, her pleasure coiled tighter.

"More," she breathed, craning her neck to see him over her shoulder.

His lips found hers and his heady taste brought a new sweet agony—she reached around and tugged his pants down until she found his arousal. She squeezed until he grunted, and then she pumped, sliding her fist up and down his satin-smooth length.

Still with their mouths on each other, but her back to his front, they increased the urgency of their loving until she could stand it no more. She needed him inside her. Now. She angled until his tip pressed against her wet, needy center. In one swift thrust, he pushed in completely. She cried out, almost flying into climax, but when he didn't move, she came back down to earth.

Oh, so now he plays, she thought amused. Her humor vanished when he refused to move, even as she squirmed and writhed in arresting torment. The sensation of him filled and stretched her deliciously. She tried to move, to thrust back into him, but he gripped onto her and forced her to still.

"What are you doing?" she murmured impatiently.

"I'm taking a picture memory."

She laughed. *Bastard*.

Only when she was panting and hot with need did his fingers wander down between her legs, rubbing and bringing her back to the edge of oblivion.

Feeling drugged on his heat, his scent, and his taste, she could do little else but let him kiss her while he expertly pleasured below, and only when that knot of sensation pulled so tight that she exploded and saw stars, did he begin to move inside her. Slow, languid thrusts that kept her orgasm cascading, curling her toes and making every limb pleasantly numb. There was no doubt in her mind that she felt loved in that moment. No doubt that whatever the test result would be tomorrow, he'd hold her with two hands, never letting go.

forty-two

SLOAN LAZARUS

THE NEXT MORNING, Sloan shuffled into the VIP room in the restaurant below their apartments. Heaven was only a short walk from her front door, but it seemed like a world away. The previous night's activities had turned every muscle in her body into a screaming bitch. That's what activity would do to you. Much easier to sleep all day than to force yourself to save the world. She'd rather have stayed in bed a few more hours, but she'd made a promise to Wyatt that she would make an effort.

The rest of the family were already seated around the enormous banquet table usually reserved for board meetings with snooty business men like Parker. As she stood at the door, in her fluffy Sailor Moon slippers, and looked for a vacant seat at the crowded table, she picked up the tail end of Evan's recount of his efforts from the previous night. Apparently the explosions that rocked the city were linked to the dude Wyatt and Misha had beef with. When the cops ended up at that Russian club, and found the dead bodies inside, they chalked it all up to some gangland weird shit. It helped that she'd left some evidence she'd gleaned from his computers out in the open.

Of course, she'd also taken a shitload of evidence for herself. Why not? The guy had ties to the Syndicate.

Someone must have said something funny because everyone laughed and she looked up at all the smiling faces.

It was good to hear that sound, and somewhere deep down inside her, there was a yearning to feel the same, but… it was like an empty chasm in there. Hollow, dry, and achy from misuse. Just like her body. But she was done feeling sorry for herself and blaming all her woes on another man. Max Johnson, who?

He was just an asshole who didn't deserve her.

Wyatt had been right. Getting outside and having purpose again snapped something inside her back to life. Pity she'd been useless last night. Mary had contributed most of the body count, while all Sloan had done was shoot a few arrows and then hid under a dead body. The edges of shame pushed at her but, to be honest, she didn't care.

Empty, remember?

She didn't even feel much about the revelation of their eldest sister being alive. Sloan was the second youngest in the family, and had no memory of Daisy, so—meh.

The only thing that held a trace of fire in her otherwise barren heart was the burning hate for Max. Seeing three of her siblings happy in love was making it clearer every day that her relationship with him had been toxic. Long distance, online, and always at the whim of his beck and call. The things she did with him over the phone would make Tony blush. Stupid, stupid things. And she knew better than anyone that your digital life was a mighty long time. You couldn't completely erase your electric fingerprint. The worst part, the reason she hated him, was because after she'd confessed her deepest secret about her true identity, he'd told Sloan he loved her and that he was quitting the army to come and be with her. Then he fucking dumped her. No explanation, no reason, just disappeared like a ghost.

She'd looked him up and discovered he'd actually arrived in town like he promised, but had left the same night.

What a jerk. Now that she saw the bigger picture, that her true mate was still out there, and it wasn't Max, he wasn't worth the scuff-grub beneath her slippers. He was all wrong for her. A lover who ran at the first sign of trouble? Not for her. She needed a man who would run headlong into danger for her, like Wyatt had for Misha.

"You going to stand there all morning with a snarl on your face?"

The deep voice had her blinking away cobwebs in her mind. She turned to Parker's disapproving stare. Like the rest of his family, he'd scrubbed up for the occasion. Suit, tie, shampoo-commercial lustrous locks.

"Swear to God, Parks. You should be on the cover of a romance novel with that hair," she said with an arch of the eyebrow.

For a moment, her giant brother blinked, shocked that she had the audacity to insult him—or rather compliment him. For serious, those locks were swoony model territory according to all the women he dated. Made no sense to her.

She could virtually see thoughts colliding behind his eyes as he took in her limp hair, fluffy slippers and pajamas. *Don't give a shit. I do what I want.* To shove it to him, she grabbed her pigtail and popped the crusty end into her mouth and then dared him with her eyes, pretending not to be grossed out by what she'd just done. She wouldn't give him the satisfaction.

Parker checked his Rolex. "You're twenty minutes late."

Standoff over, she spat out her hair and moved down the room to a vacant seat between Liza and Wyatt.

"Who does a breakfast meeting, anyway?" She plopped down and reached for a croissant. "Most normal people aren't even up at eight in the morning."

"I, for one, am glad the security firm we've hired are so diligent," Griffin added from his spot directly opposite her.

His life-mate, Lilo, was next to him. She poked her tongue at him. "Of course you would say that. You think five a.m. is a perfectly respectable time to wake up."

"That's what I was going to say," Sloan said, laughing. She liked Lilo. The woman was growing on her. Another woman growing on her was Misha and her fun-times attitude. Sloan needed more of that in her life right now.

"Where's Misha?" she asked Wyatt.

"She's not well," was all Wyatt said, and then left it at that.

The sooner this meeting was over, the better.

A knock came at the door, and in walked a tall, well-built man dressed in army fatigues and a black Henley stretched over an impressive body made for violence. Tanned, square jaw covered in scruff, sandy blond beach hair—brown familiar eyes staring right back at her. Sloan choked on her croissant and coughed it up.

Parker stood up. "Everyone, this is Maximillian Johnson from Nightingale Security. He'll be heading up our private protection. Some of you may remember serving in the Aussie SAS with him."

Tony yipped loudly and jumped to his feet, clearly over the moon as he went to his longtime friend. Parker proceeded to point around the table making introductions, but Sloan had spaced out. All she could see was a blur. All she could hear was his name turn over in her head.

Maximillian. Max.

Max.

Max.

What the fuck?

Rage, like none she'd ever known before, surged to the surface of every blood vessel in her body and the croissant crumbled to mush in her fist.

Wyatt's gaze whipped her way. "Sloan?"

She couldn't speak. Could barely think. As the rest of her traitorous family shook hands with the Australian bastard, she found she could barely breathe. And then Liza—thank the stars for Liza—snorted out a laugh.

"Max Johnson?" Another irreverent laugh. "Is that a joke?"

Relief sagged Sloan's shoulders. At least one member of her family had the sense to remember this dickwad-filled-scrotum-tasting... Argh! She couldn't even get expletives out right. Asshole. He was an asshole. *I hate you!*

"His name means big dick." Liza elbowed Sloan in the arm. "Can you believe it? Get it, Max for maximum, Johnson for dick?"

Sloan looked aghast at her sister and the reality dawned on her.

No one gave a shit.

This man they were hailing a hero to come and protect their public identities had chewed up her heart, and spat it out. And now he was there to gloat.

And no one gave a shit.

Suddenly, all the anger drained from her body to leave her cold and shivering. Then slowly, keeping her eyes on the spot just in front of her, she pushed her chair out, stood, and walked out of the room.

"Sloan."

When his rough voice called her name, she kept walking, because if she was forced to look back at him, she wouldn't be held responsible for her murderous actions.

forty-three

WYATT LAZARUS

LATER THAT MORNING, in Wyatt's apartment, he paced outside the bathroom door, waiting for Misha's test results. After she'd crashed the previous night, and spent the morning puking, they'd had precious little time to talk about anything. He'd had to go to the family meeting at Heaven and take Alek home to where the rest of the Minski family waited. Alek was instructed not to mention a thing about Misha's possible condition until she notified him, and the kid was more than happy to oblige. When all his errands were done, as per Misha's request, he'd stopped by the store to get a pregnancy test. The minute he got home, she took it and entered the bathroom.

And there they were… waiting.

His heart pounded in his throat and his palms felt clammy. She'd been in there for three minutes. That was long enough, right? Why wasn't she opening the door?

Maybe she didn't want to keep it.

The thought slammed into him with a frightening intensity and he stopped pacing. She hated the strain of looking after her brother and sister. To her, that work had robbed her of a happy youth. She'd missed out on so much. She was probably terrified of dying during childbirth like her mother.

And what did he want?

Shit.

Wyatt had never expected to have children of his own. They'd been told they were sterile, and Wyatt believed he always would be. Mary had refuted that "always" and said Gloria had designed their genetic code to resist reproduction while they were unstable in mind —without a mate to balance their sin's dark urges—because having an unhinged powerful person reproduce would only pass on the darkness.

No one had believed Mary about the mate business. It had sounded ridiculous. They all thought their sterility was a side effect of being experimented on, and that people as twisted as them, abhorred by mother nature, weren't allowed children.

Christ.

Wyatt ran a hand down his face, scratching over the stubble he'd forgotten to shave. Why wasn't she coming out?

"Misha," he prompted gently at the door.

A shuffling sound, and then the door opened. His heart leaped into his throat.

Dressed in yoga pants and a borrowed T-shirt of his, Misha came out holding the little white stick in her hand.

He held his breath, but she didn't say anything. She just looked at him with glistening eyes, so he took the stick and checked the result. Two blue lines in the window. That was positive, right?

"Positive?"

She nodded.

Suddenly, the floor shifted beneath his feet. It was her decision.

"And... how, um. I guess, how does that make you feel?" he asked.

She shot him a wry smile. "Is that your way of asking if I want to keep it?"

"It's your body. The decision is ultimately up to you."

"What do you want, though?" She sighed and slumped. "We promised we'd be honest with each other."

"You're right." Uncertainty twisted his heart. He had said they'd be honest.

"Wyatt," she said. "You can't keep being afraid that I'll run away. I'm sorry I left yesterday, it was a stupid move, and I learned my lesson, but I need you to tell me the truth. I'm asking because I will always consider your feelings. What do you want to do?"

She took the test from him and placed it on the bench in the bathroom, then came back and held both his hands. "Two hands goes for both of us, right? Tell me what you want."

But his throat closed up. "I don't know."

"What *do* you know?"

"That I want you to stay."

"I'll stay regardless of your choice."

"You say that, but…" He shook his head. She wouldn't.

When he didn't answer, she let go of his hands with a disappointed expression. "You don't want to keep it."

Alarm pricked him. "No! That's not what I said."

Cautiously, she met his eyes, a slow grin forming on her cupid's bow lips. "You *do* want to keep it?"

A wash of heat rushed him, and he realized he was embarrassed. What the fuck? He didn't get embarrassed, but… he did want it. He wanted a life with her and everything that came with it.

Of course he did. He'd always wanted the family life. The Syndicate had made them freaks of nature, and he resented them for it. Being one of the Deadly Seven always felt like a duty, but not something he would have set out to actually want. To him, being normal, or having normal things like a family or a job as a chef, was what he'd wanted. It was probably why it had hurt so bad when Sara took that choice away from him—lying to him about everything she offered and ruining his voice. He met Misha's expectant and hopeful gaze, confident that what he voiced mattered.

"Yeah, I do, but I'm worried you're afraid because of what happened with your mother. I don't want to push you into anything."

She launched at him, latching onto his body. He stumbled and almost fell backward from her sudden weight, but he caught her under her thighs.

"I want it too." She kissed him, full on the lips.

Relief washed through him so thoroughly that his knees weakened and he had to take them both to the couch and sit down. Cupping her face and spearing his fingers through her hair, he smiled down at her. "You want it."

She nodded. "Don't get me wrong, I'm freaking the hell out. This is the complete opposite to how I thought I'd ever feel, and like you said, it's scary because of the way mama died, but"—her smile turned shy—"With you, I... I don't know, I feel good. I know you'll look after us."

"Damn straight, I will."

"I guess I can close the yoga studio down for a while."

"No," he said immediately. "I don't want you to miss out on anything you don't want to. I'll stay home and look after the baby."

Her eyebrow arched. "Really?"

"Sure. I'll stay home during the day, and you can watch the kid at night. Plus, with any urgent missions, we've got a big family. Grandma Mary on my side and, what do you call your father now?"

"He'll be *dziadzio*."

"Judge-oo. Yeah. Right, so there're plenty of babysitters."

"You have it all planned, huh?"

He nodded smugly. Anything he set his mind to, he became an expert at. He wasn't cocky. It was the truth. "How hard can it be?" Her peel of harmonious laughter was infectious, and he couldn't resist smiling along with her. "What's so funny?"

Tears formed in her eyes and she wiped them with her arm. "Oh, nothing. You'll see, I guess. But thank you." She entwined her fingers in his and brought their two hands to her lips.

"For what, knocking you up?"

"For making me realize that living is worth the risk to my heart."

He frowned, hating that she once thought dying to protect her family was ever an option. "I'll protect your heart before my own."

"How about we just do it together?"

"Perfect."

She kissed him gently on the lips, then pulled back, eyes wide. "I just remembered something. I stole Grace's lab coat from downstairs."

"What for?"

She gave him a saucy look and then indicated for him to follow her to the bedroom. "If you have to ask that, are you even my boyfriend?"

"I don't need to ask." He laughed and chased after her, running toward something he loved for the first time in his life.

THE END.

join lana's vips

Subscribe to Lana's newsletter and receive a free box set, first dibs on giveaways, special printable freebies and more. You won't want to miss out.

subscribe.lanapecherczyk.com

On Facebook? Join Lana's Angels Reader Group https://www. facebook.com/groups/lanasangels

characters &
glossary

THE DEADLY SEVEN

(Appearance in order of age from youngest to eldest)

ENVY: Evan Lazarus
SLOTH: Sloan Lazarus
GLUTTONY: Tony Lazarus
GREED: Griffin Lazarus
LUST: Liza Lazarus
WRATH: Wyatt Lazarus
PRIDE: Parker Lazarus

Mary Lazarus: Adoptive Mother of the Deadly Seven and ex assassin for the Hildegard Sisterhood
Flint Lazarus: Adoptive Father of the Deadly Seven

OTHER CHARACTERS:

Dr. Grace Go: Surgeon at Cardinal City General Hospital. Mate to Evan Lazarus.

Lilo Likeke: Investigative reporter at the Cardinal Copy. Mate to Griffin Lazarus.

Misha Minski: Wyatt's mate

THE SYNDICATE

The Syndicate is a secret organization who believe the only way to save the world from its own harmful self is to eradicate all sinners, even if that means destroying half the world.

THE BOSS: Julius Allcott

SARA MADDEN: Ex-girlfriend of Wyatt Lazarus

FALCON: Enforcer for the Syndicate

THE HILDEGARD SISTERHOOD

The Hildegard Sisterhood are nuns with a history reaching back to medieval times when the original Sister Hildegard struggled against a male dominated clergy. Now the world know her as the founder of scientific history in Germany, but back then, her opinions were disregarded until she claimed to have visions from God himself. Belittling herself as a woman in order to be heard was only the beginning of the humiliation the woman faced.

So she started her own abbey filled with women. That same abbey exists today and is a place where women are celebrated and their education encouraged—minus the male influence. Records at the Sisterhood archives reveal they had a hand in the rise of many women over history from *Joan of Arc* to *Indira Gandhi*. From *Catherine the Great* to *Margaret Thatcher*.

Under the surface of the auspicious abbey lays the secret mission that no woman will ever suffer the same struggle as Hildegard and they condition a select few "Sinners" to enforce this mission. These Sinners are trained as assassins for the cause: Sinners like Mary Lazarus. A necessary evil.

In the prequel novella, *Sinner*, Mary Lazarus escaped the Sisterhood who wanted to use the children for their own gain, much like the Syndicate who created them. To this day, she is still on the run.

about the author

OMG! How do you say my name?

Lana (straight forward enough - Lah-nah) **Pecherczyk** (this is where it gets tricky - Pe-her-chick).

I've been called Lana Price-Check, Lana Pera-Chickywack, Lana Pressed-Chicken, Lana Pech…*that girl!* You name it, they said it. So if it's so hard to spell, why on earth would I use this name instead of an easy pen name?

To put it simply, it belonged to my mother. And she was my dream champion. For most of my life, I've been good at one thing – art. The world around me saw my work, and said I should do more of it, so I did. But, when at the age of eight, I said I wanted to write stories, and even though we were poor, my mother came home with a blank notebook and a pencil saying I should follow my dreams, no matter where they take me for they will make me happy. I wasn't very good at it, but it didn't matter because I had her support and I liked it.

She died when I was thirteen, and left her four daughters orphaned. Suddenly, I had lost my dream champion, I was split from my youngest two sisters and had no one to talk to about the challenge of life.

So, I wrote in secret. I poured my heart out daily to a diary and sometimes imagined that she would listen. At the end of the day, even if she couldn't hear, writing kept that dream alive.

Eventually, after having my own children (two firecrackers in the guise of little boys) and ignoring my inner voice for too long, I decided to lead by example. How could I teach my children to follow their dreams if I wasn't? I became my own dream champion and the rest is history, here I am.

When I'm not writing the next great action-packed romantic novel, or wrangling the rug rats, or rescuing GI Joe from the jaws of my Kelpie, I fight evil by moonlight, win love by daylight and never run from a real fight. I live in Australia, but I'm up for a chat anytime online. Come and find me.

Subscribe & Follow
subscribe.lanapecherczyk.com
lp@lanapecherczyk.com

facebook.com/lanapecherczykauthor

instagram.com/lana_p_author

amazon.com/-/e/B00V2TP0HG

bookbub.com/profile/lana-pecherczyk

tiktok.com/@lanapauthor

goodreads.com/lana_p_author